"I have a reactionary Army, a National Socialist Air Force, and a Christian Navy."

-Adolph Hitler

"Isn't there some way we can avoid our first exchange with a Russian submarine—almost anything but that?"

-President John F. Kennedy
October 27, 1962

Eternal Father, strong to save
Whose arm hath bound the restless wave.
Who bid'st the mighty Ocean deep its own appointed limits keeps:
O hear us when we cry to thee,
For those in peril on the sea.
Lord God, our power ever more
Who arm doth reach the ocean floor,
Dive with our men beneath the sea;
Traverse the depths protectively
O hear us when we pray to thee
For those in peril under the sea.

The Navy Hymn

OF ICE AND STEEL

D. Clayton Meadows

iUniverse, Inc.
Bloomington

OF ICE AND STEEL

iUniverse books may be ordered through booksellers or by contacting:

iUniverse
1663 Liberty Drive
Bloomington, IN 47403
www.iuniverse.com
1-800-Authors (1-800-288-4677)

Because of the dynamic nature of the Internet, any web addresses or links contained in this book may have changed since publication and may no longer be valid. The views expressed in this work are solely those of the author and do not necessarily reflect the views of the publisher, and the publisher hereby disclaims any responsibility for them.

Any people depicted in stock imagery provided by Thinkstock are models, and such images are being used for illustrative purposes only.

Certain stock imagery © Thinkstock.

ISBN: 978-1-4759-7016-6 (sc)
ISBN: 978-1-4759-7017-3 (e)

Library of Congress Control Number: 2013900062

Printed in the United States of America

iUniverse rev. date: 1/3/2013

For Carl Ballard who loves history and a good story.
To all those throughout history have sailed,
fought and died under the sea.

The Submariner

Only a submariner realizes to what great extent an entire ship depends on him as an individual. A land man doesn't understand this and it maybe difficult to comprehend, but it is true.

A submarine at sea is a different world and in consideration of the protracted and distant operations of submarines, the Navy must place responsibility and trust in the hands of those who take such ships to sea.

In each submarine, there are men who in an hour of emergency or peril at sea can turn to each other. These men are ultimately responsible to themselves and to one another for all aspects of operations of their submarine. They are the crew. They are the ship.

This is perhaps the most difficult and demanding assignment in the Navy. There is not an instance during his tour as a submariner that he can escape the grasp of responsibility. His privileges in view of his obligations are ludicrously small but it is the spur that has given the Navy its greatest mariners, those who wear the insignia of the United States Naval Submarine Service.

Acknowledgements

THE IDEA FOR THIS book was born when I was a young sailor. It was May 6, 1986. My submarine USS RAY SSN-653, along with USS ARCHERFISH SSN 678, and USS HAWKBILL SSN-666 surfaced together at the North Pole. It was the first surfacing of three submarines at the Pole.

I would like to thank my father Reverend Donald C. Meadows for instilling in me a love for writing. Without and constant urging of my mother Diane Clark *Of Ice and Steel* would have never been created. A special thanks to my Grandfather James Atkins. As a child I spent hours asking question after question about his time in the Navy. It was from this giant of a man I gained a fever for the sea and a love of the Navy.

No task however small or great can occur unless you have behind you a family that supports and encourages you. My wife Susan has been there through it all. She has played the roles of both Mommy and Daddy while I was at sea. She believed in me and put up with more than any woman should.

For the first years of my children's lives, "Daddy" was a framed picture lovingly placed by their beds. Despite my absence or maybe because of it Donnie and Andrew have become two of the finest young men I know. Donnie is an aspiring chef, while Andrew is now a Sailor in the United States Navy. I am so very proud they call me Dad.

Author's Note

This is a work of fiction. Tactics described are in no way representative of United States, NATO, or Russian tactics, past or present. Descriptions of ships, weapons, weapon systems, and other details have been purposefully modified to protect sensitive information.

1

FIRE AND ICE

"War is the science of destruction"

-John S.C. Abbot

U-761 FLOATED STILL AND silent. Her slender graceful lines and shark-like bow blurred to translucence by billows of freezing mist. Daggers of ice hung like teeth from her rails and guns. The worn gray camouflage on her sides and conning tower melded into a lifeless slate sky. She laid there the perfect predator hidden in a field of jagged, broken ice.

Shivering on the U-boat's bridge *Kapitanleutnaunt* Manfred Becker peered into an empty frozen ocean. At 34, he was one of the old gang of U-boat commanders. His five foot-nine inch frame was thin, his shoulders broad. His face was pure Prussian. A noble nose jutted from proud smooth cheeks. His thin mouth turned down to a permanent frown. Stung by the angry mist normally pale blue eyes red and swollen, strained to spot movement or shadow on the bleak dead ice. An occasional gap in the swirling clouds of mist would open like a shutter only to slam closed seconds later as the sky fumed and frothed.

"Everyone okay," he asked those with him on the bridge.

"Yes captain," each replied through chattering teeth.

Becker stepped to the open hatch. Bending slightly he peered into the submarine. Warm air rising from inside the U-boat caused a trickle of melted ice to run across his throat.

"Frimunt," Becker called.

"Captain?" A voice replied from inside the U-boat.

"How long have they been out?"

"One hour twenty minutes."

"They should be back by now."

U-761's engineer officer Chief Edel stuck his head out of the hatch, "We need to start the engines. Lube oil is getting cold. The intakes may be freezing."

"Not yet. Let's give them a few more minutes."

"Sir I think…"

Becker stopped him. "Not yet."

"Yes sir," replied the engineer. He started to slide down the ladder.

"Wait chief," Becker said bending further down. "What is our guest up to?"

"The same," Edel shrugged. "Sitting alone, staring at the clock." The engineer stuck his head farther out the hatch. "Seems nervous," Edel Shrugged.

"Me too," whispered Becker.

Edel grinned and disappeared down the hatch.

Becker was about to call for coffee when the port lookout shouted, "There they are!"

Becker saw only shadows cast from mounds of lifeless ice. He wiped his eyes clearing the mist from his face. Translucent manlike shapes appeared from the swirling mist. "Why are they running?"

His men stumbled and picked themselves up only to fall again. *U-761*'s commander tore the cap from his head, his brown hair in a wild tangle while he watched his men crawl on the ice.

"Frimunt man the guns," Becker's voice echoed off the ice. "Get men to the after casing.

Within seconds gun crews made the twin barreled 3.7cm weapons ready. Showers of ice shattered from the creaking, groaning weapons as the barrels swung over the tower side.

"Ready," the gun captain reported.

"Stand by." Becker swallowed hard at the sight of his men clawing toward the U-boat.

Only six meters from the boat all strength gone the first man collapsed. Exhausted one after another, they tumbled to the hard ice.

"Frimunt take over," Becker barked as he slid from the bridge on to the after-casing. The galley hatch clanged open. Nine of *U-761's* crew clambered up the galley hatch, slipping and sliding on the frosted deck.

Those shivering on the after-casing called to their shipmates, urged them on pleaded with them to get up. The men looked to Becker. Their bodies coiled like spring steel.

"Go," Becker, commanded.

In unison, all nine leapt from the deck to the ice.

Becker looked back to the bridge, "Contacts?"

"Nothing," Frimunt answered.

Becker stared as the nine volunteers reached their nearly frozen shipmates. It took fewer than two minutes until all lie in gasping heaps on the deck, "All on board?"

"Yes sir."

"Where is Volker?"

"Here," answered one of the shivering rescuers.

The captain stepped over two of the men and knelt by the third. Becker gently placed his hand under the gasping man's head, raising it slightly, "Volker?'

Volker's eyes fluttered half open. "Sir?" he managed in a weak thin rasp.

"What happened?"

"All dead," he managed.

"Who's dead?"

"All," he whispered.

"Volker?" Becker wiped the man's face, his lips blue from frostbite. "Lieutenant Volker."

Again, the eyes fluttered and muscles twitched with an effort to keep the eyes open. "All dead, shot-burned…."

"All hands below. Prepare to dive. " Becker shouted, "Secure the guns."

Becker slid down the galley hatch tearing off his blue-gray parka. "Diving stations!" he ordered.

Edel came forward taking his place behind the planesmen. "Three hours left on the batteries."

Becker turned to *Oberbootsmann* Hamlin, "How far to open water?"

"Twenty kilometers," Hamlin answered.

Becker looked at Edel.

"Go slow," urged Edel.

Becker nodded.

As he opened his mouth to order the dive a voice called out, "Halt!"

Every face in the control room looked at the forward hatch. SS *Sturmbannführer* Lambert Von Gerlach stepped into the control room as if walking on air, graceful, silent, and menacing. "Captain on whose authority are you submerging?" His voice was soft yet as lifeless as his black eyes.

"Our mission is over."

"Why do you say that?" asked Gerlach. His black eyes narrowed.

"Everyone is dead."

Gerlach polished his fingernails against his jacket. "All?"

"Yes all."

"Unfortunate," responded Gerlach.

"My boat is in danger." Becker stepped toward Gerlach pointing to the hatch. The *Sturmbannführer*r ducked his head under the steel circle into the next compartment with Becker close behind.

Away from the crew Becker grabbed Gerlach's collar shoving his small frame into a recess forward of the U-boat's toilet. "I command this boat," Becker hissed.

"First captain, take your hands off me." Gerlach ordered stiffly.

Becker released his grip.

"Your mission," his voice cool and lifeless, "Is over when I dismiss you." He paused as if to let the words sink in.

"Something up there is killing people."

He met Becker's eyes. "You are the captain of this ship. But until we fulfill our missions I am in charge."

"What happened out there?"

"I don't know." Gerlach's mouth cracked into a thin smile. "Trust me. If what your men say is true this ship is in no danger."

"What?" Becker asked.

"We remain here till I tell you otherwise."

Stepping back through the control room hatch, Becker slammed his fist on the chart table. "Secure from diving stations. Chief start the engines. Charge the batteries. And get some heat in this coffin!"

"Aye sir," replied Edel as he headed aft.

"Hamlin," Becker called. "You have the bridge watch. You see anything at all dive the boat."

Hamlin nodded his understanding.

The familiar welcome rumble of the U-boats twin *MANN* diesels growling to life meant air warmed by the diesel engines would soon drive the chill from the cramped hull.

Becker stepped into the tiny wardroom where the landing party shaken but alive, rested in bunks or sprawled on a thin bench. Stripped of their parkas, shirts, pants, and boots, they shivered under rough, gray blankets.

Berdy the cook ladled steaming red soup into cups held by trembling hands. Radio operator and *U-761*'s medic, Waldron Roth examined and fussed over all five men. Apart from slight exposure, exhaustion, and dehydration, the men were uninjured.

Kruger, the big torpedo mechanic from Paderborn came through the hatch, his bulky, grease smeared arms filled with bottles of apple juice. He handed a bottle to each of the landing party. "Wish it was beer huh?" Kruger grinned. "At least it is cold."

Becker smiled. "Good, Kruger." He slapped the torpedo man's back. The captain caught Roth's eye. "Volker?" he asked.

Roth's head motioned to a top bunk.

Becker gently pulled back the wool blanket, "Volker?"

"Sir?" A drop of Berdy's soup rested on his chin.

"You look better than last time I saw you," grinned Becker.

"My apologies," Volker chattered.

"No need for that. How are you feeling?"

"A bit weak but I'll be okay."

"What happened out there?"

Volker lie back, staring at the maze of pipes and cables above him. "We reached the camp and I signaled with the light. I didn't see any reply. I signaled three more times, still nothing. I thought they could not see the signal in the fog. I ordered the men forward. The entire camp was gone...," he stammered.

"Gone?"

Volker trembled. "Tents, equipment, metal buildings all blown apart. Bodies were everywhere."

"What bodies?"

"There was a large fence, or enclosure more like a cage. I counted fifteen dead."

"You mean our men?" Becker asked.

"I think they were Russian."

"POWs?"

"It looked like some escaped. I found a hole under the ice on the backside. We then found German and Russian bodies. Our men were beaten, stabbed, or shot. Russians had our weapons. I think there was a fight and someone shot a fuel tank. Outside one of those buildings was a big hole in the ice. I could smell burned petrol. I imagine that was a depot."

"You're sure everyone was dead?"

"I don't know. We checked the bodies we could. I counted seventy." Volker paused. "I thought there could still be Russians hiding in the ice. We were unarmed so I ordered the men to run."

"You did the right thing. Get some rest." Becker turned to go.

"Captain," Volker managed to pull himself to his elbows. "I went in one of the metal buildings and saw large canisters. Twelve I think. Each canister was large enough for a man. They had windows cut into the front and hoses coming from the tops." Volker's brow crinkled. "What happened?"

Becker ran his hands through his hair. "I don't know but I am going to find out. Now get some sleep." Becker moved to the hatch. "Roth, check for messages," he whispered. "Find out what the *Sturmbannführer* is doing and report to me."

"Aye sir," Roth nodded.

Becker walked forward into the torpedo room. The mechanics came to attention as he entered. Becker waved them to carry on. His men moved about in silence tending to the sinister looking fish. The sleek shapes of the torpedoes filled most of the space. Their dull bronze bodies and greenish warheads held captive by straps, secured them to the hull. The upper torpedo stow held the new secret *Leche* torpedo. This was one of the new *wonder* weapons. It measured a meter smaller than the regular G-7e torpedo. Unlike the dull steel of the other weapons, the new weapon was the color of tarnished brass with a nose of soft black rubber.

Instead of running straight to a target, this electric powered torpedo listened for its quarry then steer toward the noise. If it missed, it would turn and attack again.

Above his head heavy chains dangled from massive steel beams. Narrow bunks used only after a number of fish had been fired formed of thin steel tubing lashed up along the white painted hull. Boxes of tools lay strapped to the diamond patterned deck. To use every millimeter of space loaves of moldy bread and greasy sausages hung everywhere. Canned foods stacked and tied in neat bundles hung in rows lining whatever space remained.

The torpedo tubes stood at the head of this jumble. Becker picked his way carefully until he stood between the tubes. He peered over the maze of pipes and cables to a small space behind the equalizing valve manifold. There wrapped in a dull grey blankets was the secret cargo. Becker ran his hand over the cool damp covering. "What is this all about?"

Ducking through the hatch Becker turned toward his cabin.

Across the narrow passage, Roth sat at his folding chair hunched over the radio receiver. As Becker brushed past, he could see Roth poring over the top-secret enigma-coding machine careful to copy each letter correctly.

"Anything for us?" asked Becker.

"Just routine traffic from other boats," Roth sighed. "There is one message I don't understand."

"Oh?" Becker yawned.

"We never receive messages from the Japanese navy."

Becker turned his head, "The Japanese?"

Roth read the message,

"All Vessels of the Combined Imperial Fleet, Merchant, and Allied vessels of Japan operating in the Northern Pacific."

"Let me see that." Becker snatched the message and studied the words. "Get Frimunt," he ordered.

Roth stepped quickly around the corner and ducked through the control room hatch.

Becker read the message again. "Is this code?"

Frimunt stepped through the hatch with Roth close behind.

Becker handed him the paper. "Read it."

Frimunt cleared his throat.

"An earthquake of great intensity has occurred from the American held Aleutian Islands to the Bering Sea. This earthquake continued

along the sea of Okhotsk to the tip of the home islands. All vessels operating in these waters are warned of intense wave action including waves of Tsunami force. Vessels operating in the service of His Majesty will use all precautions. In the name of the Emperor, Admiral Mineichi Koga, Commander Combined Fleet...

What does it mean?"

"I hoped you would know." Becker took the message back. "Okay, carry on."

Becker limped to his bunk again and let his frame fall on to the thin mattress. "Here," Becker said as he handed Roth the message.

"What do you think?" Roth asked.

"That's on the other side of the world," Becker answered. "We have enough trouble on this side."

"Yes sir," Roth nodded. "TS-UN-AM-I," he sounded out the unknown word. "Captain, the *Sturmbannführer* decoded a message from Berlin."

Becker bolted upright. "Did you see it?"

"No sir. He destroyed it after decoding."

Becker jumped off his bunk. "Where is he now?"

"I don't know."

"Find him. Get the chief, Frimunt and the other officers here now." Becker heard a faint popping sound then another followed by a scream. He recognized sound of 9mm pistol rounds. A screech of high-pressure air filled the hull.

Shouts and curses were heard above the screaming air. Becker pushed through a tangle of sailors to the control room.

The control room mechanic saw the captain. "Torpedo room," he shouted.

Flying through passages and hatches Becker entered the forward most part of the ship. Two men lie on the deck wounded but alive. Mechanics searched for the valve to secure the screaming air. Then Becker saw Kruger the giant torpedoman.

The deafening scream of escaping air slowly died. Orders rang out. Kruger stood silent between the tubes only his back visible. Becker saw muscles on Kruger's back ripple and flex. Kruger's right arm slowly rose and his plate-sized hand gripped another hand, clad in black and holding a pistol.

"Kruger," Becker shouted as he ran forward. Becker grabbed the pistol. He looked over and saw Kruger had Gerlach's throat in his left hand. Kruger's fingers squeezed like bands of steel sinking into the SS man's tender neck. Gerlach's mouth opened and his tongue hung out.

"Stop!" screamed Becker as he grabbed Kruger's arm and pulled. The arm flexed again and the fingers tightened. "Kruger!" Without thinking, Becker backed up and with all his strength plowed his fist into Kruger's side.

The big man turned his head.

"Kruger let go," Becker order. "I have the gun."

The fingers relaxed. Gerlach crumpled as his tortured lungs gasped for air. Streams of crimson spit dangled from his blue lips. His head hung limp.

"What have you done?"

Gerlach gurgled.

"Get him out of here," shouted Becker.

"What do we do with him?" a voice asked.

"Tie him up in the engine room. For God's sake, put a watch on him. Where's Roth?"

"Here, sir."

"How many wounded?" Becker's own breath came in gasps.

"Two."

Another shout rang through the steel hull, "Captain!"

Becker's head turned to the voice. One of the wounded pointed to the torpedo on the upper port rack.

"The warhead, under the warhead," the wounded man rasped.

Obermechaniker Baldric the weapons warrant officer was closest to the torpedo. Leaning slightly he peered under the fish. "A bomb," he gasped.

From the corner of his eye, Becker saw Edel jump over the wounded man to the weapon. Thrusting his thin hand under the warhead, Edel grunted, strained and pulled until the bomb came loose. With one hand, holding the explosive Edel reached into his back pocket for a rag, wrapped the fuse, and pulled, but the fuse stayed. Angry wisps of gray smoke jetted from the under the dirty rag.

"Get it off the boat," Becker shouted.

"Out of the way," Baldric shot forward grabbed the bomb and in an instant was gone. Becker followed.

Men dove to the side slamming themselves against the steel hull.

At the control room ladder, Baldric reached for the rung. Suddenly the bomb slipped from his greasy sweaty fingers. With a dull thud, the explosive landed on the deck. The fuse hissed louder. With no emotion, Baldric reached down and snatched the bomb. His boots clanged loudly as he climbed the ladder into the conning tower with Becker close behind. The fuse spurted sparks and blue-white jets of fire as Baldric thrust himself to the bridge.

Becker was the last on the bridge. Just as he pulled himself to his knees the warrant officer's voice boomed across the ice.

"Get down!"

Baldric threw the bomb off the starboard side. It flew to the ice in a graceful arc.

The moment it struck the hard ice, the bomb detonated. A fireball three meters across erupted in a flash of white and dirty orange. A pressure wave moving three times the speed of sound slammed into U-761, rocking the submarine as if it were a toy.

The blast tore the air from Becker's lungs and pressed his eardrums to the point of rupture. His body lifted before gravity overcame the blast and slammed him into the deck. The explosion carried its report across the broken ice. Then silence.

Slowly those who pinned Becker rolled to the side.

"Stay down," Baldric shouted. "Cover your heads!"

Chunks of black ice rained over the U-boat. Broken ice the size of footballs smashed down onto the casing sending deadly shards in all directions.

Becker craned his neck. "Anyone hurt?"

Slowly they picked themselves up weak-kneed and dazed.

"Baldric?" asked Becker.

"Sir," he panted, "I need a new job."

"I hear the Army is hiring," Becker answered.

Baldric grinned. "Thank you I will keep that in mind."

Edel thrust his head from the hatch, "Everyone okay?"

With the help of the lookout, Becker regained his feet.

"The batteries," Becker asked.

"Another half hour," Edel grumbled.

"Good. Check for damage before we get out of here."

Edel disappeared down the hatch. Becker followed close behind.

In the control room, men staggered about, shaking their heads clearing affects of the blast.

Roth appeared by Becker's side. "I checked the wounded. None are serious." Roth paused, "I'm worried about the *Sturmbannführer*. His trachea is swelling shut."

"Damn." Becker closed his eyes. "What can you do?"

Roth chewed his thumb. "If the swelling gets worse I will have to open his throat, insert a tube for him to breathe until the swelling goes down."

"And you've done this before?" asked Becker.

"No," Roth admitted.

"Thank you," Becker nodded.

Becker sat again on his mattress. He drew the flimsy blue curtain shut.

"Captain?" a voice called.

"Yes?"

"Sir its Berdy," the voice whispered. "I brought you food."

Becker swung his feet off the bunk and pulled the curtain aside. Berdy with his infectious smile stood holding a covered tray.

"Here captain. Some corned beef with gravy. Fresh bread and a bowl of tomato stew."

"Thank you, Berdy."

The ship's cook bowed slightly. His small hand drew the curtain as he left.

Becker dug into the steaming plate. A minute later, the heaping mound of beef was gone. Suddenly the bowl of stew shook. The shaking grew worse until the submarine rocked on her beam while pitching up and down.

Becker jumped to his feet the tray, plate, and utensils crashed to the deck. He headed for the control room dodging men as they fell unable to balance.

A deep rumble ran through the hull, and grew until it drowned out the sound of the diesels.

The U-boat bucked, causing Becker to slip on the ladder. It took all his strength to regain his footing. He pushed his head over the bridge where a gale hit his face. "What is it Hamlin?" he shouted above the growing roar.

Eyes wide the young Lieutenant pointed over the bow

Blood drained from Becker's face as he saw a wall of ice growing and rushing toward them. The ice around the submarine danced as great plates lifted and fell. Large cracks opened along the ice. Each convulsion of the ice sounded like a thunderclap. The already dim atmosphere darkened. Those on the U-boat's bridge looked into the darkness. In the screaming rush of air, the 30-meter wave lifted great house-sized blocks of ice flipping them like playing cards. As if feeding on the dying ice the wave grew 40 meters high, then 50. Thousand-ton slabs of ice rolled and churned in the wave and the roar grew louder.

"Clear the bridge," Becker bellowed above the roar.

A lookout stood transfixed by the site of the mounting wave, Becker grabbed him by the arm and shoved him toward the hatch. Men tumbled down landing on each other.

"Alarm," he yelled. The wave towered over the U-boat. Becker looked one last time before slamming the hatch.

As if alive, the wave boiled, grinding the ancient ice to powder. Bullets of blue white ice crashed into the U-boat. Automobile sized boulders splashed alongside the submarine, throwing her from side to side. Each time the German submarine fought to right herself she was rocked by another boulder of ice.

Becker landed in the control room with a heavy thud. He pulled himself upright braced himself with the chart table. "Chief 200 meters now," he screamed.

"Open the vents," Edel shouted over the roar. "Stand by on the motors."

All eyes watched the depth gauge. It didn't move.

A shout rang out from the back of the control room. "Vents will not open!"

Edel's eyes widened. "Override the control. Operate them in hand."

The stern of the U-boat sank slightly, the shark-like bow jutted up as if challenging the oncoming wave.

Edel looked at the captain. Their unspoken words told the terrible truth.

"Hold on," Becker shouted.

Then a slab of three-meter thick ice slightly smaller than a city block slid under the upturned bow. The entire hull teetered then rode up over the slab.

Unable to bare the weight of the submarine, the great slab cracked and the U-boat fell two meters. As the wave rushed over, tons of ice pushed *U-761*'s hull further into the ice as more ice rained down burying her. The bow remained up, but the stern dropped. Again, the ice exploded under the U-boats weight. The millennium old frozen chunk of water resisted, but the pressure of the wave was too great. The ice started to spin. It spun faster as pressure increased.

Inside U-761, men and machines tumbled through space. The lights flickered then went out. Sparks from blown fuses lit the air in flashes.

Becker strained to hold onto the chart table. His arms felt as though they might rip from his shoulders. Over the roar, he heard screams, but couldn't tell which was his.

2

TRAPPED

"All you that would be seaman must bare a valiant heart."

Martin Parker, d 1656

IT DIED AS QUICKLY as it had come. Shuddering moaning steel quieted as the furious wave faded. The German submarine rested with a heavy port list. Ghostlike moans and whimpers filled the dark control room.

With great effort, Becker forced himself upright. His hand managed to find a valve to grab just as his boots slipped from under him.

Grudgingly lights flickered until they peaked to a sickening yellow. Becker glanced around. Charts, logbooks, broken dishes, spare parts, clothing, and men lie everywhere. Bundles of red black and green wire lay in a tangle along the deck, or dangled from broken panels as if the very guts of the submarine lay strung out.

A reeking stench of bilge water, sweaty men, and rotting food filled Becker's nose. He shook his head to clear the dizziness. "Get me damage reports!"

Men struggled to their feet.

"Where is the chief?" Becker turned almost losing his footing on the tilted deck. "Edel?"

"Here, sir." Edel wedged himself up using the silver periscope barrel for support.

"I need a full report."

"Yes, sir," Edel mumbled as he limped aft.

Becker clapped his hands. "Let's get this sty back in order," he bellowed. "Come on men, nap time is over. Frimunt," he called.

"Sir," a weak voice answered.

"Where are you?" Becker saw boots lying behind the barrel like gyrocompass. The boots moved. Frimunt rose to his knees. A trembling hand reached for the top of the compass. Frimunt groaned with effort as he pushed his shaking frame upright. "Sir ..." He staggered a step. The control room electrician dropped his tools and stepped up the sloping deck just as Frimunt's legs collapsed.

"Help here," he called out.

Two crewmembers reached out. Together they lowered Frimunt to the cold slanting deck.

Becker knelt next to the young lieutenant. Gently he pulled the oilskin hat from Frimunt's head.

Frimunt's usual light auburn hair was matted with thick oozing blood. The left side above the ear was caved inward, as drops of dark blood dripped from his left ear. His body shook and his eyes glazed.

"Frimunt," Becker shouted.

The *Oberleutnant's* legs slowly flailed on the deck. The eyes regained some color. He tried to move his head.

"Frimunt don't move," Becker whispered. "Just look at me." The captain saw Frimunt's eyes try to focus. The pupils grew smaller. "Frimunt," Becker whispered. Becker wiped blood from Frimunt's forehead. "Get Roth!" He again looked down to Frimunt. "Stay with me." Becker took the man's hand."

Frimunt's lips moved, but no words formed.

"Roth knelt to examine Frimunt's head. Some help over here," Roth called."

Two of Edel's machinists moved up the sloped deck.

"We need to get him to a bunk," Roth whispered. "Take his feet," Roth directed. "I'll support his neck and head."

Slowly, with great tenderness they carried the young officer forward.

Edel came through the hatch toward Becker. "I have a damage

list. A coolant leak in the starboard diesel, three lighting panels tore off their mounts. One cell in the forward battery cracked. Number 2 lube oil purifier has a cracked base plate. Our compressor's second stage relief valve is jammed. Fuel oil transfer pump blew a packing. And our air banks are depleted."

Becker nodded, "How long for repairs?"

Edel pulled the cap off his head and scratched the tuft of his remaining hair. "Give me two hours, three at the most."

He pulled Edel close his voice a whisper, "Are the vents open or shut?"

Edel looked at the indicator above the planesmen seat. "Open," Edel, whispered back.

"Are we submerged?"

The engineer tapped the depth gauge's glass face. He paused a moment then moved to the periscopes. Reaching high above his head his hand found the green handled valve. "Let's see if there is any water in the periscope housing." Slowly he twisted the valve and a hiss of air escaped. Edel stepped to the depth gauge valve. His hand reached for the special wrench still in its holder. Behind a maze of pipes, he fit the wrench on the valve and opened the tiny port. A faint wisp of air spurted from the valve. He leaned back, face puzzled.

"What about the control room strainer?" Becker asked.

"Good idea." Edel stepped around the periscopes, dropped to one knee to the left of the scope. He carefully removed the dull brass cap from the sea strainer, pulled the locking ring retainer, and slowly twisted the end. After three turns, the bronze plug came off. He peered into the hole, "Nothing." Edel replaced the cap and screwed it down hard. "Captain, we have no water under us." Edel stroked nervously at his wiry brown beard. "The hull must have been forced over the ice."

"The stern is down. It could still be submerged."

"Could be," Edel shrugged.

"If it is we can use the motors to back out."

"We have a way to find out." Edel spoke into the brass voice tube, "After torpedo room," he barked.

A strained voice answered back, "After torpedo room."

"Open the tube flood valve for tube-five. Then open the tube inboard vent."

A few seconds passed. "Control the valves are open."

"Is water flowing?"

A half minute passed. "Control," this time the voice seemed puzzled. "There is no flow from the vent."

Edel's eyes looked up. "We're trapped."

Becker took a full deep breath. "I'll try the periscope. See what's out there."

Edel nodded. "Use the sky scope. The attack scope is too thin. If we break that scope barrel..." He placed his hand on the frosted steel periscope. "That's an eighty centimeter hole right to the ocean."

Becker nodded his understanding, "Up scope!" Edel pushed the orange handle of the lifting hoist. The lifting cable went tight as the scope slithered up. Edel and Becker felt the scope shudder, then stop, not quite halfway up.

"Damn." Becker swore as the scope screeched to a halt. He heard the lifting ram whine, straining to lift the heavy scope.

"Probably a lot of ice to push through," explained Edel.

Becker moved the handle down. The scope slid back into its pit. "Here we go again."

When the periscope lifted, it vibrated and twisted with a crunching noise that caused the conning tower to shake. Becker grit his teeth as the scope moved higher, slowed, and then stalled.

"It stuck again." Becker was about to lower the periscope when, it screeched. Breaking free of the ice, the two-ton barrel slid to full height. Becker turned his white cap until the brim was at the back of his neck. He peered into the eyepiece. "Unbelievable!"

Edel remained quiet. He wiped his hands over his filthy shirt.

Becker moved the scope as if dancing. He swung it left, then right only to stop and swing it back.

"Well?" Edel asked.

Becker rested his arm on the black handle of the periscope letting his chin fall onto his arm. "The ice is below the scope head."

Edel gasped.

Becker motioned for him to see for himself. Edel looked into the tiny optic window. After one rotation, he hung his head. "Maybe use the cutting torch. Melt ice off bridge hatch.

Becker lifted the cap from his head. "What about a scuttling charge?

"Explosives?" mumbled Edel. How would we get them outside? Another close explosion might rupture our side."

"Is there anything we can do?" Becker asked.

Edel took in a long drag of foul air. "No."

"Get Roth," Becker snapped.

Wiping blood on a dirty towel Roth steeped through the hatch.

"Frimunt?" Becker asked

"He needs a doctor. His skull is fractured."

Becker turned to make sure no one listened. "Roth how many special pills do you have?"

Roth's eyes went wide. "Sir … I …"

"Roth, how many?" Becker insisted. "One for each man aboard?"

Roth nodded.

"Good." Becker managed a smiled. "Go back to work."

One of the mechanics stuck his head from the forward hatch, "Captain?"

The sound startled Becker, "Yes?"

"Engineer needs you in the torpedo room."

Becker's began to tremble, eyes flared with rage. His fingers curled into powerful fists and his cheeks twitched. Edel stepped from the torpedo room toward him.

"Captain, I…"

"Not now, "Becker barked. His eyes flashed of pure hate as he turned and headed aft.

Edel followed, "Captain?"

The thin passageway cleared as if by a force of nature.

He stopped at his cabin. Behind the pillow, lay Gerlach's Luger. He grabbed the weapon, and pulled the action feeding a live shell to the chamber.

Becker turned. Edel stood arms outstretched blocking the way into the passage. "Captain," he said softly.

"Out of my way," Becker shouted.

"Sir, please."

"Get out of my way." Becker's lip curled.

Edel dropped his arms. He moved his hands in front of him, palms up, "Please, captain."

Becker pushed the engineer aside. Once in the passageway his steps thumped on the deck gratings. He passed the hatch to the diesel room then ducked his head in the electric motor room.

On the starboard side, Gerlach swayed in a stinking wadded up canvas hammock. His head lay to the side propped up by a blanket, hands tightly bound over his head. His eyes watched every move through bruised and blackened lids.

Becker grabbed Gerlach's black coat below his battered throat. "Now," he hissed through clenched teeth. "You will talk or your brains will be all over my ship. Why are we here?"

His bloodshot eyes stared at Becker without emotion. Gerlach turned his head away.

"Damn you to hell," Becker shouted. He slammed Gerlach back down only to grab him up again. "Because of you my crew will die here." Becker's mouth foamed slightly. "I want to know why."

Becker shoved the black barrel into Gerlach's mouth. His eyes on fire, Becker moved his thumb and slowly brought the hammer back.

WATER BEARS

"I am a man under authority, having soldiers
under me: and I say to this man, go, and he goeth:
and to another, come, and he cometh."

Matthew, VII, IX

AUGUST 21, 1944

GERLACH GAGGED AND SPUTTERED when the Luger's barrel pressed the back of his throat. Blood dripped down his chin in long red strings from his lips.

"Bastard," Becker shouted.

Gerlach's eyes spun wildly in their sockets as if looking for salvation. He gurgled as his swollen throat took in what air it could.

Suddenly Gerlach's body went limp. He exhaled a long bubbling breath.

Becker turned his head to see Edel standing behind him.

"Give me the gun," Edel said with his hand outstretched. "This is not who we are," Edel said softly.

Gerlach's eyes blinked open as if a switch turned him back on. He focused on Becker. His lips slowly parted.

Becker lifted his finger from the trigger, and withdrew the gun's barrel from Gerlach's mouth.

"I'll take it," Edel urged.

Becker turned his head, letting the gun slide gently in the engineer's palm.

"You okay?"

"Yes." Becker nodded to the gun in Edel's hand. "Put it away."

Edel's hand closed around the gun.

"Why?" Gerlach rasped.

"You're not worth the bullet," Becker hissed.

Gerlach's bloodied lips curled into a vile grin, "True, but not the reason."

Becker rolled his head from side-to-side to stretch out the tension. "You know this is it. We'll die here." Becker looked at the hull above him. "In a day-maybe two-we'll freeze. Not much left in the batteries. No fresh air." Becker sneered. "I wanted you to enjoy it with the rest of us."

"Not a bad way to go, so I understand." Gerlach cleared his throat, turned, and spit. "Peaceful and quiet."

"Don't push me," Becker warned.

"Why didn't you kill me?" Gerlach's voice was almost a taunt.

Becker stood slowly, and rubbed the back of his neck. "Killing you is easy, to let you live is a challenge. By killing you, I become you. I let you live, I win."

"Win?"

Becker's cheek twitched, "The last bit of humanity I have."

Gerlach shrugged, "Oh come now captain. A German in the service of the fuehrer worried about his humanity?"

Becker's eyes blazed. "What else do we have you arrogant little bastard."

"Duty to the cause," rasped Gerlach.

Becker lowered his face inches from Gerlach. "You think what you and your chicken farmer boss is doing has anything to do with duty?"

Gerlach's bruised face reddened further. "You're a traitor."

"Look at my crew. These are the real Germans. Thousands of miles from home rotting in this stinking sewer pipe ready to die, die for what? So boot lickers like you can reign over the planet." Becker caught his breath. "The worst part of it is I am just as guilty. Every patrol, I take boys to sea. When I went to sea, I learned how to reef a sail, tie a bowline. What do I teach? I teach death. I give lessons in killing other young men. Does that make them acceptable Germans?"

"It is their duty to the Fatherland," Gerlach hacked.

"Duty," Becker snarled. "They cheer when our torpedoes sink a tanker or freighter. They paint flags for each ship we send to the bottom. They don't see what I do in the periscope. I see other young men-British, American, and Russian-arms torn off, legs gone, and some on fire. They fall into the ocean choosing to drown rather than burn. There will be no victory and us? We will just be a statistic."

Gerlach could not speak, the arrogance drained from his face. "Germany will lose this war. You talk of the things you have seen," Gerlach swallowed hard. "That is nothing compared with what I have witnessed."

Becker held up his hands. "I don't want to know."

Gerlach turned to face to Becker. "That's the problem," Gerlach's voice cleared. "Soon the whole world will know." Gerlach gagged again turned, and spit. "When that happens, Germany will be erased from humanity. Just like us," Gerlach whispered. "Germany is doomed. You should be grateful you won't live to see it."

"Grateful?" shouted Becker. "If there were any way to save my ship I would."

Gerlach stared, "Captain, there will be no Germany no home, nothing."

"I can't believe that. I have something you don't."

Gerlach looked puzzled. "What would that be?"

"Hope." Becker reached down and tore the party emblem from Gerlach's coat. "Not all Germans think like you. Most are good people. You think they hate the British, or Americans. Your ideals feed on hate. Hate is nothing to run a nation on. Hate for a better world?"

Gerlach rested his head against the woolen blanket. Becker rose to his feet, and turned to go.

Gerlach's eyes shot open, "captain."

"What?"

"You are right."

Becker laughed.

"Captain you don't understand. There is hope."

"Maybe in the next life, but I won't be seeing you there."

Gerlach coughed. "Maybe *I can* get us home."

Becker moved next to Gerlach and sat down.

"How?"

"You wanted to know about my mission? Gerlach coughed. "Germany is going to lose. Everyone knows that-some knew it from the beginning. Some think Hitler is way ahead of his time."

Becker looked puzzled.

"This mission was part of an experiment to preserve Hitler until the world was ready for his ideas."

Becker's eyes narrowed. "What?"

"Yes, it's true." Gerlach took a deep gurgling breath. "Have you ever heard of an animal called the water bear?"

Becker shook his head.

"A very tiny animal, so small you need a microscope to see it. These animals live in moss, under rocks, in trees, mud-everywhere, even on this boat, there are millions. They may be the oldest living creature on earth. What makes these animals important is that they never die," Gerlach said. "If you take a water bear and freeze it, the animal will shut its body down. If you starve it of oxygen, the same result. We even placed a water bear in boiling water and the little bastard just draws in its legs and goes to sleep. Breathing, heartbeat, all stop. Even frozen without air or boiled, the water bear reanimates when conditions returned to normal."

Gerlach went on. "A doctor in Munich discovered he could remove a protein that provides the water bear with this talent. Better yet, he discovered how to make the same protein."

"And used those Russians for guinea pigs," Becker mumbled.

"Yes."

Becker's features turned hard. "So when the ice camp was blown away you were to destroy all evidence of the experiment?"

"Yes."

"Are you saying that our cargo is that protein?"

"The code name for the operation is The Forever Project-not just the protein. It is combined with agents that assist an organism's survival." Gerlach beamed. "Our scientists created a gas that floods the lungs, blood, and tissues of the subject." Gerlach stopped to clear his throat. "A dog was placed in a solid block of ice for six months. The animal had no food, no water, and no air. When the ice thawed, it seemed no worse. No tissue damage."

"So this was to be the first test on humans?"

"One of the first," Gerlach replied. "We had other items we wanted to look at also."

Becker interrupted, "What if a person were injured and then frozen?"

"As long as they are not dead such as your navigator, he would remain just as he is until doctors could assist him. Once exposed to the gas cold triggers the reaction. The gas does not freeze the subject. It prompts hibernation-more correctly-we call it suspended animation. Other additives in the gas protect tissues, organs, and such."

"What if these tests succeeded?"

"If my report came out positive, leaders of the Third Reich would have been smuggled here."

Becker's jaw dropped, "In the name of God, why?"

"Dr. Goebbels convinced the fuehrer the time is not right for him, too many Jews, Communists, too many weak links in the chain. Why should Germany fight the war? Therefore, Hitler was to be placed into suspended animation. Once the leadership is hidden away, Himmler will sue for peace."

"Sue for peace? Then we will have lost."

Gerlach sat back, "Only the battle not the war."

"You don't make sense."

"How long do you think the Americans and the Russians can get along?"

"I have no idea."

"Let's just say that after peace is in place, there are those whose duty it is to help start a new world war."

Becker's mouth gaped. "What?"

Gerlach shook his head. "Oh yes, this war is just the beginning. From the ashes Germany will rise again."

"What if you reported the gas didn't work?" asked Becker.

Gerlach waved his hand. "Then the war would end and Germany will be wiped from history."

"This could save my crew. Nevertheless what would the lives of fifty men mean to the world?"

Gerlach pulled himself upright. "You have to decide."

"If this does work what will you do?"

"I told you; you were right."

"What does that mean?"

"This boat these men, this is Germany. We seem to kill more of our own than the enemy."

Becker's head dropped. "Maybe your bomb was the answer."

"No captain. The Forever Project is a gift."

"A gift?" asked Becker.

Gerlach again leaned back and shut his eyes. The bruises around his neck darkened. "That depends on you."

U-761's commander looked around. The U-boat's batteries held no more charge. The air grew worse. In dark corners, the film of ice grew to white sheets. A strange quiet hovered inside the U-boat like the silence in a tomb *U-761* was dying.

4
THE FOREVER PROJECT

*"A man is no sailor if he cannot sleep when he
turns in, and turn out when he is called."*

R H Dana Jr.,
Two Years before the Mast,
xxxiv, 1840

AUGUST 21, 1944

"How do we use the gas?" Becker asked.

Gerlach rolled his head slowly. "Time is against us. The men need to make themselves insulated from the steel hull. They need to eat as much as they can. When you are ready put one canister in each compartment and turn the handles."

"That's it?"

"Sorry it's not more technical."

"Ulrich," Becker shouted down the narrow passage between the two electric motor controllers.

"Yes Captain?"

"Give me your knife."

Ulrich handed his folding knife to Becker.

"Have officers and petty officers mustered in the torpedo room," Becker ordered.

"Yes, s-sir," he stammered.

"Hurry, man," Becker urged.

"Sorry, sir," Ulrich disappeared into the dark passageway.

Becker eyed the injured *Sturmbannführer*. "I hope you are being honest with me."

"You really have no choice," Gerlach sputtered.

"You know what this crew thinks of you. Any tricks, and I will let them tear you apart. Hold still."

Becker sliced the thick cord binding Gerlach's hands.

Gerlach's hands fell into his lap. His head shot back as he tried to lift his numbed arms.

"Can you walk?"

"Help me get up," Gerlach groaned.

Becker leaned over and took a handful of Gerlach's black parka top. Both winced as Becker pulled him to his feet.

At the torpedo room hatch, Becker helped Gerlach drag his body through. His officers and men stood like specters in the fading light.

Becker straightened the white cap on his head and let out a long slow breath of the heavy foul air. "Men, we have a plan."

Becker heard the men shift their feet as they tried to get closer. Becker saw them sway and stagger as their oxygen-starved minds slowed.

"Captain," a voice called. "What's he doing here?"

Becker squinted into the gloom of the U-boat searching for the owner of the voice. "I need you to listen. The *Sturmbannführer* will explain."

Gerlach turned to the shadow-like faces. He coughed again as his damaged throat struggled to speak.

Ten minutes later, the crew of *U-761* busied themselves with preparations. Becker assigned Volker to set the gas bottles one to each compartment. Baldric would prepare the men, issue each sheets, blankets, assign them a bunk, or place on the deck.

Berdy came around offering thick slices of sausage or cured salty pork. Most ate willingly some had to be ordered.

In the engine room, Edel and his machinists shut fuel valves and drained the cylinders of remaining fuel in order not to gum up the engines. They drained the water jacket expansion tank. If water froze inside the tank, it would rupture, leaving the engines unusable.

Roth hid the code machine and books.

Just outside his tiny cabin, Becker turned to Gerlach. "What about you?"

"I don't know." Gerlach looked at the deck, then to the overhead.

"Roth has you a place on the wardroom bench. Go."

Becker watched the SS man leave then pulled his thin curtain shut. Once comfortable he turned on his side. Next to his bunk, the yellow green canister stood braced between his bunk and the lower part of the little writing table. "Roth," he called.

"Yes, sir," came the reply out of the dark.

"Pass word forward and aft to release the gas."

"Release the gas," Roth bellowed.

All along the interior of *U-761,* voices distant, weak, and ghostlike repeated the words. Becker found the knob on the bottle next to his bunk. It took some force, but the knurled knob slowly rotated. Becker heard a faint hiss. Strange warmth filled his body. His eyes grew very heavy. Becker wrapped the wool blanket around his head and face.

The hissing continued in the darkness of the U-boat. Becker thought he heard singing or something. He could no longer tell and did not care.

His mind drifted back to Ada. He wondered what she was doing at this second. He realized how much he missed and loved her. She deserved a chance at life, a happy life with their child. Just as his eyes closed, he smiled. His mind again played the same words repeatedly, our child.

One by one, the men of *U-761* drifted off. In an hour, they had all slipped into their own dreams or nightmares. The next day the interior of the submarine reached the same temperature as the ice that trapped her.

In 1947, the ice shifted enough to move the U-boat three feet to the side, putting the submarine on a more or less even keel.

As the new millennium came the old ice bashed into a mile

long plate of ice. Cracks opened wider. Heat from the summer sun managed to warm the hull only a few degrees melting most of the ice from her upper works. A decade after that the world changed.

5
RUMORS AND REVOLUTION

*"Every society is pregnant with revolution and
force is the handmaiden of revolution."*

Karl Marx, 1818–1883

"ANY MORE INFORMATION?" ASKED Admiral Malroy, Chairman of
the Joint Chiefs.

"No sir. Just what's here," the watch officer answered.

"I'll brief the secretary, see what he says," Malroy breathed out
slowly. "Is the boss in?"

"He's at the White House."

"Great. Today just keeps getting better and better."

"Want me to wait here," the officer asked.

"No get on the horn to Fort Meade. If anything else pops up
let me know."

"Yes sir.

"Have the car brought up."

Admiral Malroy looked at his watch. "Damn, five-thirty already.
I won't get to the White House until seven." Malroy pulled out his
cell phone, hit the first button. "Margie," he said in his slow Texas
drawl. "Listen, I'm running late again."

The black four door made good time along the beltway slowing only occasionally for construction. "Not much traffic tonight."

"No sir," the young enlisted driver agreed. "We missed most of it."

As the exit approached, the car slowed, gracefully curved from the highway onto the exit ramp.

Soon the gates of the White House rose. The petty officer at the wheel made a perfect stop at the security guard's feet. The driver remained motionless-almost robot-like.

Malroy pushed the button, lowering back window. The cautious guard peered in, then snapped to attention, and saluted. He waved the driver on.

The guard stepped into the guardhouse and picked up his phone. A second passed. "This is gate one. Chairman of the Joint Chiefs is here."

When Malroy stepped from the car, the Assistant Director of National Security met him. "Bill, what the hell is going on?"

"Where is SECDEF?" Malroy asked.

"Oval Office, They're waiting on you."

"Oval Office?" asked the admiral.

"Yeah, Bill. This thing is taking on a life of its own. We don't even know if it's real."

"What's State saying?"

"Nothing, we can't get through to the embassies."

Malroy stopped. "What?"

"See what I mean? This just didn't happen. It was planned and damn well executed."

Malroy shook his head. "Okay we have to keep this low key for now."

Hayes chuckled, "Low key? It's gonna hit the fan and fast."

"Damn." Malroy stepped off again his pace quickened.

Just outside the Oval Office, the president's personal secretary greeted Malroy.

"Hello admiral. The president is waiting. Please go in."

Malroy nodded as the door to the Oval Office opened.

The president forced a grin as he looked up. Admiral Malroy could see the fatigue in his eyes. He looked older than he had last year. Last year, the long shot republican candidate all energy and drive, now he seemed weighed down by the burden.

The secretary of defense rose from his chair opposite the great oak desk. "Jim, glad you're here."

"Thank you," replied Malroy.

The president stood, "Jim, what's happening?"

"What we know is at 3 a.m. Moscow time units of the 173rd Armored Guards took over the Kremlin. Shortly after, all television radio everything went off the air."

"At the same time?" asked the president.

"Within ten minutes."

"What about military frequencies?" SECDEV asked.

"They still operate, but what we get doesn't make sense."

"Like what," asked the president.

"Crazy really, lots of name-calling among ships of the Northern Fleet. Fighters, bombers you name it flying to and from bases in no order and without authorization. As I see it there is no command and control."

The president shut his eyes. "What does it mean?"

The Chairman of the Joint Chiefs paused. "Sir, we think this is a coup. We believe this is the first stage of an attempt to rekindle the Soviet Union."

The president dropped heavily into his leather chair. "What do we do gentlemen?"

"Mr. President, we have very little information now. To do anything might provoke a response we don't want."

"True, but if we do nothing we could get sucker-punched."

Malroy's eyes met the president's. We have few options right now."

"Jim, give me those options."

"We can move naval units over the next week to within range of most major Russian bases." Malroy started.

"What if this thing goes to hell before then?"

Malroy chose his words carefully. "We do have forces capable of a response."

The president placed his arms on the desk. "What if we need to hit them first?"

SECDEV lowered into a chair opposite the president. "Sir, this coup or revolution is internal. Why get involved? Besides, Kenshanko might have enough force to put it down."

"Kenshanko is a puppet. He was part of a deal." The president leaned into the high backed chair. "I played a bad hand."

"Jesus," Malroy sighed.

"What are my options for a limited conventional first strike?" asked the president.

"Sir?" managed Malroy.

"What if I needed to remove the new leadership?"

The president's eyes narrowed. "Gentlemen Russia is now the largest, most well-armed Mafia in the world."

"What?" Malroy shuddered.

"You mean Paslav?" SECDEV asked.

"Yes." the president answered.

"Can someone fill me in?" Malroy asked.

The president folded his hands. "My campaign was based on making a safer America, by making a safer world. The Middle East will always be a problem. China is more or less playing along. The only wild card was Russia. Too many loose ends left over from the Soviet days."

"Who is Paslav?" Malroy asked.

As the president opened his mouth, the intercom buzzed. "Excuse me," he punched a button to activate the intercom. "Yes?"

"Mr. President, FBI Director on line one, sir."

"Put him through." The president picked up the receiver. "Fritz?

When, who found them? Okay, what about the UN? Can we keep this quiet until I tell you otherwise? Okay, let me know." He slowly placed it back on the hook.

"What's happened now?" SECDEV asked.

The president filled his lungs then slowly let out a long breath, "Russian Ambassador Deniska and his family were found dead."

"Where," Malroy grunted.

"His house in Arlington, the housekeeper found them."

"Was the housekeeper one of ours?"

"I don't know. I hope so. This whole thing is going to go sky high soon."

"What the hell is going on?" Malroy demanded none too formally.

"Jim, you're a military man," SEDEV answered. "We may have

to dust off our scenarios. This may happen or it may not, but truth is I don't have a clue."

He raised his head. "Mr. President, I recommend we move to DEFCON 3."

Malroy didn't believe it. Five hours ago, his biggest worry was supplying five new tanks to a unit in Iraq.

The president rose and stepped to the window. "Move to DEFCON 3."

Malroy nodded. "We will activate the war room here, Mr. President."

"Gentlemen, you have a lot to do, I have some calls to make."

Ten minutes after leaving the oval office the military might of the United States began to stir. Responding to coded messages American submarines crept up from their hiding places. At mid-west air bases, B-1 and the stealthy B-2 bombers readied. United States Army divisional commanders recalled troops. Supply sergeants shuffled thousands of requests, trucks fueled, cargoes loaded.

Within three hours, a division of Marines boarded the amphibious assault ship USS Tarawa.

Other warships, sleek destroyers, and larger deadly Ticonderoga class cruisers from bases around the world moved to sea.

Miles above earth, satellites moved to new locations. Highly sensitive lens refocused and transmitted streams of data.

THE WAR ROOM
OCTOBER 12TH

Reports came through, problems addressed and decisions made by generals, admirals and their staffs.

At the head of it all Jim Malroy sat quietly letting his team do their jobs. Information he needed appeared on his computer screen. Malroy reviewed it and either saved the information to the main frame or sent it to the hundred other screens in the pale light of the war room.

"Admiral?" a voice called.

Malroy turned to his left. A young Air Force captain stood before him. "Yes?"

"Sir, there is a scheduled launch of a TITAN 3 booster on the eighteenth."

"Payload?" he asked.

"New type of ice mapping bird used to estimate ice melting at the pole."

"Has it been on the boards?"

"Yes sir, three months now. All notifications have been sent and acknowledged."

"What time is the launch?" Malroy asked.

The young officer looked at his watch "17:35 Zulu."

"That makes it eleven-thirty here. Tell Cheyenne Mountain to keep their eyes open."

"Will do, sir," the captain nodded.

"Okay," Malroy announced to the room. Let's see where we are. I want a brief in ten minutes."

Ten minutes passed and the room hushed. The Joint Chiefs sat at their respective places around the oval table, Malroy at the head.

"Gentlemen," Malroy started, "I have just as much information as you." Malroy opened his briefing notebook. "Army, where are we?"

"Admiral, the Army is prepared to deploy three divisions of mechanized infantry from Germany. These divisions include a battalion of heavy armor, along with artillery support. Another three divisions are being readied for deployment and can be on the ground in seventy-two hours."

"Good," responded Malroy.

In turn, each branch commander reported the readiness of the immense fighting power of the United States.

After the chiefs finished, Malroy looked around the room. "Ladies and gentlemen, I need each of you to think outside the box. We don't have a clue where this is going."

"You think there will be a move against NATO?" An Air Force general asked.

"Anything is possible," Malroy shrugged.

The deputy chief pushed back from the table. "We'll contain a ground action for 48 hours, after that…" his voice tapered off"

"I hope so," "I sure as hell hope so."

6

AMBUSH

"The sea is his and he made it."

Psalm XCV

RUSSIAN AKULA CLASS, CLASS NUCLEAR
ATTACK SUBMARINE K-157 (VEPR)
SIXTY-EIGHT NAUTICAL MILES NORTH WEST OF
THE KOLA PENINSULA
OCTOBER 15TH

IN HIS STATEROOM, CAPTAIN First Rank Valerik Danyankov watched the digital numbers of the depth gauge move between five and seven meters. Lord over K-157 and everyone in her Danyankov ruled without pity. At 6 foot 3 inches, Danyankov's powerful build was as intimidating as the permanent scow chiseled on his slender face. His pale eyes could in an instant turn cold as the sea surrounding *Vepr*. If not for his closely cropped reddish blonde hair, Danyankov was the picture of an ancient Spartan warrior.

Like her commanding officer, *K-157* was powerfully and purpose built. Her streamlined hull parted the frigid azure hued sea without effort and in total silence. Graceful lines flowed from her hull and sail into one sinister shape, a perfect underwater killing machine. Perfect except for one critical flaw.

Danyankov checked his watch. It should only take forty-five seconds to acquire the satellite thirty to query for traffic, and another twenty to download messages.

Fifty meters above *K-157*, the sun made its final appearance for the day. Shafts of glowing orange fanned across the gently rolling waves. *Vepr* eased up from the depths into the fading light. As she neared the surface the submarine's receiving antenna pierced the waves.

Seconds later the small speaker next to his desk hissed with static. "Captain, we received orders from Fleet Command. Also in receipt of emergency messages," replied a calm voice.

"I'm coming." Danyankov growled He made his way down the cream-colored passages as nervous eyes followed him.

"Captain in control," a voice shouted when Danyankov entered *Vepr*'s command center. "Contacts," he asked?"

"No, Captain," replied the watch officer.

"Remain at this depth," he ordered.

"Yes sir."

Danyankov moved aft until he stood at the heavy steel door leading to the radio room. A digital lock with illuminated red letters reading, ENTER CODE glowed up at him as his thick fingers stabbed at the numbered buttons. The lock accepted his code with a faint click.

The radio room was bathed in blue light, designed to preserve the radio operator's night vision. Inside the compartment, the temperature fell. The vast array of communication equipment radiated heat, which could damage delicate circuitry if over heated.

Two men, an officer and a technician, operated the radio room. The officer stood and held out a covered clipboard to the captain.

"All messages on board," the radio officer said.

"Took you long enough," Danyankov snarled.

"Captain, atmosphere…"

"I don't need excuses." Danyankov hissed.

The radio officer's eyes fluttered, "Yes, sir."

"Line up for transmitting," Danyankov ordered.

Danyankov sat at the small folding table hinged to the left of the mast control levers. He opened the folder. His eyes studied the received messages.

From: Commander 7th Submarine Squadron
Northern Red Banner Fleet
To: Commander Submarine K-157 (VEPR)
SUBJECT: CHANGE OF GOVERNMENT

1. A change of leadership has occurred. As of 0452 Moscow time, President Kenshanko was removed from office by force of arms. 2. I expect each officer and crewmember to continue serving the motherland.

Fleet Admiral
Sergi Litoniska, Commander Naval Forces

Danyankov carefully folded the message, tucked it neatly in a sealed recess within the folder. He took the next message. His eyes moved quickly over the lines and he smiled.

(URGENT AND MOST SECRET)
To: COMMANDER SUBMARINE K-157 (*VEPR*)
From: COMMANDER SUBSQD 7
SUBJECT: RETURN TO PORT
1.) Submarine *K-157* is to make best speed to return to port. Caution is urged along *K-157*'s track at point 34.54. It is believed a friendly submarine has turned rogue. At 1922 local, the frigate *GROZYYASHCHIY* was torpedoed and sunk with the loss of all hands.

Sevenov Sends

"Watch Officer," Danyankov bellowed. "Transmit an acknowledgment."

"Yes, s-sir," he stammered.

Vepr's captain rose gingerly from the small chair. Danyankov stepped to the door. "You have two minutes."

The officer continued setting the teletype, sweat pouring down his young round face. He jumped when the door slammed behind him.

One minute and eighteen seconds later, Danyankov stood in the command center. The silence was that of a tomb. "Sonar," a microphone mounted in the maze of wire runs and pipes in the control overhead picked up his voice.

"Sonar," answered a voice through a speaker near the captain's chair.

"We will return to patrol depth in the next two minutes. Get the array deployed."

"Yes sir."

"Navigator, when we are at patrol depth, set a course for Chart 1–5–6, and put us in a modified patrol box."

"Aye sir," replied the navigator.

"Radio, what is status of the message?" Danyankov's voice not loud but still abrasive.

"Ready to transmit," came the voice over the speaker.

Danyankov crossed his arms. "I want officers in the wardroom in five minutes."

The sun sank into the dark Arctic Ocean when *Vepr* left the surface. The Akula's massive hull faded as her deep blue gray matched the surrounding sea. Atop the rudder a teardrop-shaped pod, roughly the size of a small bus held the sonar-towed array. Inside the pod, a cable reel rotated, extending a thin black wire. Along the wire tiny but highly sensitive hydrophones listened. At nine-hundred meters, the entire array trailed behind the Russian submarine. Without noise from her the hull and machines the digital array could detect and classify any surface or submerged object within fifty kilometers.

At the steering and diving control station, the young control operator kept the boat on depth and level by gentle adjustment to the stern planes. He studied the angle indicator and depth gauges. His thumbs rested on tops of the black handles that directed the stern planes. He found it harder to keep the boat from rising. The control handle seemed a bit sluggish. He looked to his left at the servo indicator. Its green glow meant the system operated normally. He checked the plane's angle indicator, saw the planes move up very slowly. He countered the rise with a small thumb wheel that controlled trim tabs on the trailing edges of the stern planes.

Hydraulic pressure gauges read normal. Still, the planes wanted to rise, which usually meant someone left the automatic depth-keeping system engaged. The young operator opened the automatic depth-keeper cover saw the indicator lights out and the power handle in off position. Quietly, he shut the cover.

At midnight, *Vepr* reached the edge of the area where the rogue submarine was supposed to be hiding. Danyankov slowed to allow his sonar to search above and below a layer of warm water.

At 0300, *Vepr* was just above the thermal layer, ninety meters below the surface, when the towed array heard a faint noise off the starboard quarter.

"Contact," the operator called. His fingers adjusted the gain allowing the sound to flow to his trained ear. The blue dot-faint, but clear lay over the computer generated bearing lines on the screen.

"Bearing to new contact is 332 degrees, possible-submerged contact."

Again, the towed sonar operator let his fingers dance over the hundreds of buttons. "Sending the contact to class," he said as his finger touched the enter button.

Danyankov heard the report from his stateroom and was in the command center seconds later. "What is the bearing drift?" he growled.

"Contact is on the left, drawing right," answered the sonar officer.

Danyankov had put *Vepr* on target. "Give me a range."

"Estimated range based on signal to noise is 2000 meters."

"Narrowband classification," Danyankov barked.

"We hold 240 and 320 Hertz on that bearing. Contact classified as Russian built Type 877EKM diesel submarine.

"Ah," Danyankov hissed. "Diving command, five degrees, right rudder, new course is north."

If the other submarine detected *Vepr*, he would also change course.

"Contact remains on course 332, speed constant, no change in depth."

"Good, come to course 350," he barked. He closed the range and to put *Vepr* into a perfect position on the stern of the unwary submarine, code-named Kilo by Western navies

"What is the range now?"

"Range is closing, 1100 meters."

"Officer of the watch, man battle stations."

One minute and thirty seconds later readiness reports flowed into the command center. At two minutes, fifteen seconds, *K-157* was ready for combat.

Danyankov held course letting the range slowly close. As they approached, the conformal passive bow, sonar picked up the slightest sound coming from the target. Information on range, bearing, course, and speed entered into the fire-control computers and displayed on the screen of the weapon's control officer. Each time the bearing changed, new information fed into the waiting torpedoes.

Danyankov brought his submarine above the thermal layer at 175 meters since there was a possibility of the Kilo getting a shot off before she died. Positioned above the layer a torpedo directed at *Vepr* would be a poorly aimed bearing only shot. A thousand meters from the target Danyankov ordered two of her six torpedo tubes flooded. The outer caps swung silently open.

The silent contest neared its final act when a small warning light lit up next to the sonar officer. He punched two buttons, a two dimensional graphic of *Vepr* filled the screen. A tiny red lightning symbol appeared next to the port stern plane.

"Captain, self-noise monitor has alerted at the stern," The officer reported.

"What is it," demanded Danyankov.

The officer adjusted his screen. "Sounds like a grinding coming from the control surface. The noise is slight, no detection threat."

"Planesmen, use no angle," Danyankov ordered.

The stern planes locked in place with a hinge called the pintle. The pintle ran through the plane into the hull and linked to the yoke arm that operated the stern plane. Unknown to Danyankov, during fabrication of *Vepr*'s plane, molecules of sulfur remained embedded in the steel. When submerged in seawater the contaminated high carbon stainless steel started to break down. Sulfur formed hydrochloric acid that began a slow but effective attack on the surrounding steel. This attack both wore away the metal and changed the atomic structure into a base metal. Galvanic reaction took over. Two unlike metals fought for atoms. Seawater acted as a conductor, as the differing electric charges slowly ate the core of the pintle. The erosion spread to the bearing surface of the tube-like pintle.

As Danyankov maneuvered *Vepr* for her shot at the still unsuspecting Kilo, the last of the rotted steel pintle collapsed.

At 650 meters from the target, *K-157* launched her weapons. Both homing torpedoes left the tubes at over 40 knots. Two hundred meters later, the acoustic heads within each weapon switched on.

It was obvious the rouge submarines heard torpedoes leaving *Vepr*'s tubes. She suddenly went to full speed. In her wake, two noise-making decoys filled the sea with bubbles, hoping to hide the Kilo from the incoming torpedoes. The range was too short giving the noisemakers no chance of luring away the closing weapons.

As programmed, the first torpedo turned 40 degrees to the left, and pitched up until it pushed through the thermal layer. Noise of the fleeing submarine's wildly spinning propeller enabled the torpedo to lock. Just below the layer, the second weapon also had also picked up tonal information from the whirring of the Kilo's struggling electric motors. The first weapon closed the doomed submarine from the aft quarter. At 100 meters the warhead armed, and signaled the motor to go to full power. Now making fifty knots the distance closed to twenty meters. In the torpedoes nose electromagnetic sensors detected the targets steel hull.

It happened in a blinding flash. The expanding explosion generated a massive over-pressure that the hull of the Kilo could not stand. Death came quick as pressure from the explosion tore through the ruptured hull. Although not needed, the second torpedo detonated under the dying submarine' battery compartment.

Sections of the Kilo not vaporized by torpedoes shattered, into fist size chunks from detonations of the dead submarine's own weapons. From the center of the boiling angry ocean bits of the dead submarine rained toward the sea floor.

Vepr had turned and diving deeper when the stern plane pintle fell apart. With no guide bearing and no support, gravity caused the plane to droop. Hydraulic pressure could no longer move the sagging plane. A signal sent to the control valve required too much pressure to move the control surface. A separate signal went to the plane control station that caused the control panel alarm to flash a warning. When pressure in the systems spiked, another valve opened and emptied the fluid into the emergency reserve system. Automatically the plane control now shifted operating modes.

During the two-second delay, the wobbly plane slipped from the yoke assembly and jammed at a fifteen-degree dive angle.

In the command center, the planesman yelled his controls no longer responded. The automatic system engaged and again pressure built. The control surface jammed and twisted the control arm, which fractured then splintered like an old log. The emergency system, never designed for this emergency, continued to pressurize while the hydraulic lines swelled. One after another, the lines ruptured.

Atomized hydraulic fluid filled the engine room. With no

hydraulic pressure, the control surfaces flapped uselessly in the slipstream of water.

With no way to control the 12,000 ton, submarine *Vepr* heeled to the right, causing her nose to pitch down.

"All back emergency," Danyankov screamed.

"Emergency plane's control not working," shouted the watch officer.

Danyankov looked at the depth gauge. The digital numbers blurred past190 meters.

The propeller stopped, shuddered, and started in reverse.

"Captain," a voice shouted. "The array is out."

The engineer grew pale. "Hydraulic rupture in the engine room," he yelled above all the other noise, "Permission to activate fire suppression?"

"Activate fire suppression," he barked.

"The array," a voice shouted.

Vepr backed over the array. Like a giant bobbin, the long wire wound its way around the screw as the submarine reversed.

"Jettison the cable!"

The sonar officer activated the release mechanism, but the array wrapped tighter around the spinning propeller. As the end whipped, it lodged against the hanging stern plane. It held tight. Again, the propeller shuddered and stopped. *Vepr* had no propulsion, no way to steer or control her angle. Pressure on the hull grew and she picked up speed as she dove toward the bottom.

Inside the Akula men held on to what they could. The angle increased to twenty-five degrees.

Anything not attached or restrained crashed to the decks. The falling submarine passed 210 meters. "Fire emergency ballast system blow forward trim five seconds then open vents by hand," Danyankov ordered.

In the ballast tanks, gas generators fired. Water flashed to steam driving the remaining water from the tanks. Mechanics stood by to operate the forward vents when the angle of the ship reduced. As the water left the main ballast tanks, *Vepr* grew lighter. The descent slowed and the angle eased.

"Open forward vents," Danyankov ordered as the bow reared up.

With the tank vents now open massive bubbles of air boiled from the submarine. Her ballast tanks now empty, K-157 lifted toward the surface.

"Surface contacts?" Danyankov shouted over the sound house-sized bubbles.

"Sonar is blanked out, I can't hear a thing," responded the sonar officer.

Twenty seconds later, *Vepr* broke the surface. Her hull heaved itself clear of the ocean, only to fall back again with a thunderous smack.

There in the moonless cold night she bobbed in the slight swell. Shaken men went about repairing what they could.

"Radio to captain," answered a voice over the speaker, "Ready to transmit our action report."

"Good," responded Danyankov. "Come up on clear voice from the satellite. Tell them we need a tow and an escort."

7

WORLD AFFAIRS

*"Which of you intending to build a tower
sitteth not down first and counteth the cost
whether he have sufficient to finish it?"*

Luke, III, 5

SATELLITE NEWS TODAY (SNT) interrupted the eleven-forty weather report with breaking news. The attractive weather reporter's pleasant face switched to the news desk. A stern faced anchor sat before the camera with the proper air of seriousness. "We have a breaking story just in to SNT. Earlier today in what can only be called a coup, Russian President Kenshanko was removed from office by military force. We are still trying to get more information on this story. We have some video we can show you."

The screen showed shaky images of Russian T-80 tanks rolling along on an unknown highway on the outskirts of Moscow. The scene then cut to pictures of droning HIND attack choppers nervously darting across the gray sky.

The video faded and the anchor looked into the camera. "We have now on the phone our Moscow correspondent Dale Shevley. Dale, can you fill in any details?"

"Brent, can you hear me?" a voice asked.

"We can hear you, Dale. What can you tell us?"

"This is a scene right out of 1917. Russian forces have taken over the Kremlin. Tanks are inside the walls and gates are blocked. Earlier we heard small arms and tank fire. The shooting is sporadic now.

I can see the top of the Kremlin, and yes-yes, the red flag with the hammer and sickle now flies at the flagstaff. I am sure it is the flag of the Soviet Union."

"Dale, have you talked with anyone in government?"

"We have not been able to move far from the hotel until now. Streets are empty of people and traffic. We will try to get more on this when as it develops."

"Thank you, Dale. We now have Pam Brenner, our associate in London."

Again, the screen flashed to the attractive yet business-like face of long time reporter Pam Brenner.

"This is indeed a revolution. Governments of Latvia, Georgia, Belarus, and Russia have been overthrown by military force. Fighting was intense earlier, but now there is a strange quiet. I'm getting word that a military spokesman in Latvia is declaring his country and Russia are merging."

"Pam, what does this all mean?" The anchor asked.

After a pause in the satellite transmission Brenner continued. "Dale, for years the nations of the former Soviet Union have struggled with capitalism and free market. Crime is rampant, and living is hand to mouth at best. All the signs point to a rejection of Western ideals. It looks like the Soviet Union has returned."

The image flashed back to the news desk. "Thank you, Pam." He turned toward another camera. "It is unclear what this means to the world and to the United States. One thing we can be sure of, this news is not what the administration needed right now. We will have more as the day goes on. This is SNT."

IRAN

In Tehran, the revolutionary ruling council discussed the matter of the new Soviet Union. This Russian affair could go two ways. If the United States suddenly found itself distracted by a war with Russia, the way could open for Iran to join its brothers in Iraq. The dream of one holy Islamic nation could come true. Surely, the United States would have its hands full and no desire for two wars at the same time. Conversely, Russia would be hungry for oil. Tehran had a good working relationship with Moscow, but this new leader might see the American weakness and take the oil. That scenario would place Iran in the uncomfortable position of asking help from the United States. Still this was at most a setback for Iran. She had her own plans.

PYONGYANG, NORTH KOREA

The Great Leader reviewed his options and strike plans. Generals sat nervously hoping that this mad man would let this crisis pass. Unfortunately, the Great Leader went further. North Korea possessed two missiles capable of hitting the West coast of the United States with 25 megatons each. A strike on Bremerton, Washington, or San Diego, would cause a devastating blow to the Pacific military might of the United States. Destroy Bremerton with its nuclear missile submarine base and San Diego home to American Naval and air combat units. The Great Leader hypothesized with most of its Pacific assets turned into radioactive ashes America would not retaliate. The Americans would want to protect what was left should the Russians get out of hand. A wounded America so weakened would do little to stop an invasion of the South. Why stop at South Korea? Maybe now would be the time to extract a long sought revenge on the Japanese.

From hidden mountain caves, mobile launchers emerged. The heavy trucks had no lights, and no markings to identify their purpose or cargo. Upon leaving their secure underground facilities, the launcher vehicles split up. They crawled along shabby worn roads, to remote locations. Once on station the crews began fueling long-range nuclear tipped missiles.

BEIJING, CHINA

It rained when the Chinese met. The talks were heated and frank. Some members welcomed the new Russia and demanded China throws vast military support behind the movement. Other more practical thinkers called for no reaction. They reminded the war hawks that China was very much-though regretfully dependent on American trade. Any move that put that relationship at risk was financial suicide. Finally, the talks calmed and the council agreed China would sit the sidelines and see how the game played out. One quiet member reminded his fellow party members that a new Soviet

Union emboldened with victory might as before challenge China's rule of the Pacific. China went on alert.

United Kingdom

The House of Lords filled with shouts that afternoon. The Prime Minister reported on events and British reaction. Questions of blame and bad policy argued back and forth. Most knew that like the U.S., British markets would be at the mercy of news from Russia. Little headway was made during all the shouting, although England had already made some moves unknown to the general population.

From Faslane, Scotland, three of England's Trident armed submarines slipped quietly into the Firth of Forth. From Portsmouth and Plymouth, sleek warships of Her Majesty's Navy moved into the English Channel. Once cleared of the harbor, the ships divided into Hunter-Killer groups, one group sailed south, and the other north.

From air bases around the United Kingdom maritime patrol aircraft lifted from the runways. Airborne tankers followed ready to keep as many aircraft aloft as needed.

NATO Headquarters
Brussels

Stung by the lack of forewarning, NATO held an emergency conference. Each member nation placed what assets it could afford in the allied order of battle. Polish tank brigades rolled toward her border. Spain deployed her single aircraft carrier, and escorting frigates to guard the approaches to Gibraltar, lest a Russian submarine ambush supply or warships entering the narrow chokepoint. The United States redeployed the new aircraft carrier George H. Bush to an operating area south of Norway. Four battalions of Italian mountain troops mustered at air bases around Italy awaited orders. The German navy deployed to protect shipping lanes to and from the Baltic.

Lieutenant General Evgeni Moiseev strode to the great doors of the president's office. His boots still muddied, thudded with sharp reports on the worn marble tile. Guards at the door, attired in shoddy wrinkled suits, made from cheap wool stared under black heavy brows, their faces pocked and scared and hands, thick and powerful, hung at their sides.

"Tell your boss I need to see him," the general barked.

The guard to the right appraised the general and reluctantly took a walkie-talkie from his belt. "Moiseev is here."

"Send him in," a voice spoke back.

The man on the left opened the ancient door. "General."

Moiseev entered the office, the heavy doors clang shut behind him. The stench of Cuban cigars, and cheap cologne, filled his nostrils. The heavy smoke made the already dimly lit room even darker.

At the great desk sat Viktor Paslav, a tall stout man with deep kind eyes that betrayed a cold ruthless soul.

"General," Paslav smiled warmly. "How goes the war?"

Moiseev did not return the smile. "My units have control over most of the country. There was resistance in an area of Kiev, but nothing too troubling. Still we may have an issue."

"Oh?"

"The North is a concern. The army mostly does as it is told, same as the air force. The navy is another story. The Pacific Fleet is under control, but we have problems in the Kola."

Paslav's eyes narrowed. "What kind of problems?"

"A diesel submarine has refused to return. A frigate sent to find it was sunk. Fleet air is divided they do not know who to follow. Our biggest worry is the *Kuznetsov* is making for open water. Her intentions are unknown."

"This *Kuznetsov*, Is it a big ship?" asked Paslav.

Moiseev shook his head in disbelief. "It's an aircraft carrier, so yes it is rather large. She sailed with her escort last night. Two cruisers, three Udoly destroyers, and her supply ship."

"Umm," Paslav grunted. "Tell me, what does that mean?"

General Moiseev removed his hat. "That we have a hell of a lot of fire power loose."

"What will they do?" Paslav asked.

"I don't know. They could launch strikes at our supplies or our troops. I just don't know."

Paslav looked around the room. "Will they return to port as ordered?"

Moiseev scratched his pale forehead. "You have no idea what you're doing do you?"

Paslav's eyes narrowed and the smile faded. "General, I'm no politician or a military leader. I am a businessman. I surround myself with those who have answers. I thought you would be the man to handle my military affairs. So far, you have done the job. I wonder if you can carry it through."

"Don't threaten me," Moiseev hissed. "It was my tanks that got you here. Look out your window. Those tanks sitting in the yard have bigger guns than these thugs do. I am the one with my finger on the trigger."

"General, come now." Paslav smiled. "We are in this together. When it's all over, we're going to be very wealthy men."

Moiseev leaned over the desk, his arms rested on the antique wood, his face inches from Paslav. "I am not in this for money. I want my country back."

Paslav leaned back in the great chair. "General, *I am* in this for the money. Your patriotic notions mean little to me. In a few weeks, maybe a month, there will be a *free election* and I will step down. Of course the new president will be one who, shall we say, tends to overlook certain activities."

"Do you think the world is turning a blind eye to this?"

"What are you talking about?"

"You've set the whole planet on its ears. There are three United States aircraft carrier battle groups on the way. Oh, and those are also very big ships."

"This is none of their business," Paslav shouted.

"Well comrade, I suggest you tell them that," Moiseev laughed.

"You make a good point. I am the leader of Russia and I should speak for Russia," Paslav stood and stared at the line of T-80s just below the window. "So, what would you have me do?"

"Talk to the world. Tell them you are a man of peace. You had to commit to this to save Russia from corruption and financial ruin. You are a good liar you can pull this off. The longer you wait the more nervous people get."

"I have done nothing to anyone outside Russia."

Moiseev rubbed his temple. "Are you that ignorant? What you have done is upset the balance. "The West had an acceptable relationship with us. Of course, the relationship was one-sided. Nevertheless that is gone."

Paslav looked puzzled. "So the West is in it for the money also?"

"Money is the cause of most wars," Moiseev shrugged.

Paslav cocked his head. "War, you think this could lead to a war?"

Again Moiseev laughed. "I can guarantee it."

"Hmm, I see. I will make an announcement. Give them a smile."

"Why not hand carry, a message to the Americans?"

"That will not be possible," Paslav responded with ice in his voice. "Our ambassador was a weak link in my plans. He had second thoughts. He might have given us all up."

Moiseev took a deep breath. "So he is dead?"

Paslav raised his chin and loosened his tie. "Yes."

"You better have a silver tongue Paslav." The General shook his head. "If you are linked to killing the ambassador you lose all credibility," Moiseev let his words taper off. "Oh, I might also suggest you do more research on your victims."

"Why is that?" Paslav sighed.

"The ambassador was uncle to the commander of the *Kuznetsov* battle force."

A sudden look of fear crossed Paslav's face."

The general squared the cap back on his head. "I'll be looking forward to your announcement."

Paslav said nothing as Moiseev turned for the door. Moiseev stopped. "Oh, I almost forgot. Should anything happen to me, say some *unforeseen accident*, those tanks on the parade grounds have orders to crush you like an insect."

Paslav remained silent as the door shut. Even with the doors closed; those in the great office of power heard his boots thudding down the long marble hall.

Paslav returned to the seat. Others in the room stared at him, waiting for direction. The leader of the revolutionary Soviet state picked up his phone. "Get Troschinsky," he spoke into the mouthpiece.

"Colonel, I think maybe you are the man for minister of defense. Moiseev seems to be having second thoughts.

THE WHITE HOUSE
OCTOBER 16TH

The president was up before daylight. Around him, advisors waited his decision. An emergency meeting of the United Nations Security Council was to begin in three hours.

"We can't trust him," the president started. "This whole thing is a sham."

The national security advisor nodded his head. "I agree Mr. President but what are the options?"

Farther down the long table, the White House press secretary waved her hand. "Listen, if we don't say anything the folks over at the UN will have a field day. The offer seems reasonable. Everyone pulls their forces back."

The defense secretary spoke next. "Problem is Paslav has no idea of what he's doing. He is a thug, and using this to kill off other thugs. This revolution against crime and poverty makes good press. What we have to worry about is who really is in charge. The army may have been duped, but someone is using Paslav."

The president looked to the Secretary of State, "What does the world think?"

"Mixed sir, NATO has doubts. I have a feeling we may wind up with a new world order. All it will take is a mistaken border crossing, an accidental bomb release, or some Russian private taking a piss on the wrong side of the fence."

"Okay," the president sighed. We will officially accept the offer of a pull back of forces. I want open communications with Paslav. CIA and state get to work on finding out what is really going on."

8

FRIENDS AND FOES

"Set ye Uriah in the forefront of the hottest battle."

II Samuel, XI, 15

HER GRACEFULLY CURVED BOW lifted and fell in a moderate swell as *Kuznetsov* turned into the wind. Heeling slightly to port, the giant ship brought the fifteen knots of wind over her flight deck. Once steady on course, the shriek of jet engines pierced the evening stillness. One by one, *SU-25 Frog Foot* ground attack jets lifted from the carrier's deck. Once in the air the attack planes formed tight wedge-shaped formations of four aircraft. Three wedges formed, and began a slow orbit of the carrier.

Once the bombers were aloft stiletto shaped, fighters raced from the ski slope bow of the carrier. Like the *Frog Foots,* the fighter wing of SU-27 Flankers formed formations in curved defensive arcs. Twenty-six aircraft circled the carrier. The fighters rose to their stations at 18,000 feet. Once at altitude the fighters split into two elements.

One-hundred miles northwest of *Kuznetsov*, an American four-engine *P-3C Orion*, code-named ANVIL 23 hung in the sky.

In the cockpit, the pilot eased back on the throttles. "She checked the fuel status. " Good for another three hours."

"Slow circles to nowhere" replied the co-pilot.

She glanced out her side window as the sea and sky merged in shades of dark purple.

"Commander?" a voice called through her headset.

"Go ahead."

"Looks like, the carrier, just launched."

"Okay, people looks like we have some activity," she called into her throat microphone.

"Count is twenty-six fast movers on course 045 true."

"Roger that. What about classifying?"

"We have no detection of radar emissions. These guys are staying quiet."

"Stay on top of it, we don't need any surprises. Radio, send our data to LINK so TWEETY can see."

"Roger that Commander. TWEETY is now on line," answered another voice, with a deep southern drawl.

Six hundred miles from the lone *P-3, an E-3A AWACS* also circled. Code-named TWEETY the large jet was filled with highly sophisticated radar and communications equipment. Atop the fuselage, a twenty-foot diameter saucer slowly rotated, feeding raw data to various stations along the *AWACS* interior. TWEETY could monitor air traffic for a thousand square miles. At her present position just north of the Faeroes Islands, TWEETY scanned almost the entire North Sea. With ANVIL 23 sending a LINK, the AWACS could see even further.

"ANVIL 23, this is TWEETY," a voice came over the radio.

"Go ahead, TWEETY," the pilot answered.

"Roger ANVIL 23. We have good copy of your LINK."

"TWEETY, understand. Break. What is the situation?"

"ANVIL 23, we are analyzing."

Again, the *P-3* pilot keyed her microphone. "Roger TWEETY-ANVIL 23 out."

"Analyzing? Does that translate into We don't have a clue," the co-pilot asked.

"I'm afraid so."

"Commander," a voice almost screamed into her headset. "Ten boogies at seventeen miles, course 220. Fast fliers headed our way."

"Can you classify?"

"Negative Commander," answered the *elint* operator.

"Are they from the carrier?"

"No, these are larger aircraft. The contacts have increased speed. Wait. Now I have six more from the carrier," the radar operator suddenly sounded nervous. "One element has broken away from the carrier's first launch. New course of those aircraft is 310. They will intercept our track in three minutes."

"Patch me to TWEETY," she ordered.

"Hard to make contact, we're being jammed," the radio operator reported.

"Get on COMSAT, they can't jam that."

Seconds later the radio operator reported. "Okay we're on with TWEETY."

"TWEETY this is ANVIL 23."

"ANVIL 23, ANVIL 23, this is TWEETY we see. Maintain course and altitude."

"Classified," the male voice with the southern drawl, yelled. "New contacts are classified Land based *TU-160* bombers. Classification based on DOWN BEAT Radar."

"Bombers?" she asked. "They're going after the carrier," she shouted.

The male voice reported. "SLOT BACK radar just lit off."

"SLOT BACK?" she asked.

"Carried on *SU-27* and *MIG-29* fighters," the male voice reminded her. "Commander, they're lighting us up."

Neely pressed her microphone, "TWEETY this is ANVIL 23, we are being painted by SLOT BACK radar."

"ANVIL 23, this is TWEETY come to new course South, descend to angels 2," the voice directed.

The nimble *Orion* obeyed at once, turning in a graceful arc south.

Descending rapidly toward the ocean, the *P-3* was twenty degrees from her new course when the co-pilot screamed.

"Pull up, Pull up!"

"What is it?"

The answer showed itself a second later. The sleek razor-like shape of a *TU-160* bomber pulled alongside her. She looked over to her co-pilot. Another giant bomber rode the right wing. Leaning forward, she looked up. She let out a yelp as her eyes focused on the glowing exhaust of a third Russian bomber.

"We're surrounded."

"Commander BEE HIND gun control radar from the bombers has us."

"I can't maneuver," she announced. "TWEETY, this is ANVIL 23. I am surrounded by bogies."

"ANVIL 23, wait," came the reply.

"Wait, wait for what?"

"ANVIL 23, ANVIL 23, this is TWEETY, hang on. Norwegian F-16s have been scrambled."

"Commander second group of SLOT BACKS are painting the bombers," the ELINT operator announced.

"They're using us as cover," the co-pilot shouted.

"What?"

"The bombers hope no one will risk hitting us."

A long slow exhalation came over the intercom. "Commander I now hold PLATE STEER air search and targeting radar from the carrier." His voice rose in a higher pitch, "Multiple missile control radars just came on. Radars are high pulse mode. Believe these radars to be also from the carrier and two Kresta class cruisers."

"How far are we from the carrier?"

On this course we are forty miles."

"Okay these boys wanna fight it out, fine. I'm not sticking around. I'm going to slow down and nudge our way out of here," announced the thirty-two year old mother of two.

When her hands reached for the throttles, the missile warning alarm flashed.

Now the ELINT operator screamed, "Inbound missiles. Count is eighteen-no wait, six more. Too many to classify, some are from the carrier groups, most are air-to-air."

"TWEETY, this is ANVIL 23 we are under attack."

"ANVIL 23, this is TWEETY. Evade, evade."

A blinding flash lit the sky. A missile had found one of the bombers.

Her eyes widened as the sharp nose of the dying bomber lifted then tore from the fuselage. Flames shot from the decapitated body as the right wing crumbled then erupted in a fireball.

The turbo-prop bucked and swayed as the pilot fought to keep the *P-3* from colliding with the remaining bombers. Three great flashes again blinded her.

"Bombers have launched missiles," the ELINT operator yelled. "Based on radar these are classified AS-7 KERRY anti-ship missiles."

The bomber flying over the left wing banked away from the *P-3*, when it was hit with another huge explosion. One of the Flankers scored with an AA-11 ARCHER air-to-air missile.

The blazing jet rolled toward the *Orion,* She slammed the control column forward, as the burning plane passed fifteen feet over her head.

It was then the wounded Russian bomber tore apart.

Chunks of aluminum slashed into the *P-3*. Warning lights flashed. The right wing dipped. More explosions lit the sky around American plane. She heard a rush of air in the cockpit. Another flash lit the right wing. Fighting for control she looked over to see the entire right side of the cockpit gone, only the lower part of the co-pilot's body remained.

"Mayday, mayday," she screamed.

The roll continued until the *P-3* was almost on its back. The flaming wing folded back until it crashed into the tail severing the *Orion* in two. Another flash of light billowed as the fuel cells exploded. Her crew knew nothing more.

VITUS

"A man trusts his ears less than his eyes."

Herodotus, 484–424 B.C., Clio, I, 8

Twenty-four minutes after launch from the Kennedy Space Center, the payload section of the TITAN III booster carrying a new satellite separated into four sections. The satellite emerged and a second smaller rocket fired.

Three-hundred-twenty miles above the Arctic the new satellite named VITUS stabilized in a perfect geostationary orbit. Energy from the sun collected on thirty-foot solar panels feeding electricity to the satellite's hungry batteries. Deep inside VITUS's exterior shell a maze of circuits and components felt the tingle of the power from the sun. One by one, the satellite's operating and navigation systems came alive.

The Kennedy Space Center, Florida

Bored and yawning reporters from a few papers and two local stations waited just outside the launch control room. Determined to make the best of a lousy story they perked up when Flight Director Ted Rawlings approached the small podium.

A pretty, young reporter managed to get the first question. "Mr. Rawlings? I am Brenda Santos, WJSC-TV 9. Can you tell us what VITUS is about?"

"Of course, VITUS carries with her a new mapping system. This machine will show the Arctic in a way never seen before. We will be able to see in three dimensions, ice formations, ice movement, and thickness."

"Why is that important," Santos asked.

"VITUS will be a vital for weather forecasting, answering questions about global warming and just how old ice formations are."

"What does the word VITUS mean?"

"VITUS is named after an early explorer of the Arctic."

As a smiling, Rawlings answered the questions. Nelson Evers designer of VITUS was in the control room explaining to a Navy liaison how his creation worked.

"It is not only the hardware but an advanced software application to drive and control the pulse length thus causing a fan shape beam of laser light. The energy is the same, but the light pattern covers a wider area. When the laser hits the surface, it penetrates and expands. It's a matter of recording the wavelengths of reflected light, and computing those with the pulse length. The colors reflected indicate ice thickness. The information is processed and displayed in three dimensions on our printouts and at the same time overlaid on a virtual chart."

Evers looked at the control room clock. Mapping will start in about ten minutes. Solar panels are out batteries are almost at full charge."

The Navy liaison, a young commander nodded.

Eight minutes later Evers scanned his screen. "Okay, folks, this is it."

Around the room technicians monitored their screens and computers.

Evers took a deep breath, "In five-four-three-two-one, firing." Evers pushed the execute button.

In seconds, data flowed across the screen.

The display showed a perfectly modeled narrow strip of Arctic ice. Evers peered into the frozen ocean as if it were split down the center. On the screen shades of blue, orange and violet marked ice thickness to the millimeter.

"Look, the blue indicates one meter thickness all the way to 15 meters here," Evers bubbled. "Switch to a profile view," he ordered. A few seconds passed before the image changed. Evers gasped, "Look at this!"

The image showed the bottom of the ice to its surface. "This section of ice extends to eighteen meters. Look, you can see where ice plates slide under other plates."

Chuck Rawlings stepped up. "Nelson how big of an area is on the screen?"

Evers held up a finger. "Wait, let's see." He punched a few buttons. Numbers appeared next to the glowing image of the ice. "We have data on about fifty-eight square miles."

"Wow," exclaimed Rawlings.

"All right, I am moving the map grid to 12.32–584. Now, we wait so VITUS can focus."

His monitor showed the cursor move toward the new map grid. A green light indicated VITUS lined up and ready. "Here we go again in 5–4–3–2–1 firing, he announced.

New data flowed, and again an image of the ice projected onto the chart. "Nice picture Evers purred. " Looks like eighty miles."

From behind him, the Navy commander leaned over the screen, "What's that?"

"What is what?" Evers asked.

"That dark shape, there on the upper left side of the screen."

"Humm," Evers sighed "Looks like something blocked the light reflection. Here, let me magnify it."

The computer updated the requested information. A fuzzy image appeared-long and narrow tapered at each ends.

"Interesting," Evers said calmly. "It appears man-made." Evers pointed to his glowing model. "Only steel or iron could absorb or block light that way. If it were wood the image would show some light."

"Can you tell how long it is?"

Evers typed a function into the computer, numbers flashed across the bottom of the image. "I'd say anywhere from two to three hundred feet."

"What it is?"

Evers looked again. "No idea could be an old shipwreck, a lost whaler ... who knows?"

"Is there any way to tell where it is in the ice? I mean, on top or under the ice?"

"Sure just a second," moments later numbers alongside the image changed and filled empty places on the screen. "Uh, hard to tell, but I'd say it's under the ice."

The commander tilted his head, when his eyes widened with sudden realization He walked to Rawlings small desk. "Is there a secure phone I can use?"

"Sure," Rawlings smiled. "In the preparations area," Rawlings nodded to a door at the end of the room.

Thirty seconds later the commander was speaking with the watch officer at the National Security Agency.

"I have an image taken from the VITUS satellite. Sir, this bird snapped an image of what I think is a Russian boomer snuggled up under the ice, about 350 miles North of Bear Island.—yes sir I can hold."

The commander bit his lower lip. "Yes sir, I'm still here. Are you sure, we have accounted for all Russian SSBNs? Sir, this is a submarine no doubt about it. I think it may be a *Delta III*. I know the Russians agreed to pull back. Captain, I have high confidence in this image. We may be in the cross hairs of a first strike. The image sits right next to a good-sized polinya. Yes, captain. If this is a Russian boat, all she has to do is pop up and launch her missiles. Yes sir that will put me back at 22:30."

Three hours later, the commander touched down on a special runway at the West end of Dulles Airport. An hour later analysts at Fort Meade looked at the image. A half-hour later phones rang in Washington, D.C., Norfolk, Virginia, and Groton, Connecticut.

10
SECOND CHANCES

"He that ruleth over men must be just."

II Samual, XXIII

RAIN PATTERED AROUND THEM, as they stood silent at the head of the pier. Rear Admiral Burke Tarrent had a long history with this pier. Most of the boats he served on made their home here at one time or another.

The rain continued as mist slid from the surrounding hills into the Thames River. Soon sailors; line handlers from the surrounding submarines walked onto the concrete pier.

An officer appeared from the gloom his patent leather shoes splashing along the rain soaked pier. Captain Cavin T. Farmer stepped up and saluted. "Sir, the families have been briefed."

"Thanks Gav. Any problems?" asked Tarrent.

"No sir," Famer nodded. We have arranged for the body to be taken up the hill for autopsy."

Tarrent looked at the puddles around his shoes. "I want him released to the family as soon as possible."

"Of course," Farmer replied sadly.

"Damn it," Tarrent swore, "Of all things."

An ambulance pulled onto the pier.

"Master Chief?" called Tarrent.

"Yes, sir," Nick Bisetti answered.

"There are going to be lots of questions. Questions best answered by someone besides me."

"I know. I have it covered."

The mist thickened. Although just short of noon, a damp darkness crept around them. In the channel, the water seemed to evaporate as fog settled over it.

Out of the fog, USS Miami SSN 755 emerged. Two powerful tugboats tied with thick lines to her cleats gently nudged her through the narrow waterway. With short hoots from their whistles, the tugs expertly handled Miami's 360-foot length. Another short toot and the tugboat pushed the 6,900-ton submarine toward the pier. The second tug cast off the starboard side, reversed its engine, and drew astern. Once clear, its diesels rumbled as it moved forward to aid its sister.

From the curved deck, heaving lines snaked through the air. Those on the pier caught the lines and attached them to the mooring lines. Within minutes, Miami was home.

A crane lowered a dull aluminum brow to the sub's deck. A whistle blew. The ship's Ensign climbed to the tip of the flagpole, then slowly lowered to half-mast. The crew moved about rigging the topside for port. The men moved quickly and with purpose. They lashed canvases emblazoned with **USS *MIAMI* SSN 755** to the cold aluminum brow. Absent were the usual smiles and jokes when a boat comes in. With their tasks complete, the sailors disappeared back into the submarine. Only one remained, the Topside Watch .

Tarrent approached the young sailor with a thin smile. "Hello Petty Officer Barkley."

"Mornin' sir," Barkley noticed Bisetti and Captain Farmer. "Master Chief, Captain," he said with a nod.

Bisetti stepped forward and clamped the young petty officer on the shoulder. "You okay?"

Petty Officer Barkley looked down at his rain soaked shoes. "I been in the Navy three years and this is the worst day ever," Barkley said in his deep Boston accent. "He pinned on my dolphins."

"I know. Trust me, I know. He was engineer when I was on *Saint Louis*," responded the Master Chief.

"You need to see the XO?" Barkley asked.

"Yes, we do," Tarrent, answered.

Barkley picked up the microphone for the general announcing system or 1MC. "Submarine Group Six arriving," he announced. "Come aboard admiral. The officers and chiefs are in the wardroom."

"Thanks," Tarrent offered.

Bisetti and the Farmer followed Tarrent down the rain slick brow. At the narrow hatch aft of *Miami's* sail, the men lowered themselves into the submarine. After a ten-foot climb, they landed in operations compartment middle level directly behind the crew's mess. Chief of the Boat, Danny Norse waited for them.

"Hello admiral," Norse said and motioned for them to proceed.

"COB," Tarrent offered his hand, "Your guys did a great job bringing her in."

"Thank you, sir."

Tarrent walked forward. Master Chief Bisetti waited until the officers passed then gently tugged at Norse's arm.

"How's the crew Danny?"

"Pretty shook up but these guys will get through it."

"What the hell happened?"

Norse moved out of earshot of the crew's mess.

"We surfaced in a state four sea, pretty rough. Radar picked up a merchant at 11,000 yards closing our track. The Officer of the Deck maneuvered to open the range but the contact maneuvered toward us. We slowed, and damned if the contact didn't turn toward us. The OOD called for the skipper. Captain came out of his stateroom, and went up the ladder. About three rungs from the top, the boat took a big wave over the sail. I guess he slipped and fell. He was dead by the time Doc got to him."

"Jesus," exclaimed Bisetti.

"Doc did everything he could but the skipper's head was smashed."

"Okay Danny let's get this over with and put your people on the beach."

After meeting with the officers and speaking with crew, Tarrent returned to the pier. The crew of *Miami* came topside. Each officer, chief, and Sailor wore dress blues. They formed two lines from the weapons shipping hatch along the sail and off the brow ending at the waiting ambulance.

The flag-draped body of Commander Joshua K. Upman passed gently hand to hand along the submarine. Each member of the crew worked as a team to bring their skipper ashore for the last time.

As the body left the brow, Petty Officer Barkley sounded the ships bell. Four sharp but solemn rings echoed off the fog mist and rain. Barkley placed his mouth next to the 1MC, and pushed the button, "*Miami* departing."

The rain fell harder. A stiff breeze swept up the river and caused fog to swirl. It grew darker. Bisetti drove the white sedan. Admiral Tarrent and Captain Farmer sat in the back.

"Miserable day," remarked Farmer.

Tarrent stared out the window.

Captain Farmer looked toward Tarrent, "Admiral?"

"We have a problem," the admiral muttered.

"Yes, sir we do."

"I can't hand this mission to just anyone. Sending another boat won't work either, too many commitments too few submarines." Tarrent removed his hat.

We need someone with Arctic experience."

"That's a tall order these days we all but stopped going under the ice when the Russians cried uncle."

"The world changed. We are so caught up in shallow water operations, Special Forces delivery, and fifty types of specops. We forget the basics. How were we to know?"

Tarrent remained quiet. The car passed the Navy Exchange, eased around the corner, and headed up Hospital Hill road.

"There is one man," Tarrent said.

Farmer turned to the admiral. "You mean McKinnon?"

"He's qualified for command. I think he is still down the hill at Sub School. Teaching navigation last I heard."

"But Sir, I…"

Tarrent cut him off, "God knows he has time under the ice."

Farmer shook his head. "Admiral this mission …I mean this is dicey."

"I've known Grant McKinnon since he was a Junior Officer on *Pogy*. That's been what-twenty years?"

"But admiral," Farmer argued.

"But what," Tarrent growled.

"Isn't McKinnon *damaged* goods?"

"Yes he is," the admiral glanced at Farmer. "I'm the one who damaged him."

Basic Submarine Officer Training Building
Naval Submarine Base, Groton, Connecticut

Alone at his desk, Grant McKinnon pored over charts for the next day's class. A man of medium height, narrow build McKinnon would look at home in any environment, be it a corporate office, a little league ball game, or on the conn of a nuclear submarine. His high forehead and receding gray hair accented green eyes that though kind held a spark.

McKinnon swiveled in his chair. He could hear the faint rap of footsteps outside his office.

The petty officer on watch stuck his head in the door. "We're about to lock up sir."

Commander McKinnon looked at his watch. "19:30. Wow. Okay I'll be finished in a second."

"Thanks commander."

With his charts secured in a heavy steel safe, Grant McKinnon picked up his hat and keys. Outside his office, he checked the door, then turned and went down the steps to the Quarterdeck. The watch sat at his tiny desk the duty phone to his ear. McKinnon smiled and waved goodnight as he opened the door to the parking lot.

"Wait, commander," called the petty officer.

McKinnon turned and walked toward the watch.

"Yes sir, he's here." The petty officer said as he handed the phone to McKinnon, "For you, sir."

McKinnon put the phone to his ear. "Commander McKinnon."

Office of Admiral Burke Tarrent
Commanding Officer, Submarine Group 6

"Grant why haven't you ever called me a son-of-a-bitch?" Tarrent asked.

"Never thought the term fit," McKinnon answered.

"I sure as hell felt like one."

McKinnon frowned. "Drop it admiral. We've been down this road."

"Commander I need answers." Tarrent leaned back in his chair causing the springs to groan slightly. "Why did you stay in the Navy?"

McKinnon leaned forward. "Burke, what are you doing? There is nothing to forgive."

"Forgive? I'm not looking for forgiveness," Tarrent said softly.

"Then what," McKinnon responded.

"Why did you stay in? You knew you would never command."

"This is all I've ever known."

Tarrent shrugged, "That it?"

"Okay, listen, I stay because I wanted you to know you made a mistake. I respect the hell out of you and you made a tough call. When you pulled my recommendation for command, it was the wrong call. Hell Burke I wanted to you to know that for once in your life you were wrong."

Admiral Tarrent folded his arms across his chest. "Maybe I am looking for forgiveness."

"My wife and son were dead for three months before you told me. For three months you knew that my life would never be the same." McKinnon hissed. "What could you do?" he asked. "You remember where we were? Sitting on the bottom of the White Sea watching Russian boomers launch SS-N-20s. Was it worth it? I think so. Our Intel gave President Reagan what he needed. Brought the Russians to the table again, maybe I hope, made the world safer."

"I pulled your recommendation because if it had been me, I would have killed someone. I would have never been right-again. The Navy shrinks agreed. Trust me Grant it was not easy. I had to think of the crews and the fact you might carry around a thousand mega-tons of nuclear weapons. And believe it or not I did it for you."

McKinnon lowered his eyes. "I know that and I won't lie to you, Burke. It was hell, pure unending hell. The first year, I was a basket case. However, I managed. I never blamed you or the Navy."

Tarrent stood and put his coat on. "Now I'm the admiral again so listen up. I'm giving you *Miami*."

"Sir?" he managed to mumble.

"You are the only one I trust with *Miami's* next mission. Maybe it will make my record of good decisions perfect again."

"When?" asked McKinnon.

"We'll bury Josh Thursday. Monday morning, I want you on that boat. You sail on Tuesday."

"What will Admiral Jennings say?" McKinnon asked.

Tarrent chuckled. "Grant the president of these United States approved your orders three hours ago."

"How did you know I would accept?"

Tarrent's smile faded. "I don't remember asking you... This won't be easy Grant." He picked up his phone. "Gav I need you in here."

Captain Farmer stepped through the door, his left hand holding a chart his other held a plain leather briefcase.

"Commander McKinnon," Farmer smiled.

McKinnon returned the smile "Captain good to see you."

Farmer extended his hand. "Congratulations and well done." He reached in his coat pocket. Farmer handed Admiral Tarrent a small box covered in rich blue satin.

"First things first," Tarrent opened the box. "Commander Grant McKinnon, I take great pride in awarding you the Command Star. You are now duly authorized by the Chief of Naval Operations to command a warship in the naval service of the United States of America." Tarrent held up the star. "Grant this is long overdue." He pinned the gold five-sided star on McKinnon's shirt.

"Okay guys sit down." Tarrent motioned them to the chairs in front of his desk. "Now Gav let's show Grant what he signed on for."

Captain Farmer pulled an image from the briefcase. "Last night the VITUS satellite took this image."

McKinnon stared at the image. "I read VITUS only mapped ice?"

"That's what it was supposed to do. This was unexpected," responded Farmer.

"Unexpected but fortunate," Tarrent added.

"That's a submarine." His finger jabbed on the fuzzy image. "I thought the Russians agreed to pull back?"

"We know their track record for keeping promises," Tarrent grunted.

The new commanding officer of the *Miami* leaned close. "Too small for a Typhoon, maybe a Delta 1 or 2, I don't know … something's not right. It may be the angle but the shape isn't right for a boomer, not a Russian boomer anyway," McKinnon answered.

Farmer sat back, "If not Russian what?"

"Like I said, it might be the angle. We have any intel about this, maybe more shots from VITUS?"

"They all come out about the same. What has us worried is if you look she sits right next to a polinya."

"I see it now," nodded McKinnon. "Of course you've already gotten a count of the world's missile boats?"

"Everybody's accounted for."

"Maybe not," sighed McKinnon.

Captain Farmer slipped the image back into the briefcase. "We've plotted the location of that unknown. It's here." He pointed to the chart.

"Bad place for a boomer."

"Why is that?" Tarrent asked.

"It's at the edge of the Hopen Rise," he stated. "The Lofoten basin meets the rise exactly where our bogie sits. Noise transients would echo off the walls of the basin. You'd be able to hear a fart from two-hundred miles."

"You mean that is the last place you would put a missile boat?" asked Farmer.

"Yes sir too quiet. Not even the sounds of the ice would do you much good. There is a shallow layer there. Any noise below the ice will head straight down that basin nothing to stop it. You'll have a huge negative gradient."

"So this guy is either the dumbest skipper in the Russian navy or a genius," Tarrent stated.

"Genius?" McKinnon asked.

The admiral crossed his arms. "It would be the last place we would look for him."

"The very last," McKinnon sighed.

Tarrent sat up. "Commander McKinnon you will take *Miami* and find that sub."

"Admiral what are my rules of engagement?"

"Grant we don't know who is pulling this guy's string. Hell, he may be a defector waiting for the heat to wear off. We cannot take that chance. If that boat makes a false move you spank her ass."

"There will be a briefing with you, the XO, and the navigator tomorrow at 0800. Squadron Two will handle your store's load," added Farmer.

"Okay enough for tonight," Tarrent stood. "That will be all."

On the road, Grant McKinnon steered his steel-blue Lexus up North I-95. At the Mystic exit, McKinnon left the highway. A mile later, he passed Mystic Seaport Museum. He crossed the old drawbridge, where he took a left. He traveled two blocks and turned into his small driveway. He shut off the lights and the engine and sat in silence.

11

OUR OWN

"I am sure you will be on your guard against the capital fault of letting diplomacy get ahead of naval preparedness."

Winston Churchill

VEPR LAY CRADLED IN the rusty gray dry dock. In the frigid air a mixed stench of rotting fish, diesel fuel, paint, and welding, surrounded those at work on the damaged submarine.

Gantry cranes set scaffolds around the twisted stern plane. Electric generators roared to life along with compressors and welding units.

Inside the stinking dock, Valerik Danyankov stepped over cables and around equipment and made his way to the stern of his submarine. The dry dock manager, tried to keep up, but his feet were not as nimble.

"Captain, it is not possible to predict when repairs will be complete," argued the dock manager. "Parts are a problem. Rail shipments don't arrive," he moaned.

Danyankov's face went cold as the Arctic air. "That is not my problem. I want a firm date and hour for completion."

"Sir, what you ask."

"I ask nothing," Danyankov exploded. "That is a front line submarine you have in your filthy box. Do you know what is going on in the world?"

The manager could only stare. Above the clank of tools and the hiss of steam, a deep forceful voice called out, "Captain Danyankov!"

Both men turned to see Admiral Zivon Vitenka at the edge of the dry dock.

Again, the baritone voice called, "Captain a word please!"

Vepr's captain looked down his nose at the trembling manager.

"You find a way. Get my ship back in the water." He walked to the admiral and offered a halfhearted salute.

"Captain, leave the men to their work."

"The man is an imbecile. All excuses," Danyankov countered.

Vitenka chuckled. "Maybe, but he's the best imbecile we have to repair your boat. Come Valerik walk with me." They walked through a riveted steel door cut into the fifty-year-old dry dock. Once outside the noise and smell died away.

Admiral Vitenka glanced toward the rounded tops of the low hills. "Winter looks like it might come early."

"We both have better things to do than talk about the weather."

The commander of Submarine Squadron Seven turned to Danyankov. "True. We have much to do."

The rather short but firmly built Vitenka stepped off. Danyankov held back a few paces then followed. "Then sir if I may ask?"

"You may not ask Valerik," His voice soft. "You may however listen."

Somewhat disarmed Vepr's commander remained silent.

The admiral stopped short of a ribbon of narrow rutted pavement. "You remember your history Valerik?"

"Some," Danyankov answered cautiously.

"You did well last week."

"Thank you sir, I serve the Motherland."

"Do you?"

"Of course."

A small convoy of trucks approached the intersection. The

large vehicles bounced and thudded along the miserable path that intersected the equally bad pavement. The first dull tan truck passed, Danyankov saw men crammed into the back. They wore no coats only dirty yellow shirts. The epaulettes on their shoulders identified them as officers.

The next carried a platoon of Naval Marines. They sat stone-faced their hands held tightly to dull muzzles of AK-47 rifles. Civilians, large men with shovels and spades rode in the last truck.

"What is that about?" asked Danyankov.

Admiral Vitenka looked down. "Those are surviving officers of *Kuznetsov*."

As though lightning struck him, Danyankov stared as the trucks struggled up a small hill and disappeared down the other side, "Admiral?"

"Yes it is sad." Vitenka sighed.

Danyankov's face trembled, "And the men?"

"They are safe. They followed orders. Most never knew what happened."

"How many survivors," Danyankov asked.

The Admiral looked to the hill, "Three hundred men, and fifteen officers."

"*Kuznetsov* carried 2,600 men!"

"Let's not talk about that." He waved his hand. "You and I have other matters to discuss."

"Such as," Danyankov whispered.

"Valerik, I am greatly troubled by all that has happened thus far." Vitenka stopped "My loyalties as I hope yours have always been with the Motherland."

"You know that as fact admiral."

"These new leaders in Moscow where do you suppose their loyalties are?"

"What are you saying?"

"These leaders have no concern for the Russian people. Will this revolution feed our people? I think this is the path to destruction."

The rattle of AK-47 rifles echoed off the snowcapped hills. Danyankov winced.

Admiral Vitenka lowered his head. "Again we kill our own," he whispered.

The echo of the gunfire faded again silence surrounded them. Vitenka stepped forward Danyankov at his side.

"I am afraid, Valerik."

"But I thought…"

"We have been yet again used and lied to," Vitenka interrupted. "This new leader is a murderer. Most politicians are; but this man— this man serves only himself. He is very dangerous."

"Where does that leave us?

"Alone."

"What about the defense ministry?"

"Gone, replaced by men who never served a day. They are drones, no minds of their own. Russia is in danger from the inside and out. As for the outside we have an agreement with the West."

"What kind of agreement?"

"During the fight over *Kuznetsov* an American *P-3* was destroyed. The war could have begun then. Our fighters and Norwegian F-16s almost came to blows. Fortunately the NATO commander had insight enough not to make a bad situation worse," Vitenka paused. "I just worry such insight is not at work on our side. It is anyone's guess what will happen in the next days, weeks, or months." Vitenka continued, "I just want you to remember the Russian navy has always served the motherland not the politicians."

"I will remember sir."

"Good then you will understand what I tell you. Should this whole mess get out of hand, I will hold your boat in reserve."

"I don't understand."

"Amateurs now rule Russia. Unless they get an education very quickly this nation is headed for war."

"If it is war then I should be out there."

Vitenka's short but powerful arms went to his side. "What is in the minds of these men in Moscow? Who is loyal to whom? There has been little communications among branches of the armed services. One false move one careless action one overt act and it will be over."

"You sound like a defeatist," Danyankov snapped.

"No my dear Valerik I am a realist. The Americans have three battle groups circling in the Atlantic as we speak." He paused. "How many submarines do you think prowl out there now? If I were they,

I would say screw the agreement. They never trusted us, why should they now?"

"Still if it comes to that I …"

"Look out there Valerik." the Admiral interrupted and pointed across the base. "See those undermanned rust buckets. That's what I have to fight with."

"But why hold me in reserve?"

"When the shooting starts we will lose half, maybe more. It is then that you will best serve the motherland. You may be all that is left. Many of those boats will sail, fight, and die bravely but there are those who will reason life is too precious to be thrown away for a government that couldn't care less."

"You mean mutiny?"

"That has crossed my mind. For what cause is there to fight? We kill our own there is little pay, less food."

"Still the numbers do not add up. There is another reason."

Vitenka's eyes widened. "Yes. The Russian mind does not consider losing. I fear this may lead to a nuclear exchange."

"The Americans would not dare." Danyankov countered.

"It is not the Americans I fear."

Danyankov stared over the harbor. "What are my orders?"

"When I and only I issue you the order," he paused. "You will render our ballistic missile submarines combat ineffective."

Danyankov's eyes turned to the hill over which the doomed officers had just taken leave of their lives. "You have been like a father to me admiral. I trust you and will do as you say."

Admiral Zivon Vitenka looked into Danyankov's eyes, "As do I." Vitenka cocked his head. "There is another issue that has been brought to my attention again and again," he said smiling. "Evelina asks about you."

Danyankov almost gasped. "Sir, I really don't think…"

Vitenka cut him off. "I know you don't think. None of us is getting younger and I want grandchildren. What is my daughter not good enough for you?"

"No, I mean yes. She is good enough but my work, my boat…." Danyankov stammered only to be cut off again.

"She adores you and I don't think you're half bad," Vitenka thundered. "So Captain Danyankov you will report to my dacha at 1930 tonight for dinner. And do clean up a bit."

Back in the dry dock, the manager climbed the shaky scaffold to the edge of the twisted stern plane. The damage to the Russian submarine was extensive. The control arm shaft bent to forty-five degrees held the eight-ton stern plane. Tons of hydrodynamic force caused the plane to smash into the control surface trim tab tearing out huge gouges in the high-grade steel. What remained of the faulty pintle welded itself to the trailing edge of the control surface.

"How long to repair," the dock manager yelled over the noise.

The supervisor took a long drag from his cigarette then rubbed his temple. "Three weeks."

"Three weeks," shouted the dry dock manager over the sudden blast of a compressor's relief valve.

"I have material to repair the control surface. We can bend the plane back with the press but control shafts are special to this class. I don't have raw stock to make them."

"What do you have?"

The supervisor leaned on the scaffold and tossed his smoke over dry dock's side. "We can repair hydraulic lines and servos. The screw is chewed up but I have one more." He lifted his finger. "Bearings are no problem but that shaft and pintle are a worry."

"Captain Danyankov wants his boat back in three days."

"Okay," he frowned. "I have a shaft from the missile boat we did last year. Not the same metal though. I could use welding rods to coat the shaft then turn it down on the lathe."

"Can you do that?"

"Sure but I don't know how long it will last. The coating will wear off quickly."

"So?"

The supervisor rolled his eyes. "Then you'll have the same problem."

"Just do it."

"You're the boss." The supervisor slid down the scaffold.

Danyankov arrived at the dacha exactly on time. Evelina met him at the door "So it takes my father to get you here?"

Vepr's commander offered only a shy grin.

"Do come in captain." Evelina motioned with her delicate hands.

Danyankov stood transfixed by her sparkling blue eyes and her blond hair upsweep exposing her tender neck. He admired the flowered dress that clung to her slender body. When he followed her to the dining room, his eyes traced a line down her shapely legs.

12
DOWN TO THE SEA

"…mighty men of valor."

Joshua, 1, 9

USS MIAMI SSN 755
GROTON CONNECTICUT
OCTOBER 24TH

WELL BEFORE DAWN, *MIAMI'S* crew brought the nuclear submarine to life. Throughout the ship each department, each division and each man made ready for sea.

The sun inched over the hills of Groton Heights when Grant McKinnon walked onto the pier He greeted the topside watch with a sharp salute. "Morning," his smile stretched across his face.

"Morning sir and welcome," the watch responded.

"Is she ready?"

"Not yet. Soon as I get off watch, I'll take the vent covers off and remove the sanitation fitting. We'll get outta here on time though. Always have."

"Good," replied McKinnon."

Stepping down the ladder to the operations compartment Grant McKinnon smelled the fresh brewed pots of coffee. In the crews' mess, a jumble of boxes and frozen foods covered the tables. Mess specialists in checkered pants and blue cotton shirts stored each item according to preset menus.

McKinnon stepped in the pantry behind the wardroom.

"Morning skipper," the pantry supervisor smiled. "Care for a cup of Joe?"

"Sure would," smiled McKinnon. "I will take cream and sugar if you please."

"Oh yeah, blonde and sweet, Just like I like the ladies. Here you go sir, and welcome. *Miami* is a fine boat."

McKinnon entered the wardroom and saw his officers seated around the table. "Good morning gentlemen," McKinnon started. "Most of us know one another from other boats or from school so we can hold the introductions. First things first, this mission will not be easy. You will need to learn or re-learn skills. We will conduct extended operations under the ice. For how long, no one knows. We have information that a Russian boomer has staked out a place under the ice."

"I thought they agreed to pull back?" asked the weapons officer.

The Captain pulled out the VITUS map. "They did but, there she sits fat, dumb and happy. Our job is to nose around and see what she is doing. As you know, tensions run high. That boomer is in a pretty good firing position."

"Sir, the Russians are really paranoid about their missile boats. They always have a Victor III, or Akula riding shotgun. Any sniff of an escort?" *Miami's* navigator asked.

"None detected, which means we have a few possibilities. One, this boat operates without orders. Two, she waits for her escort. Three, they plan a first strike. Truth is we don't know."

"Now let's clear the air." He sipped his coffee. "I talked to some of the crew. Morale is still high and from your record of inspections, *Miami* is top ship in Group 6. I ask your help to maintain that record." McKinnon paused. "I know what a loss you've suffered. I knew Commander Upman since we were both no older than Ensign Kolter there." He pointed to the reactor officer. "I have no intentions of reinventing the wheel, business as usual. I will have my standing orders to you soon after we dive. Men, this mission may be the most important submarine operation ever. Keep on your toes. That is all."

At 0815, with lifelines and anything that would generate noise was removed or stowed. *Miami's*, 6,900 tons of steel, radiation, and enough explosives to level an area, ten square miles, was ready. The line handlers stood at parade rest waiting the word to cast off.

With a soft growl of powerful diesels the twin tugboats splashed up the river, their blunt bows shoved the river aside in a gush of foam and spray. With nimbleness so unlike their squat appearance the tugs swung into the slip and stopped short of *Miami's* hull.

Thick nylon lines from the tugs looped around sturdy T-shaped cleats along the submarine's back.

Standing in the tiny crowded bridge, Grant McKinnon gave the proper air of distraction. "Captain," the young office of the deck said. "The ship is ready to get underway. Request permission to remove the brow and cast off."

McKinnon looked at the young officer. Get the ship underway."

"Get the ship underway. Aye sir,"

The yellow crane grumbled to life, slowly and carefully it lifted away the bridge between land and *USS Miami*.

"Single all lines," the officer of the deck called.

On deck the line handlers led by the Chief of the Boat, removed wraps of mooring line that secured the boat to the pier.

One by one, the mooring lines slumped and splashed into the water. The harbor pilot spoke into his radio. At once, the tugs churned and growled as they pulled *Miami* into the channel.

In the center of the transit lane, the tugs cast off. Under her own power, *Miami* moved effortlessly toward the sea.

As his ship began to glide down the river, McKinnon noticed wives and children of the crew as once again, they watched husbands, and fathers venture into the unknown. They stood behind the chain link fence that separated the pier from the rest of lower base. In the chill of an early Connecticut fall the families watched their men slide down the Thames river. Grant McKinnon had to turn away.

AUXILIARY NAVAL BASE PECHENGA RUSSIA

The two officers met well past midnight under one of the countless neglected wharves. Each puffed on stale, powerful cigarettes. As they talked, small dark waves slapped gently at the rotten timbers of the wharf.

"You know what will happen if we are found out?" asked Junior Lieutenant Sergi Cheslav.

Captain Third Rank Igor Rurik blew a cloud of smoke into the cold Arctic night. "I know very well."

"Are you sure this has any chance of working?"

"That's up to us," Rurik answered. "Can you deliver the package?"

"Of course I can deliver."

"Then we are half way to becoming very wealthy men," shrugged Rurik.

"What is the plan?"

"We sail under orders to the North. I figure it will take some time before we are noticed. Then we tell them we have radio problems," Rurik explained.

"Yes and then," Cheslav puffed faster on his cigarette.

"When we reach the marginal ice zone we make all speed to international waters."

"They'll sink us."

"I think not," Rurik replied coolly. "When we reach international waters we broadcast our intent to defect. NATO will welcome us with open arms."

"How can we deliver our cargo if a NATO ship picks us up?" he demanded.

"We will suddenly have a fire onboard. Of course a distress signal will be sent," Captain Rurik, grinned.

"This is suicide."

"Our savior is even now sailing up the coast of Norway. An Iranian freighter will happen on the scene. It is there we deliver our package and are taken to France where we quickly disappear."

Cheslav scratched his head through the itchy rabbit fur hat, "And what about our money?"

Our fee will be deposited in four separate Swiss banks."

"It sounds like a simple plan."

"The best plans are."

"One thing you did not mention."

"What would that be?" asked Rurik.

"What about the crew?"

Captain Rurik took a long drag on his cigarette, then dropped the glowing butt to the ground and smashed it with his boot. "I told you there will be a sudden fire."

Cheslav's eyes went wide. "You mean we'll be the only survivors?"

Rurik grinned, "Unless you want to share one-hundred-million U.S. dollars with them."

"I understand." Cheslav smiled. "Are you sure they'll pay?"

"Oh yes, I am very sure. For them, it is a bargain. One-hundred-million for a 200-kiloton nuclear warhead, that works out to 5000 dollars per kiloton."

13
DESIGN AND DECEIT

"...this horrid disturber of the peace of mankind.

-Lord St. Vincent: Letter, 1812

VIKTOR IVANOVICH PASLAV SMILED. He slicked back his gray hair. "Good morning."

General Eugni Moiseev approached the new despot appraised him coldly as he sat in the chair across from the great desk. "Mr. Chairman, comrade, your royal highness, or whatever you call yourself," the general said with as much sarcasm as politeness would allow.

"Always a ray of sunshine," Paslav huffed.

"You executed the *Kuznetsov* survivors?"

Paslav returned to his seat, "Of course. They were traitors."

"Traitors against whom?" whispered Moiseev.

The smile left Paslav's face. "Russia."

"Russia? You have no idea of what you have done." His eyes narrowed.

Paslav slapped his hands on the desk. "What I have done, is send a message."

"That you did. Let me assure you the message eliminated a threat, but created a thousand more. Remember what I told you?"

"What do you mean?" His brow furrowed.

"Rumors have already started." Moiseev pointed his gloved finger at Paslav. "You are going to lose it all if you don't listen."

"Listen to you?" Paslav laughed. "You don't seem to have your heart in this general."

"My heart is for the motherland."

"This is a most complicated situation." Paslav nodded. "I am not ashamed to say my own interests play a part."

"Let someone take over before it's too late."

The new leader of Russia laughed heartily. "Take over? General now what would the people think? Indeed, what would the world think if they saw a uniformed Russian in the Kremlin?"

"Paslav, you are a dangerous ignorant man," Moiseev said calmly. "I am not sure which is worse the danger or the ignorance."

"You're right I have made mistakes. I am but a man. I promise you I will correct those mistakes." Paslav relaxed in the huge leather chair. "You will see."

"I hope so."

"You need proof? I can understand that. I've learned much from you."

Paslav motioned for one of his men. The man handed Paslav a folder. His fingers ran over the soft brown leather then laid it on the desk. "Your tank crews have done their duty bravely. I watch them you know. I must say I somewhat envy them. Their only duty is to those steel monsters and to you. They are professionals. I see them eat and sleep on those tanks. At night they gather around the warmth of their cookers and they sing, laugh and they never seem to wonder why," Paslav shrugged. "They just salute and do as they are told."

Paslav pushed the folder toward the general.

"Take a look, I have awarded each officer and enlisted man, The Order of the New Soviet Republic. Of course, the medals have yet to be made. Will this help to bridge the gap?"

"It will," responded Moiseev.

"Good, will you present these as soon as possible?"

"Why don't you?"

Paslav thought a moment then nodded. "Okay, I will."

"When?"

Paslav again paused, "Would now be a good time?"

Moiseev checked at his watch. "Yes, in ten minutes."

"Why ten minutes?"

"I thought you watched my men?"

"I have," Paslav shrugged.

"Then you know my afternoon briefing is ten minutes from now."

"Ah general, you should have been a politician."

"No Paslav, I know my limits."

"So you do." He motioned for his aid, an unshaven scruffy looking man with a dark pock marked face and wearing a suit not much better. "Make the arrangements."

The man merely nodded his understanding to Paslav. He stepped to the back of the room and whispered to the guards.

"General," Paslav stood. "I will see you and your men in ten minutes. As I said, I hope to correct a few of my errors."

USS MIAMI SSN 755

Miami slipped through the dark cold sea. Making more than twenty knots, the distance between the American submarine and the unknown closed rapidly.

New to this ship, Grant McKinnon was somewhat bewildered at the mound of paperwork on his desk. Even the daily routine of the ship required his authority. When McKinnon finished reviewing the various logs, reports and charts, he stretched his legs.

He stepped into the small passageway outside his stateroom. He turned to the right and made the three steps into the control room. "Conn-sonar" announced a voice over the 27 MC speakers.

"Sonar gained new contact on passive broadband. Designate contact as sierra-22 bearing 232. Range by bottom bounce is three-three-thousands yards. Contact on the right, drawing right. Contact classified as merchant doing 1–2–5 RPMs on one four bladed screw."

"Very well, sonar," responded the OOD.

"Afternoon," McKinnon smiled.

"Hello captain. We've been busy sir."

"Busy is good," McKinnon nodded, "Makes the watch go by faster."

"Sure does captain. Care to review our position report as of 1630 Zulu?"

McKinnon stepped over the slightly raised area of the control room known as the conn. "Show me."

The navigation department worked behind the conn. Two large plot tables took up most of the narrow space. McKinnon leaned over the starboard plot to look at the chart. "So far we have made less than 400 miles. Average speed is seventeen knots."

"Closest land is now Desert Rock, Maine." The officer of the deck explained. After we make our trip to periscope depth, we'll come east three degrees."

"Very well," McKinnon nodded.

THE KREMLIN

"As always general, I am impressed," Paslav whispered as he and Moiseev walked to the small reviewing stand.

Moiseev said nothing. He glanced to his left to where his men and tanks stood in neat ranks. The deadly looking T-80s sat like great insects; turrets square, gun tubes elevated, perfectly aligned. The crews stood in front of their tanks, unruffled by the cold October wind.

Paslav approached a hastily set-up microphone. "Good afternoon men. I am here today to right a wrong and take care of unfinished business. Our struggle for freedom has only begun. I want to thank each of you for the part you have played in this epic event in the history of our nation. This new government could not have occurred had it not been your dedication and your loyalty to General Moiseev. It is for that loyalty that I award you the following."

Paslav's bodyguard inched his way behind the General. In a flash, the bodyguard drew his automatic pistol placed it at the base of Moiseev's skull. An instant later, the general's head exploded in a thick red mist. The tank crews stood stunned and confused.

From behind the Kremlin walls masked gunmen opened fire. The men ran to safety of their tanks, others tried to dive behind the tracks while heavy caliber machine gun bullets from office windows cut them to pieces.

It was over in two minutes. The echo of the guns faded and the wind blew away the cloud of cordite smoke that hung like a pall over the dead and dying.

Paslav stood emotionless looking at the heaps of dead surrounded by blotches of red spattered snow. He turned to his bodyguard. "Finish them."

The guard nodded and motioned for the other man to join him. They trotted to where the tankers lay, kicking each for signs of life. When a few wounded moaned in pain, pistol shots rang in the air. Within minutes, one hundred and twenty-five men lie dead in the parade grounds. Their tanks stood over them their guns still raised and their battalion flag still flying.

When silence fell, Paslav took a cell phone from his pocket and dialed. "Colonel Trochinsky well done, I have appointed you minister of defense."

"You've heard?" asked Lieutenant Cheslav.

Captain Third Rank Igor Rurik looked over the harbor from *Barsuk's* rusting, obsolescent wheelhouse. "The whole country has heard," Rurik whispered. "But it makes no difference."

"These murders make our job easier," observed Cheslav. "I've heard the crew and even some officers' talk. There is fear."

Rurik shrugged. "Yes, but security may tighten. If we have to make our move earlier than planned can you still get the warhead?"

"It may take a bit more influence, but it will not be that difficult."

"Influence?" asked Rurik.

"Yes. It seems Colonel Sevornon has an addiction to certain pain medications."

"And you keep him supplied?"

"Oh yes, supplied and thoroughly blackmailed," Cheslav said coldly. "He'll play along."

"Why do you think that?' Rurik asked.

"I promised him a cut and he can go with us when we sail."

Rurik spun and shouted, "You what?"

"Don't worry. The colonel will never make it out of the harbor."

The *Barsuk's* commander looked at the young lieutenant with cold eyes. "Seems I've made a monster out of you," Rurik observed.

"No," responded Cheslav, "poverty did that."

Lapadnaya Lista
Russian Submarine Base
Dry Dock 9

"There is no time," shouted the repair supervisor. "I'm three days late. Each day Danyankov has a breakfast of eggs, ham, tomato juice and my ass."

"If you don't let me do X-rays of the welds Danyankov might have more than your skinny ass," the supervisor growled. "I don't even know if the control shaft will last outside the harbor."

"I understand, really I do. However, I also understand both Danyankov and fleet command are all over me, and now you. The first two I have no control over, but you I do."

"We've worked together ten years now. I just want you to cover both our asses."

"Fine but that boat must be in the water tonight."

At 2100, Dry Dock Number 9 filled slowly. With measured care, *Vepr* eased back into the dark water of the harbor. On the bridge, Danyankov looked for signs of trouble. The water rose to the keel. "Reports," Danyankov demanded.

"All compartments report normal."

"Docking officer," he shouted. "Increase the flow rate," Danyankov commanded. "We'll be here all night."

Vepr's commander glanced over the side. A new rush of water spilled into the sinking dock. Danyankov looked over the stern of his ship and strained his eyes in the darkness at the building-size conning towers of six Typhoon class submarines.

The water reached the halfway marker Danyankov felt a slight shudder underfoot as the Akula floated off the wooden keel blocks.

Danyankov breathed in the cold damp air. "Where are the tugs?" he bellowed.

"Tugs are assisting another unit," replied the docking officer.

"Another unit, what could be more important? Get their asses here."

Water inched over the bow planes. Lines that held *Vepr* centered in the dry dock, went tight.

"Captain, the tugs en route," reported a very relieved docking officer.

"Damn well time." Danyankov looked at his watch. "This boat had better be safe at her berth in a half hour or their asses will hang off my periscope."

The docking officer looked queasy. "Yes sir, I am doing my best."

"Your best?" jeered Danyankov. "That's what worries me."

The rough clatter of engines echoed off the low hills of Lapadnya Lista. Four tugs, all in desperate need of paint, fumed up to the submerged dry dock.

"Captain, the dock is flooded, the tugs are ready," reported the docking officer.

"Good," smiled Danyankov. "Pass the stern lines to the tugs."

"Aye sir," nodded the docking officer.

"Be sure you understand," Danyankov sneered. "If you so much as scratch the paint on my boat, I'll use your ass as a dry dock for my foot."

The officer trembled.

The stern lines passed over to the waiting tugs. When directed the ancient tugs reversed. On top of the dry dock walls, powerful capstans eased the forward lines holding the submarine centered. As the Russian attack submarine backed out of the dry dock, new lines were sent from the deck to the other tugs. The capstan lines cast off splashing into the icy water.

Ten minutes later, *Vepr* safely rested next to her pier.

14

SABER RATTLES

"Ye shall hear of wars and rumors of wars."

-*Matthew, XXIV, 6*

A WEARY GROUP OF officers piled into *Miami's* wardroom.

"Good evening gentlemen or good morning I should say," McKinnon smiled.

The officers around the wardroom table nodded.

"I'll make this quick so you guys can get some rack time. Tomorrow I expect to reach the ice pack. Most of you have never operated under the ice. Two words," McKinnon held up two fingers. "Be careful. I want the under ice sonar manned continually after 0600. Put your best people on it," McKinnon nodded to the weapon's officer. "We'll enter the pack here." McKinnon pointed to a spot on the chart. "This time of year the ice moves a lot, makes a lot of noise. We have no idea whether or not that boomer has an escort. If we get a sniff of an escort, we want to slip around nice and quiet. The noise from the ice should be enough to cover us. Okay, anything else?" he paused. "Get some sleep. You're going to need it."

300 Kilometers from Moscow
0245L

A Russian *AN-12BP CUB* transport aircraft bounced in the turbulent black sky over the desolate steppe. Flying high enough to avoid power lines the lumbering plane pushed south against a ten knot wind.

In the dark cavern of the *CUB's* cargo hold, Admiral Zivon Vitenka looked at his watch. So far, he was on schedule. Holding a penlight in his teeth, Vitenka spread his map along his lap. His gloved finger traced a line along the aircraft's route. Another hour and the Volga River will come into view, a twenty-degree right turn, then, other fifty-kilometers to Moscow. He looked at the air defense areas marked in large red circles. At any moment, Air Defense Command Moscow Military District would pick up the squat ugly aircraft on radar.

"Admiral?" a voice called over the rhythmic humming of the Cub's engines.

"Yes?" Vitenka replied.

Commander of the 35th Guards Spetsnaz stepped forward bracing himself against the wallowing airplane. Dressed not in a uniform, but in jeans and a heavy sweater the commando plopped himself roughly next to Vitenka. He pulled the large dull orange cap from his head. "Sir, I would like to prepare the men. Do a final check."

"Your men know what we might expect?" Vitenka asked.

"They do."

"Your communication man does he fully understand?"

"He does."

"Good. Prepare the men."

Lapadnaya Lista
Russian Submarine Base

Snow fell as Valerik Danyankov came topside. The crew stood in neat lines according to department. "Men of *Vepr* it has been what now—three week?" He asked. "Three weeks, since you had your lazy asses at sea. The rest of this rusting fleet can sit here—Oh, but not us. We have work to do. We will sit here next to this pier and we will train." He hoped his forced smile covered the truth. "Some of you may have heard what has happened over the past few days. That is what happens when you have no training. I will drill you until you want to die. Weapons will be loaded and tested. Engineering systems, communications this entire submarine will be tested. It will be as if we are at sea. Radio will monitor all frequencies. I know there are no questions so get to it. You have ten minutes to report readiness."

"Sir?" a voice from behind called. Danyankov turned to see his weapons officer saluting. "What is it?" he growled.

"Captain, is it your intention to load live weapons in port?"

"It is," responded Danyankov.

"That is forbidden," the weapons officer said.

"Dismiss the men," Danyankov growled. "Walk with me," Danyankov ordered as he started toward the end of the pier.

Five minutes later, they returned to the deck of *Vepr*. "I can count on you then?" Danyankov asked softly.

"I serve the motherland and *Vepr*," the weapons officer answered. "And I serve you."

Danyankov nodded. "Now get your ass below."

THE KREMLIN

"So now what," Paslav asked.

Minister of Defense Trochinsky shrugged. "We finish getting the military in line. After that we make this nation what it once was."

"I have also been in contact with several friendly governments. Three nations in South America are ready to talk. The Iranians are about to piss on themselves."

"What about our navy? I still have bad feelings about them."

"We'll start taking care of that today. Actually Admiral Vitenka is here to see you."

"Who the hell is that?"

"He commands our Northern Fleet submarines."

"What does he want?" Paslav grumbled.

"Oh, I suppose he'll bitch about something." Trochinsky answered mockingly.

"What do I do with him?"

"Unlike other services the navy has a different set of unspoken rules."

Paslav raised his eyebrows. "Can't you just answer a question? What are you talking about?"

"If he never returns the message will be loud and clear," Trochinsky grinned.

"What about our other problem."

"The Americans won't do anything we don't want. They're too afraid of what the rest of the world will think."

"I trust you, Trochinsky. Now show the admiral in."

LAPADNAYA LISTA
NOVEMBER 2ND

His crew scrambled from one drill to the next. Danyankov orchestrated the entire evolution from *Vepr's* bridge. The wind dropped some, but the snow still fell. Danyankov glanced around to see if any one was watching.

From his heavy coat, he took a small notebook. Looking west, he noted the location of the Typhoon piers. He checked his watch and picked up the bridge microphone. "Communication officer to the bridge," he ordered.

Soon he heard the metallic clank of boots on the bridge ladder. "Permission to come up?" a voice asked.

"Come up," Danyankov growled.

"You sent for me captain?"

"Are all frequencies monitored?"

The communications officer looked puzzled. "Of course, as you ordered."

Danyankov looked at the shivering officer. "I expect one of two messages."

"Yes sir?"

"As soon as you get one of the messages I need to know that moment. Do you understand?"

"I do."

"The messages will contain only one word. The words are *Pandora* or *Dove*."

"Pandora or Dove," the communications officer repeated.

"Now get below and wait."

"Admiral, tell us what can we do for the navy?" Paslav smiled as phony and cheap as his wrinkled suit.

Vitenka stood emotionless his eyes fixed on Paslav.

One of Paslav's thugs moved behind the admiral.

"You will now as of this moment step down as President of Russia," he said quietly.

The ten or so men around the admiral laughed.

Once the sound had died off, Vitenka continued, "Minister of Defense Trochinsky you are under arrest and will face charges."

Trochinsky still seated, his legs crossed, chuckled, "And what are the charges?"

"There are many, among them are treason, murder, crimes against the Russian people."

Again the men laughed. "Who sent you?"

"The Russian people," Vitenka answered coldly. "Time is short. I need you to leave now."

"Leave? Why should I leave?"

"I tell you if you want to live you will walk out the door."

Paslav's smile disappeared. He gave a slight nod to the bodyguard. "You are a fool admiral. Why should I be afraid of you? You are one man. I don't think demands about such matters are up to you," Paslav shouted.

Vitenka remained motionless his expression unchanged. "Then you refuse?"

"Yes admiral I refuse."

The bodyguard stood less than two meters behind Vitenka.

"Unfortunate," Vitenka whispered.

"Yes unfortunate for you," Paslav hissed.

The guard snatched his pistol from its hidden holster brought it up and extended his arm, the muzzle even with the Admiral's head.

Suddenly a pop and a tiny hole appeared in the window glass. The bodyguard's gun crashed to the floor his body sprawled beside it as a jet of blood spurted from the side of his head. Vitenka turned away from the window and squatted just as the three panes of heavy glass shattered in a deafening explosion. Men clad in black descended into the room with automatic weapons spitting bullets at the men surrounding their president.

As bodies cluttered the floor, Paslav remained in his chair. The automatic weapon fire subsided. One of the commandos pointed his weapon directly at Paslav. "Keep your hands on the table."

Out of either pride or stupidity, Paslav reached for his open desk drawer. A single muffled shot rang out and Paslav's term as President of Russia ended.

LAPADNAYA LISTA

"Your village must be missing its idiot," Danyankov yelled. "How long do you expose your scope?"

"I...I...," stammered the young watch officer.

"You what, you want the ship blown to hell because you got fixated on a target?"

Seven seconds, seven seconds. That is all you have. Now try it again," Danyankov snapped. "Launch control. Set up the scenario …."

The communications officer interrupted. "Sir, the message you wanted."

Danyankov grabbed the folded paper, tearing it open. There was only one word; DOVE. Danyankov closed his eyes. "Thank you," he said softly. "Secure from drills, all officers in the wardroom."

16

SEARCH

"Wisdom is better than weapons of war."

-Ecclesiates, IX, 18

GUNFIRE ECHOED THROUGH THE halls as the assault team finished off the last of Paslav's diehards. Thick smoke and the stench of gunpowder hung in the office. Knowing each second mattered Vitenka threw Paslav's body to the floor and reached for the special phone secreted in a false drawer on the inside of the desk.

The initial connection was nothing but static, but soon the line was clear.

"This is Chairman of the Joint Chiefs, James Malroy. With whom am I speaking?"

"Admiral Malroy I am Zivon Vitenka, I speak to you sailor-to-sailor." Vitenka said in clipped but understandable English. "Admiral Malroy, Paslav is gone."

"What did you just say?"

"Paslav is dead." Vitenka said slowly. "For now, I am in charge."

"You've taken over the Kremlin?"

"Yes. I need help. I have not told anyone of this. The country would panic," Vitenka explained. "I, like you am a sailor who does his duty. You must believe—I have no political ambitions. You must give me time to get control over the military."

"Admiral Vitenka, how am I to know what I am hearing is the truth?" Malroy asked.

"You don't. I have no way to prove to you the truth. You can trust me, or you may not. If you do not, we are all in great danger. I have no control, yet of the air force or strategic rocket forces. If they perceive a threat, I cannot tell what will happen. Again you must give me time."

By now, Admiral Zivon Vitenka's dossier was open on Malroy's desk. He flipped through the pages. "Trust, let's see about trust. We have indications that a Russian ballistic missile submarine is sitting under the ice pack. What can you tell me about that?"

"Admiral, I have no knowledge that any of our strategic units are at sea. Surely, your Keyhole satellites have accounted for our submarines. But if this is true ... destroy it."

"What?"

"If what you say is true, I have been lied to. A submarine under the ice may have its missiles aimed at Russia rather than the United States."

"Well," breathed Malroy. "I guess that makes sense."

"Admiral Malroy I ask that you brief our United Nation's ambassador then fly him here."

"Why?" Malroy asked.

"What reaction would there be if the people saw a man in uniform leading Russia?" Vitenka asked.

"I see your point," Malroy agreed. "Okay, I'll take care of that. You understand I will have to brief my president?"

"Of course but I deal with only you-sailor to sailor until the ambassador arrives."

"Agreed, what else do you need?"

"Luck."

USS MIAMI

"Fellas now we hunt," the sonar officer announced. "Just so we all understand we are looking for a type 2/3 Russian boomer."

"Don't let me catch anyone in this shack nappin," the chief warned.

In the control room, Commander McKinnon stood on the periscope stand. "XO let's go to ultra-quiet."

In every compartment, any equipment with the remotest chance of making noise was switched off. Ventilation fans, hot water re-circulation pumps, oxygen generator, bilge pumps, even the galley oven went cold. Those crewmembers not actually on watch climbed into their racks.

"Ship is rigged for ultra-quiet," whispered the chief of the watch.

"Officer of the deck, make turns for five knots," McKinnon ordered. He turned to the chief sitting the dive station, "Diving officer no angles greater than five degrees."

McKinnon poked his head through the sonar room door. Pale blue light bathed the small cramped space. "We're about ten miles from his last datum. You set in here?"

"Good-to-go, skipper."

"Chief, this is all sonar now."

"Roger that. We'll bag this guy, no sweat."

Three hundred feet above the submarine, the ice creaked, crashed, moaned, and hissed. The BSY-2 sonar system filtered what it could of the unwanted noise. The automatic tracker for broadband adjusted constantly. Even the towed array sent confused and unusable information.

Three hours later, *Miami* approached the area where the unknown submarine was supposed to be.

"Officer of the deck hold a large opening in the ice," the BQS-13 under ice operator reported.

"Very well, plot that opening," the OOD ordered.

McKinnon checked the chart and pulled out a clear plastic overlay made from the satellites image. The numbers matched.

An hour passed with only the sound of a billion tons of thousand-year-old ice crashing.

"Chief," called one of the sonar operators.

"Got something?"

"No, it's what I don't have."

"Huh?"

"Here on bearing 094. Sounds like all the ice is screaming. Except this one area," the operator explained. He touched the area of the screen at a steady dimus line.

"Put me on that bearing." The sonar chief put his headset on and listened. "Like a hole in all the noise. Could be our boy," he shrugged

McKinnon was in sonar in less than five seconds. "Talk to me, chief."

"Skipper, there is a lack of background noise at 092. Might be him-might not."

"Anything on narrow-band?" asked McKinnon.

"Nothing, but if this joker runs at reduced power-maybe on one reactor we'll not pick up any narrow band for another 2,000 yards. Two-K from a Russian boomer is getting mighty close."

"I'll start a slow turn to 005. Let the array stabilize, then maybe we can get a sniff."

"Sounds like a plan."

McKinnon turned *Miami* slowly north. He allowed the arrays ten minutes to catch up.

A half hour passed. McKinnon again checked the plot. If pictures from VITUS were accurate, the mystery submarine sat less than five miles away. "You're out there," he whispered to no one. "I can feel you. I just wonder if you are alone.

THE WHITE HOUSE
NOVEMBER 4TH

"Mr. President Paslav is dead," the secretary of defense announced.

"Dead?" asked the president.

"Killed by this man," from his briefcase, Admiral Malroy pulled Zivon Vitenka's dossier. "Mr. President, please look at this." He handed the folder across the wide oak desk.

The president leafed through the inch thick stack of papers. "Who is he?"

"Until yesterday, Vitenka commanded Russia's Northern Fleet submarines." Malroy inhaled. "Now he's interim president of Russia."

"How do you know that?"

"He called and told us." Malroy shrugged.

"You've confirmed this?"

"As far as we can," Malroy nodded

A worried look came over the president's face. "When this gets out, it'll be pure hell."

"So far, Vitenka has kept it quiet. On our side, only about ten people know." SECDEV said.

"Mr. President, Vitenka is legit." Malroy waited for a reaction. "He asks for the Russian UN ambassador put on a plane to Moscow. We have to help him."

I concur, Mr. President. I believe this is the real deal. Those folks have command and control issues; this may be an out for everyone."

The president lifted the dossier. "He's a submariner right?"

Yes sir," answered Malroy.

"Sneaky bastards," the president sighed, "No offense admiral."

"None taken, but you're right."

"What if this leaks before the ambassador lands? This could really go south."

The secretary of defense waved his hand "It's about as far south now as it can get-well almost."

Leaning forward, the president picked up his phone. "Anita, where is Secretary of State? Yes, give him a call and tell him to be here in half an hour."

USS MIAMI
NOVEMBER 5TH

McKinnon kept *Miami* three thousand yards from the position of the unknown submarine.

The watch section changed. *Miami's* engineer now had the deck and conn.

The executive officer slipped silently into the control room. "Captain, looks like you could use some down time," he said out of the corner of his mouth.

McKinnon looked up from the nav-plot. "I could use some coffee. I'll get some from the wardroom. I need to stretch my legs a bit."

"Yes sir."

"Eng..." McKinnon said softly. "I'll be in the wardroom." He descended the ladder in the Nav-center.

The engineer looked at the XO. "What you think?

"About what," the exec asked without looking up from the chart.

"The Old Man," the engineer whispered.

"I don't know. He seems all right-knows the boat," the XO shrugged.

"What about the crew?"

"Jury's still out. He's no Josh Upman, but who could be?"

KENNEDY INTERNATIONAL AIRPORT
0230 NOVEMBER 6TH

"It will be... all right," Ambassador Sergi Atopov smiled to his wife.

"Why are they taking us away?" she asked her voice full of fear.

"Kira, you ask questions I cannot answer right now." Atopov said gently.

"Have you done something?"

"No," Sergi Atopov assured his wife.

At the end of dim hallway the small party stopped. Two secret service agents stood in front of a dull green security door. A veteran of fifteen years, the agent-in-charge could tell the tiny woman with jet-black hair and the chin of a boxer was about to panic. "Mrs. Atopov, your husband is in no danger."

"Please, can you tell me why this is happening?" she asked.

Ambassador Atopov wrapped his arm tenderly around her neck. "Please, no more questions."

"Was it all my speeding tickets?"

"Uh, speeding tickets? No ma'am."

The agent at the door lifted his small two-way radio nodded to the agent-in-charge.

"Here we go." He motioned toward the door. "There is going to be a lot of noise. Follow these men, and keep your heads low."

The door opened to a hurricane-like wind caused by the rotor wash of a Navy Sea-King helicopter. She faltered for a moment until the agent gently but firmly placed his hand in the small of her back and pushed. Ducking they walked toward the waiting helicopter. Other agents lined the way their faces turned outward.

A minute later, the ambassador and his terrified wife were

strapped in. The aircraft lifted off while gracefully turning north. From New York, the Sea King followed the coast. Two hours later, it touched down in Brunswick Maine. The passengers bundled out, and rushed to a waiting C-9B Skytrain II jet. They had no more than sat down when the whining engines pushed the sleek silver and white jet toward the runway.

Flight time to Norway lasted just under four hours. Once landed a heavily escorted, Soviet era IL-20 Coot-A ferried the new Russian president to Moscow.

USS MIAMI SSN-755

"Opinions... ideas?" asked McKinnon.

"I don't know, skipper," shrugged the sonar chief.

"Maybe they moved the damned thing."

"We've reconstructed the search, didn't see squat," said the weapons officer.

The XO lifted his hands. "Where would they have moved?"

Next, the navigator spoke "We also have to ask why a boomer would need to move?"

"Good question" sighed McKinnon. "One thing we know for sure; its not here."

"We need to update our Intel. Maybe that bird has a new picture," the weapons officer yawned.

"I was thinking the same thing," McKinnon agreed. "We need to put up a mast."

"If you're thinking of using that big hole out there, I would be very careful," warned the chief. "We never got closer than three-thousand yards. That big bastard might be sitting surfaced. The ice around that little lake is four or five feet thick. A boomer at reduced power would not make a peep. The ice absorbs even a small tonal," he explained.

McKinnon paused. "We'll scout close to the polinya. Go deep and listen. Then come up on a reciprocal course, rising two-hundred feet at each pass. At one-hundred feet, I'll use the scope see if I can pick him up visually. If he's not there we'll put up the BRA-34."

17

DISCOVERY

"War is the realm of the unexpected."

-B.H. Liddell Hart:
Defense of the West, 1950

RETIRED CHIEF MACHINIST MATE Carl Blevins sat alone at his computer. He clicked his favorite web sites. "Crap! Not updated since June?" he mumbled. "Come on Ping wanna go to the shop?" In a flash, the four-year old Labrador was at the door, tail wagging.

"I'm coming." He rubbed the dog's cinnamon head and opened the door to the chilly November air.

Ping darted outside. Blevins walked slowly in the dim light of evening to a very attractive little building the size of a small garage built in the style of a traditional New England barn. Blevins wiped his feet and turned his key. The side door of the shop swung silently open. Ping followed behind sniffing the ground. Blevins flipped a knife switch to the breaker box and overhead bulbs flickered to life.

The first half of the shop appeared more like a museum than work area. Neatly built pine shelves held bits of submarine memorabilia. On the wall opposite the door hung his medals. Awards accumulated over twenty-six years of active service in the United States submarine force.

Blevins walked toward the back where another door stood. He twisted the knob, and pushed. Ping sneezed at the smell of raw fiberglass.

"Sorry about that," Blevins smiled.

Ping retreated out the door, and stretched out on the rug in front of the recliner. The retired CPO sat at a stool in front of a long sturdy workbench. On the bench sat his pride and joy, a seven-foot model of a German Type-IXC U-boat perfect in every detail. Carefully he removed the deck and set it aside. Inside the hull, a maze of wires, pumps, and electronics stared back. "Looks dry," he said aloud. "Let's see if that hinge works."

Through a tiny hole in the clear plastic pressure hull Blevins pushed a small button. Next, he reached for his radio transmitter. He operated the control stick, watching the rudder turn left and right.

"Good now the torpedo tubes." His fingers pushed the joystick. The tubes opened and shut at his command. "Yeah she is looking real good." He switched the radio off. "Another week and you'll be in the water."

USS MIAMI SSN 755
NOVEMBER 7TH

"This is the captain. I have the deck and the conn," McKinnon announced. "Dive, mark your depth."

"Eight-hundred feet," the diving officer replied. "Ship is rigged for deep submergence."

"Very well, dive." McKinnon looked at the status board.

Satisfied with the ship McKinnon grasped the stainless steel rail lining the periscope stand. "Rig control for black."

The control room lights went out leaving only the dim glow of the ships control panel.

"Helm left three degrees rudder steady course two-five-eight," he ordered. "Okay, fellas, this is it."

In the cold blackness of the Arctic Ocean, *Miami* swung slowly to her new course.

"Quartermaster-distance to point alpha," McKinnon asked.

"One-five hundred yards," the quartermaster responded.

"Mark every five-hundred yards."

"Conn, sonar, the second you hear or see anything—call it out."

"Sonar aye"

McKinnon watched the remote sonar screen so far nothing.

"Five hundred yards," the quartermaster reported.

McKinnon's eyes remained fixed on the screen, "Aye."

"Conn-Sonar—contact, bearing zero-two-four. Hold contact on passive broadband tracker three..."

"Sonar-Conn, I don't think this guy would be a broadband contact."

"Conn, sonar—waits one," answered the sonar supervisor. His voice echoed the frustration they all felt. "Conn, sonar, disregards contact report; heavy biologics down that bearing."

"Conn aye," McKinnon sighed.

"One-thousand yards," the quartermaster called off.

"Anything sonar?"

"Negative, sonar holds no contacts."

Weapons officer, take over." McKinnon ordered."

In the darkness of *Miami's* control room, McKinnon put his hand on the XO's shoulder. "Come to my stateroom," he whispered.

McKinnon lowered himself onto his bunk. The XO stood. McKinnon leaned back and turned on the small red reading light. "What do you think?"

"Don't know," the XO shrugged. "Maybe they moved."

"Why though? Two weeks—they sat here for two weeks. Then we get in the area and they vanish."

"You think the navy might have a security leak?"

"Wouldn't be the first time," McKinnon shrugged.

"There is another possibility."

"What's that?" McKinnon asked.

"Maybe it was never here."

"I thought of that. You saw those images. What else could it be?"

"Don't know. All I know he's not here."

McKinnon opened his eyes. "Let me ask you a question," McKinnon rested his elbows on his knees. "I'm not Josh and don't want to be. What do you think he would do?"

"Exactly what you're doing," the XO whispered.

McKinnon grinned. "I hoped you would say that."

"So now what," the XO asked.

"We'll go up in an hour. Stick the antenna up—see if there is any new Intel."

"Stanley Cup playoffs started last week, maybe they have some scores."

"Maybe," McKinnon chuckled. "Stand down the extra sonar watches. Have the weps review the near ice operations procedures."

LAPADNAYA LISTA

Valerik Danyankov enjoyed these late dinners with Evelina. The roast duck in lemon sauce was outstanding.

Evelina cleared the few dishes from the table refusing, Danyankov's offer to help. She returned quickly, her white calf length skirt flowed as she walked. "Valerik, we always sit at the table after dinner. Can we go to the parlor tonight?" she asked softly.

Danyankov's eyes fluttered, "Of course."

"Good," she cooed. With a grin, she took his hand and led him to the warm, cozy parlor, furnished with items that might have been new when Breshnev was in power.

"Sit with me," Evelina whispered.

When Danyankov sat beside her, the ancient springs squealed slightly. "I've been feeding you too much," she giggled.

"Maybe so," he smiled.

"I've been very worried these past few days." She looked at her shoes. "My father... do you think he is in danger?"

"Your father is a smart man. He will be fine."

"I don't know what I would do if I lost him," She said sadly. Evelina Vitenka took his hand, lifted his arm, and placed it around her shoulder. "I don't know what I would do if I lost you either." She brought her lips to his.

USS MIAMI SSN 755

Miami rose slowly, making a huge spiral in the black sea. At three-hundred feet, the blackness changed to dark blue. Two-hundred feet from the ice, the sea turned a light blue.

"On ordered depth one-five-zero feet," The diving officer announced.

"Very well," answered the officer of the deck. "Dive, trim the ship," he ordered as he pushed a button marked CO on the intercom.

"Sir, ship is at one-five-zero feet," The OOD reported.

"Very well—I'm on the way."

Seconds later, McKinnon was in the control room "How we looking Dive?" asked McKinnon.

"Almost there," The diving officer responded. "I want a little extra weight in after trim."

"Tell me when you're ready."

McKinnon turned to the nav plot, "Quartermaster how far to the center of point alpha?"

"Thousand yards on this bearing," the QM on watch responded

"Sonar," the captain called. "What's it looking like up there?"

"Conn—sonar, the polinya is roughly four thousand yards wide and six long. The floes seem to move all over the place. Recommend coming to periscope depth dead center."

"Sonar, conn, aye," McKinnon glanced at the XO. "Helm, all stop."

"Maneuvering answers all stop," the helmsman reported.

"Very well helm." McKinnon reached for the orange ring that controlled the periscope hoist. "Raising number-two periscope," he twisted the ring and the silver pole slid up silently.

Miami hung in the ocean her 6,900 tons perfectly balanced. Above the hovering submarine, a clear patch of water shimmered in the Arctic afternoon.

When the periscope limit switch clicked, McKinnon pulled the handles down, and peered through the scope. "Looks clear," he announced. "Officer of the deck, bring the ship to periscope depth."

"Proceed to periscope depth, aye sir. Dive, make your depth five-four feet."

"Five-four feet," the diving officer repeated.

Conn sonar ice getting louder, it might blank the spherical passive," warned the voice over the 27MC.

"One-three-zero," the dive called out.

"Very well sonar. Very well dive," McKinnon responded.

"I want all traffic onboard as soon as the mast breaks the surface. Line up on voice for me also," McKinnon, ordered.

As his eyes struggled to focus through the tiny eyepiece, shapes formed. The bottom of the ice came into view. Rough and jagged edges hung like knives in the sea.

Sea pressure around the hull eased. *Miami* ascended faster. McKinnon saw ice floes grind and smash into one another when the submarine passed under. "Wind must be strong."

"Nine-zero feet," the diving officer called out.

"Officer of the deck, maintain the main engines in the ahead direction. I might have to get out of here real quick." McKinnon ordered. He twisted the handle of the periscope until he looked almost directly up to see the waves inside the polinya.

"Conn-sonar, passive is blanked out due to ice noise."

"Sonar-conn aye," McKinnon replied softly.

"Six-eight feet," reported the diving officer.

"Scope is breaking," McKinnon called as a curtain of seawater fell away from the periscope's optic window. "All stations conn, ship is at periscope depth." He swung the scope quickly around a full 360 degrees. "No contacts."

"Conn-radio, have acquired the satellite, downloading traffic," came the report.

"Very well," McKinnon swung the scope around. "Winds from the north-west speed—I'd say thirty, maybe forty knots, overcast, heavy fog, or mist. I can just make out the edge of the ice."

"Conn-radio, all traffic on board. Buffer is printing."

McKinnon looked away from the scope. "What are the subject lines?"

"One is an Intel update, rest are routine."

McKinnon looked over at the XO. "Radio, did we get any scores?"

"I'll have those sent to the XO soon as they print out."

"Thanks radio," the exec smiled.

"Radio, bring the Intel update message to the conn," McKinnon ordered.

The radioman of the watch came around the corner, a clipboard in his right hand.

McKinnon pulled his eyes away from the scope. "Ensign Kolter," McKinnon called. "Take the scope."

"Yes sir," the young officer answered.

McKinnon took the clipboard, and scanned the message traffic. "Nothing new," he sighed.

It was then that Ensign Kolter spun on his heels. "Contact," he yelled.

"What?" McKinnon dropped the message board and took the periscope handles. Through the scope, he saw only the swirling mist. "Where?"

"Bearing 005 along the edge of the ice," Kolter pointed at the bearing indicator.

McKinnon swiveled the periscope ever so slightly to the blurred object. He clicked the handle to increase magnification. A gray shape jutted from the ice. As the mist cleared, the silhouette of a submarine appeared. The shape took form, the details crisp.

"What is it?" the XO called.

"Surfaced submarine," responded McKinnon. "It's a submarine, but not a boomer, too small. It's not even in the water. Take a look."

The XO stepped to the periscope. "What is that?"

"Looks like a Whiskey class," McKinnon shrugged.

"Those went out of service in the seventies," the XO offered. "Whatever it is it's stuck; torpedo tubes are out of the water."

"How did it get here?" McKinnon asked no one in particular. "This far in the ice, it has to be a nuke."

"If that is nuke boat, the Russians dumped it here. God only knows what went very, very wrong," the XO reasoned.

"What if it's not a nuke? Same scenario, but add a nuclear weapon. Maybe they had a problem with a weapon and dumped it here."

"Why bring a problem like that up here? Just sink the damn thing."

"There are two more possibilities," McKinnon sighed. "One, maybe what's on that boat has to be in the deep freeze. Maybe they had biological weapon. A bug that went bad," McKinnon whispered.

The XO shook his head. "I never thought of that."

"Two, maybe these guys tried to get away wandered in the ice, got stuck."

The XO rubbed his chin. "Hmm skipper, I don't know. Think we should call this one in?"

McKinnon shook his head "If we transmit we might be detected."

"True but we need to figure out just what this is before we call home. It's risky either way."

"That's what this business is all about," McKinnon smiled.

"Aye, captain that it is," the XO shrugged.

"We'll creep up and get a better look."

"Want me to start a message draft on what we know so far?"

"Not a bad idea, we might have to call for help in a hurry."

"What about battle stations?"

"Not till we know more."

18
SMALL BOATS

"The impossible can only be overborne by the unprecedented."

-Sir Ian Hamilton:
Gallipoli Diary, 1, 1920

HMS SWIFT
420 MILES FROM SCAPA FLOW
NOVEMBER 7TH

"BLOODY HELL," LIEUTENANT KIRBY exclaimed. "Never knew this part of the ocean to be so rough."

"Rare, but it does happen. How is the crew holding up?" Commander Ladd smiled.

Kirby wiped the icy saltwater from his face. "Half look like they're dying."

"The other half," Ladd asked.

"Looks like they already died."

"They'll get used to it," he chuckled.

"We'll be out of this tonight. We'll scout around the marginal ice."

Kirby moved to steady himself as the small ship rolled. "Marginal ice zone, never been that far north."

"We've been tasked with guarding a group—*oh excuse me*, a pod of migrating whales."

"Whales?" Kirby head turned as if he did not understand.

"Yes, lieutenant, whales."

"It will give us a chance to conduct some navigation training."

HMS Swift climbed the crest of another twenty-foot wave. "Hold on."

The small frigate hung at the top of the wave for what seemed minutes. Gravity took over and the bow dropped smashing into the next wave.

USS MIAMI

"Watch the ice," sonar warned.

"Sonar aye," replied McKinnon. "XO, raise number-one scope—keep an eye on those floes."

Miami inched forward. McKinnon locked his eyes on the strange submarine. "Range?"

"One-thousand yards," answered the fire control operator.

"No movement, just sitting there." "Helm, all stop."

"What do you think?" the XO whispered

"I want to see it. At least do a radiation survey," said McKinnon.

"You mean go out there?"

"If this thing is a hazard we need to know."

Fifteen minutes later *Miami* surfaced into the choppy ice filled water. Gusts of Arctic wind pushed the improved 688 across the polinya. McKinnon ordered the small secondary propulsion motor lowered to keep *Miami* in one spot.

"Listen up," McKinnon briefed those going topside. "I'm going to the bridge with Chief Berry. He will use the AN-PDR-27 radiac. If he gets a good reading, COB you'll take your team topside."

"I want those exposure suits zipped up tight," Chief of the Boat Norse warned. "No grab ass'n."

"COB, get the raft over the side. When I give the word, head for that boat. Once aboard, take a look around." McKinnon pointed at the off watch reactor operator. "Petty Officer Jiminez, see if that boat has radiation coming from it."

"Anything happens, get back here. Understand?"

"Understand," Norse nodded.

"Let's go," McKinnon ordered.

"Captain to the bridge," called the chief of the watch.

A sudden gust almost tore the hatch out of McKinnon's hand. He grunted and hefted himself up into the Arctic air. Instinctively he scanned the horizon. "Come up," he called down the hatch.

One by one, the others wiggled their way through the small bridge hatch.

"Chief Berry." McKinnon pointed at the gray lifeless submarine, "There it is. I need those readings," McKinnon urged "

Berry opened the cover of the radiac. He held the probe over his head and kept his eyes on the meter. He used the probe to sniff the icy air in all directions, "Nothing sir, no indication of radiation above background."

"You sure," McKinnon asked.

"Yes sir."

"Good. Get below. Have the COB lay topside."

"Aye Captain," Berry stole one last look. Suddenly he stopped and turned peering at the mysterious submarine. "Captain, do the Russians have deck guns?"

"Guns, where?"

"There on the sail inside that railing."

"Russian submarines don't carry guns," McKinnon puzzled.

By now, Norse assembled his team aft of the sail. Norse leaned over and pulled the cord. With a whoosh of compressed gas the raft inflated.

McKinnon looked down from the bridge. "Go."

Norse stepped carefully down the ladder, into the bobbing rubber boat. His hand steadied the small boat. Chief Torpedoman Wendell Rance, Nuclear Machinist Mate First Class, Devin Childers, and Second Class Sonar Justin Maurizio, followed.

They pushed away from the side of the surfaced American submarine. The wind died off and only an occasional gust whistled through *Miami's* bridge. McKinnon watched the raft plod along, the oars chopping at the water.

Norse leaned over the front moving large blocks of ice out of their path. Halfway to the submarine they stopped. Childers sampled the air for radiation.

"Keep your eyes open," Norse whispered. "Move us closer to the stern. There aft of the sail."

Skidding awkwardly the inflatable moved along the hull. Norse held out his hand keeping the boat from contacting the strange submarine. "Okay, that's good." Norse grabbed one of the limber holes and tied off the forward line. "Rance tie up your end."

"I feel like a pirate," Maurizio chuckled.

"Quiet," Norse snapped. "You get any reading, Childers?"

"Nothing."

"Sit tight. I'm calling the skipper." Norse unzipped his exposure suit and took out his radio, "Captain?"

"Go ahead, COB," McKinnon replied.

"Skipper there is no radioactivity, no movement, nothing."

"Roger COB, any damage to the hull?"

"None that I see," Norse responded.

"Can you get topside?" McKinnon asked.

Norse looked around. "Yes sir. The deck is about three feet over my head."

"Take one man. Have Rance cover you."

"Will do," Norse answered. "Maurizio you're with me."

"Me?" Maurizio pointed at his chest.

"Childers has the radiac, Chief Rance has the rifle. That leaves you Maurizio."

"I feel like I'm in a very badly written novel," Maurizio mumbled.

Norse balanced himself as he slowly raised his body until his eyes could see along the exposed part of the deck. "It's clear. Follow me." He pulled himself onto the deck.

Maurizio followed, "See anything?"

"No," Norse whispered.

"Hey look," Maurizio pulled up a small splinter of wood. "This deck is wood."

Norse held it up turning it over between his gloved fingers.

"Well?" Maurizio whispered.

"Well what?"

"Don't you think that's strange?"

"This whole day is strange." He tossed the sliver over the side. "Let's check out the bridge."

They moved slowly to the base of the conning tower. Norse looked up at the twin double-barreled guns.

"Those ain't for hunting ducks," Maurizio quipped.

"Quiet," Norse cautioned. He slid between the railings staying as low as possible. With Maurizio behind him, Norse duck-walked forward to another railing with a small deck. "How many floors does this thing have?" He peeked over the bottom rail. "There's the bridge."

Norse turned his head when something caught his eye. He turned to Maurizio and held his index finger to his lips. "There's a hatch," he whispered.

Maurizio leaned over for a better view. "Okay now what?"

"Go up further take a look over the bridge. I'll radio the skipper."

"What? Me go up there?"

"Maurizio will you shut up and go?"

"I better get a medal for this," Maurizio shivered, "I don't mean posthumously either."

Norse grimaced then jabbed his finger toward the bridge.

"All right I'm going." Crouching low, he slowly stepped forward.

Suddenly the submarine's deck trembled violently. Norse fell onto his side. Maurizio hung onto the rail. Then it stopped.

"What was that?" Maurizio huffed.

"The ice shifted... I hope," Norse replied.

"You okay COB?"

"Fine... busted my lip on the rail."

Norse glanced back. Chief Rance looked a little shaken. "Get up there and take a look."

He again pulled out his bridge-to-bridge. "Captain?" he said into the small radio.

"Is everyone okay?" McKinnon asked.

"We're good here. I think the ice is shifting."

"It is. We saw it from here. Have you found anything?"

"Negative, we're on the bridge now. Maurizio checked out the forward deck. This thing is dead."

"COB, see if there is anyone on board."

Maurizio returned, "Nothing."

"Skipper wants to see if anyone's down there."

"What?"

"Quiet," Norse grabbed Maurizio's shoulder. "Calm down. I'll go to the far side of the hatch. You knock real loud."

"Knock? You mean like on a door?"

"Yes like a door."

"What happens if someone answers?" Maurizio chagrined. "What do I say? Hi there, we're new in the neighborhood or can we borrow a cup of sugar?"

Norse laughed. "I thought you Italians were macho?"

"Not all," Maurizio replied.

"Go on, I've got you covered," Norse urged.

"I turn twenty-one next Friday," Maurizio grumbled but he crawled toward the hatch. "That is if I live through this. I want a medal and my own rack in the wardroom."

Norse took off his right glove let his hand fall to the grip of the 9mm at his side. "Okay, now."

Maurizio raised his gloved hand and let it fall on the hatch with only a muffled thud. "Looks like nobody's home. Can we go now?" he whispered hopefully.

"Get out of the way." Norse pulled the pistol and released the clip. He ejected the round still in the chamber, and turned the weapon around. "Look out," he warned as he brought the base of the grip down on the steel hatch. The clanging seemed to echo the length of the submarine. "Watch the hatch and listen."

They both watched for movement. Norse shoved the clip back in the Beretta. "Here hold this."

Maurizio took the gun. "COB, what are you doing?"

"Like the skipper said, we're going to see if anyone is down there." Norse put both hands on the hand wheel for the hatch. He twisted. "Put the gun down and help me."

Maurizio set the gun next to his left knee, wrapped his fingers around the wheel. Both men strained until a hiss escaped around the hatch.

"Move back," Norse shouted as the hatch flew open. A stream of ugly orange tinted air rushed up like an erupting volcano. The air rose high above the submarine before the wind whipped it to nothing.

"What was that?" Maurizio panted.

"I don't know," Norse, answered. "It's gone now. Maybe built up pressure or an air flask let go."

Norse took out a small flashlight. "Remember it's not just a job. It's an adventure."

"I've had all the adventure I want for today," Maurizio whined.

"Everything okay," McKinnon asked over the radio.

"We're good," Norse responded. "I opened the hatch."

"Can you see anything?"

"Not yet."

"Watch yourselves. I want you back here in fifteen minutes.

"Roger that."

Norse crawled toward the open hatch. "Come on Maurizio."

Let's make this fast." Norse aimed his flashlight. "Nothing moving," he whispered. The white light reflected off the buff-colored interior. "There's a ladder. It goes about six feet down then another hatch."

Maurizio pushed his face over the open hatch. "Smells like a submarine."

Norse looked around at Maurizio. "They all smell the same. I'm going in. You follow." Norse moved around until his body was in line with the hatch. "Seems small," he whispered. Legs first Norse tested the ladder then lowered himself down the hatch. "This thing is ancient." The beam of light illuminated the interior. At the front end the silver tube, unmistakably the barrel of a periscope reflected the light of their flashlights. Norse looked to the right and saw instruments through the light coat of frost.

The young sonar technician from Oyster Bay, Long Island stepped down the ladder. "This gives me the creeps," he whispered in the still air of the unknown submarine.

"Me too," Norse replied. He turned and shined the light into the next hatch. "That must be the control room." His light reflected off the dull stainless steel of the floor.

"Where did these guys go?" Maurizio asked.

"I don't know." *Miami's* Chief of the Boat slipped down the next hatch, carefully testing each rung until his feet landed on a solid steel deck.

Norse squinted as his light shined around the space.

"You see anybody?" Maurizio asked nervously.

"No."

His light danced across a wide flat table. "That must be the nav plot."

Maurizio descended the ladder, his own flashlight bobbing nervously. "I don't see any damage."

"We need to hurry this up." Norse shivered. "I'll go forward— you go aft."

"Alone?"

"Look Maurizio it's about ten below in here. I don't think anyone is going to reach out and grab you. Now move."

"I'm going," Maurizio, sighed. He shined his light toward the after-end of the control room when he noticed something. "Hey COB, look at the lettering on that valve."

Norse's eyes followed the beam of light to the valve.

"It says *öffnen*," Maurizio said curiously. "That's not Russian, it's German. It means open."

Norse shined his light around the dark control room. More stenciled signs came into view. "It's all in German." He stepped to the plot table. A leather binder sat neatly in the center. Norse looked down at binder's black leather cover. Carefully, he brushed away a thin layer of frost. Its black leather was embossed gold wording *Wir Fahren gegan Engeland*. Norse gently opened the book. The next page was of good quality heavy linen paper. At the top of the page, more words-*Befatzung U 761 am 24.3.1943*.

"What is it, COB?" Maurizio asked.

"It's a U-boat, a German U-boat."

"You mean—as in World War Two German U-boat?"

"Looks like it," responded Norse.

"How did it get here?"

"Hell if I know," Norse shrugged. "Come on, let's check it out."

Maurizio, scratched his head, "You sure about that COB?"

"Move Maurizio."

The sonar technician stood in darkness, "Which way?"

"Forward." He stepped toward a larger hatch.

"Right behind you," Maurizio whispered.

Norse shined his light into the next compartment. Carefully he stepped through the opening. "Look how well everything is preserved."

"The cold must have done that," offered Maurizio.

"Hey, these wood panels are real." Norse ran his fingers over the rich woodwork.

Maurizio stepped into a small opening. "What's this?" His light illuminated a blue curtain. He reached for the flimsy looking fabric and gently pulled it back. "Hey COB, check this out."

"What is it?" Norse asked.

"Don't know looks like the CO's stateroom. Look at the bunk with all the blankets."

"That bottle there, what is that?" Norse said aiming his light at the small cylinder.

Maurizio shrugged, "Maybe oxygen?"

"I don't think so. These guys didn't carry O2."

"Hey there's another," Maurizio said as his light fell on an identical container on the other side.

"This fabric is like new." Norse took hold on the corner of one of the blankets.

Maurizio reached over and felt the cloth. "Strange." He pulled a little more.

The cover fell to the side. Maurizio pointed the flashlight at the top of the bunk. "My God," he screamed.

Norse spun around just in time to catch him as he fell backwards. "What is wrong?"

Maurizio trembled. He slowly raised his finger. "Look."

Norse moved the beam of his light up. A face looked back at him.

19

QUARANTINE

"What is a ship but a prison?"

-Robert Burton:
Anatomy of Melancholy, 1621

Norse found it harder and harder to lift the radio. "It's cold Skipper," he mumbled. "Have you heard anything yet?"

"Not yet but hang on. Huddle together and save you batteries, we'll figure something out."

"I have an idea. Shoot over a messenger line. We can pull batteries and food across."

"Great idea," McKinnon said over the radio. "Hang tight; be ready to receive the line."

"I'm not going anywhere," Norse responded weakly.

"COB," called a voice from inside the U-boat.

Norse looked down to see Devin Childers, the nuclear machinist staring up out of the dark, "Yeah?"

"Come down," Childers said waving his gloved hand.

Norse slowly and painfully lowered himself down the hatch. "What you got?"

"I found the *how to* manuals on operating this thing," Childers wiped his nose.

"Good, we can burn those for some heat."

"No listen. These manuals are mostly pictures. I think we can start the engines."

"You *think*, or you *can*?" Norse asked.

"I can try, what else can we do?"

"You're right."

Childers turned and picked his way aft.

"Where's Maurizio?" Norse asked.

"Here COB," a voice came from the forward end of the control room.

"You okay?"

"I think so," Maurizio mumbled. "COB something's not right here."

"There's a lot not right," Norse chuckled.

"No, look at this." Maurizio motioned with his light.

Norse moved toward the forward hatch, and stuck his head through. "What's wrong?"

Maurizio moved his light to the face lying peacefully in the bunk. "How cold you think it is?"

"I don't know—maybe ten, fifteen below?"

"Watch this." Maurizio stepped toward the body.

"Hey, what are you doing?" Norse asked with alarm. "This is probably a war grave."

"Hang on." Maurizio moved the blanket, picked up the body's arm he raised it, and let it fall. "See? These guys should be frozen stiff—but they're not."

THE PENTAGON
0545

"Yeah," Malroy huffed into the phone. "What? Are we sure about this? Get the staff up and in. I want that captain from Bethesda in my office in an hour. You know—the bio-weapon guy—Okay, make the calls and set up the situation room for a phone conference." He dropped the receiver back into its cradle.

Within the hour, Malroy took his seat when the rest of the group entered.

"Gentlemen thank you for coming in early." Admiral Malroy

looked at the secure voice telephone speaker. "Admiral Tarrent?" he asked.

"Here sir," came Tarrent's voice on the speaker.

"CNO?"

"Here Mr. Chairman."

"Fort Meade?"

"We're on line admiral."

"Good." Malroy grunted. "I have here my staff and Captain Ranon an expert in chemical and biological weapons. Let's start by bringing everyone up to speed. Admiral Tarrent if you will?"

"Yes, sir," Tarrent replied, "At 1620 Zulu, *USS Miami*, located an unknown object locked in the ice, forty-three miles inside the ice pack. At 1650, *Miami* surfaced. The unknown object was a submarine ..." Tarrent was cut off by murmurs of disbelief.

"Quiet," Malroy said. "Let Admiral Tarrent finish."

"Commander McKinnon believed the submarine to be a stranded Russian Whiskey class diesel boat. Four of *Miami's* crew went aboard. After opening the hatch, they discovered the boat was not Russian, but a German U-boat from the Second World War. Uh, the *U-761* it seems. Upon further investigation, the boarding party found twelve canisters, contents unknown.

"Given the nature of her location and the unknown canisters *Miami's* corpsman thought the canisters might contain a chemical or biological agent. The four crewmen remain on the German submarine to avoid contamination or infection of *Miami's* crew."

"How long have they been onboard," Captain Ranon asked.

"Almost eight hours," replied the CNO.

"What's the temperature?" asked Ranon.

"Oh, I say about ten below," Tarrent's answered.

"They don't have long," Ranon said softly.

"Captain, what do you think would be in those containers?" asked the CNO.

"That's almost impossible to answer. I know the Germans experimented with a few chemical agents but not much in that area. They spent most of the war developing a nuke."

"So those guys are safe?" Malroy asked.

"No I didn't say that. The corpsman did the right thing. That leads me to think maybe a biological agent. The Germans didn't seem interested in that either. Of course there is one possibility,"

Ranon raised his finger. The Japanese were into bio-weapons quite extensively. They spread plague in Shanghai they still have outbreaks from it."

"A Japanese bio-weapon on a German submarine, I'm afraid you've lost me, Doctor," commented the CNO.

Ranon sighed. "The Germans and Japanese shared technology. Germany shipped uranium to Japan. They sent over jet fighter parts. The Japanese even bought a Tiger tank. Maybe this submarine was bringing something home. Something dangerous that got out."

"So how long can a plague live?" Malroy asked.

Captain Ranon shook his head. "Indefinite if the conditions are right. Japan had an entire complex setup to find and develop biological agents. They cooked up some very nasty bugs. If that U-boat carried one of those agents, the only way to know is from samples."

"Have the men on that submarine reported any unusual looking weapons?" he asked.

"Not that I know of," Malroy answered.

"Gentlemen what we may have here is a submarine that was on its way to deliver an agent to the coast of the United States. On the way something happened and the crew—well I don't know," Ranon reasoned.

"Could that submarine have reached the coast?" Malroy asked.

"Oh hell yeah," the CNO exclaimed. "They damn near blasted us out of the war in '42. My Dad told me stories of seeing ships torpedoed within sight of the beaches."

"Okay, so we need to know about the weapons and about the boat it's self." Malroy turned to his communications officer. "Get McKinnon on the horn. Does anyone know an expert on U-boats?"

"What about the Germans?" one of his aides asked.

"This can't get out until we know what we're dealing with. Is that clear to everyone? This gets out and the media will eat it up. Don't forget, we're not even supposed to be up there."

"I have a man," Tarrent said. "He's a retired A-ganger. He knows everything about the damn things. He even knows some of the old U-boat skippers."

"Okay, bring him onboard. We will meet again at 1030. Captain Ranon, I'll need you to stick around."

"There goes my golf game," Ranon smiled.

"Doctors," Malroy huffed.

"I'll brief the secretary. He's going to love this," Malroy shook his head. "Gentlemen, if there is nothing else we're adjourned."

Groton, Connecticut
1130 November 8th

Captain Farmer drove up the steep winding lane. "How does he get up here in winter?" he mumbled. The trees overhanging the narrow road opened, Farmer could see the roof of the house. It was a small and inviting place, charming in its simplicity and natural in the surrounding woods. He brought the truck to a halt next to a sun and salt worn Bronco. He stepped out and went to the door. About to knock he noticed a small hand carved sign hanging from the antique door handle, "AT THE LAKE."

Farmer saw a path leading around the house. Following the grass lined path, he passed the workshop, and continued down a small hill. A glimmer of water shimmered through the trees. He stepped carefully over the loose stones and jutting roots that lined the path. "This place is gorgeous," he whispered. He spotted a clearing at the water's edge. In his customary blue-flannel, shirt and paint-stained denims stood Carl Blevins. "Carl?" he called.

With a radio control transmitter in his hand, Blevins turned his head, "Captain Farmer," he smiled. "How are you?"

"Good and you?"

"Playing with my new toy—check it out."

Farmer raised his hand over his eyes to block the glare from off the water. Forty feet from shore the sleek outline of a submarine cut through the water. From where he stood, the model looked like the real deal. "Wow."

"Took me almost a year to build," Blevins said proudly. "Now watch this." He nudged one of the transmitter's controls, and the submarine dipped beneath the cool lake waters. The miniature periscope left a very realistic feather of water behind it.

"I'll be damned," Famer smiled.

"Get a load of this little feature."

The periscope turned and headed across the small lake. Farmer watched as it stopped and slowly sank.

"Take a final bearing and shoot," Blevins said as he pushed one of the joysticks forward.

Farmer chuckled smiled as wake of white bubbles trailed behind a tiny model torpedo.

Blevins's aim was perfect. The little torpedo headed straight for a peacefully sleeping mallard. The torpedo struck under the duck's tail feathers. It let out a loud squawk before lifting off the surface complaining, and flapping wildly.

"Great shot," Farmer laughed.

Blevins manipulated the transmitter. The victorious U-boat surfaced and set a course for home. "What brings you out this way?"

Ping ran from out of the woods his tail whipped in circles. He came to Farmer, demanding his head be rubbed. "Hey there Ping, how you doin' boy?" Asked Farmer, as he obliged the big Lab. "Carl, I need help."

"With what," Blevins asked as his U-boat gently put its nose on the sandy lakeshore.

"With one of those," Farmer said pointing to the model submarine.

"You want one of these?"

"No chief. We've found one."

Blevins turned around. "Found what, a U-boat?"

"That's right."

"Divers find it?" Blevins asked. "Seems more and more of them are turning up. Still there are about twenty or so not accounted for. Bet it was in the Gulf of Mexico, right?"

"No Carl," he paused scanned the lake, to make sure no one could hear. "*Miami* found it last night."

"The *Miami*?" asked Blevins.

"It's been stuck in the ice north of the marginal ice zone. Frozen since '44, crew is still aboard."

Blevins's mouth fell open. "What? I mean how?"

"That's why we need your help," Farmer said quietly.

U-761
NOVEMBER 8TH

Thankful to receive the supplies, the four men from the *Miami* sat in *U-761's* control room eating grilled ham and cheese. They warmed their hands on hot cups of coffee.

"I don't like coffee but this is good." Maurizio said as he sipped the steaming brew.

"Wonder how many Americans this thing killed?" Chief Rance queried.

"Never thought of it like that." Norse looked around as he munched on a third sandwich. "It was a long time ago. We're all friends now, remember?"

"I know but, still makes you think," Rance observed.

"Only thing I'm thinking about is getting off this pig and back to my nice warm rack." The COB drained his coffee.

"Wonder why they were concerned about the torpedoes?" Maurizio asked.

"Explosives become unstable with age," answered Rance. "When I was stationed in Charleston they were all the time finding unexploded live shells from the Civil War. Damn things would blow up if you looked at them wrong."

"Wonderful," Maurizio rolled his eyes. "I'm on a submarine stuck in the ice. It's ten below zero. I've been exposed to God knows what. I'm stuck with fifty-four dead guys and thirteen-thousand two-hundred pounds of unstable explosives. My Mother would die."

"How long till you can try the engines," Norse asked.

"I want to finish checking the injectors and intakes. Give me a half hour. I tell you for being as old as it is this boat is almost like new," Childers said as he ran his gloved hand along the bare steel hull.

THE PENTAGON
2230

"What do we know?" The Chairman of the Joint Chiefs asked.

"I have here Chief Carl Blevins an expert on U-boats. He did some digging for us," Admiral Tarrent said over the speakerphone.

"Welcome chief," Malroy said pleasantly. "What have you found?"

"Admiral, *U-761* is a Type IX-C U-boat, built by Blomm and Voss in 1943. She made six war patrols. Her only commander was Manfred Becker...."

"Becker, Becker," interrupted the CNO. "I know that name."

Blevins continued, "She sank a total of twelve ships during her patrols. The records list her as missing in August of 1944-cause unknown. I made a call to the U-boat archive in Kiel. My contact pulled the file on *U-761*. Everything was normal except for a handwritten note."

"I thought those records were destroyed?" the CNO asked.

"Some were." Blevins answered. "Himmler himself took an interest in *U-761*. He wrote a small note that said, *Approved to proceed with The Forever Project, H.-Himmler*"

"What about this Forever Project?" Malroy asked.

"That is the big unknown," Blevins responded. "But I think I can find out. The SS cross-referenced their documents. If anything related to this project they mentioned survived it could be in the archives in Berlin," Blevins stated.

"Can you get into those archives?" the CNO asked.

"I am pretty sure, yes, sir."

"Tarrent, arrange a flight for Chief Blevins," Malroy ordered. "Chief you understand how important this is and how it must remain secret?"

"I do," answered Blevins.

"What about the weapons?" The CNO asked.

"From what Captain Farmer told me, *U-761* carries her wartime load-out of G7e torpedoes. That smaller one in the bow sounds like the Zaunkönig II, one of if not the first acoustic homing torpedoes.

"What?" Malroy stammered. "The Germans had smart weapons?"

"Yes sir," Blevins answered.

Malroy then turned to Captain Ranon. "Captain you have anything new?"

"If the men were exposed to a toxin or bio-agent they would have been symptomatic by now."

"Could the cold prevent the germs from becoming active?" asked Tarrent.

"I recommend you get the men back to the *Miami* and leave the thing alone till we can get a team up there to take a look."

"Maybe we just sink the damn thing," Tarrent growled.

"For God's sake no," Ranon answered. "That might release an agent to the four winds."

"I almost wish it had been a Russian boomer," the CNO added dryly.

20
WARMTH

"The wise man in the storm prays God not for safety, but for deliverance from fear."

-Ralph Waldo Emerson

"IS EVERYTHING READY LIEUTENANT?" Rurik asked.

"It is done," smiled Cheslav. "The warhead has been removed from the missile. For all they know, it is just a training simulator. The paperwork matches the false serial number. Now it is just a matter of moving the false warhead instead of the real thing."

"Your colonel, is he still playing?"

"He made the arrangements as I instructed. Delivery will be in two days," Cheslav said quietly.

"Good. Our customer is very anxious." Rurik flipped a cigarette butt in the slush of the harbor.

"Do you have orders to sail?" The young lieutenant asked.

"It doesn't matter. We will sail regardless."

"Just think," Cheslav looked into the cold black sky, "A month from now we'll be where it is warm all the time."

"I have thought of that," Rurik grinned.

Cheslav drew his top coat tight around his neck. "One month

and I'll never be cold again." He turned and walked off *Barsuk's* quarterdeck.

"In a month you'll be dead," Rurik said under his breath.

U-761
NOVEMBER 9TH

"Maurizio, when you hear the engine start you pull those two handles straight down. Understand?" Childers asked. "That's the main air induction. Without air the engine won't run and we freeze."

"I got it." The sonar technician pointed at the two green handles.

"Here we go." Norse held the flashlight as Childers pulled the starting handle. The huge diesel sputtered and shook the steel decking under their feet. A puff of air gasped out of the engine. The camshaft rolled over then a pop. The shaft moved a turn more and another pop. Slowly as if yawning, the great Mann diesel chugged to life.

Childers moved along the length of the engine adjusting an intake or an injector nozzle. The roar of the engine smoothed into a steady rhythmic drone.

"Runs a little rough," Rance, yelled over the roar.

"She'll settle out," Childers replied. "Check that RPM gauge." He pointed to the panel behind his left shoulder. "If it holds fifteen-hundred I can get the motor generator on line." Childers removed his glove and let his hand rest on the giant valve cover. The steel warmed under his nearly frozen fingers.

Norse smiled when he heard the engine rumble. A breeze of warm air drifted from the after control room hatch. Norse tore the hood from around his head and let the warmth flow around his face. "We might make it through this."

USS MIAMI

"Would you look at that?" the XO smiled as *U-761's* engine sent a cloud of condensed vapor high over the U-boat.

"Next thing you know the COB will want to sail the thing back to Groton," McKinnon beamed.

"Captain?" a voice called from the dark bridge hatch. "Flash message sir."

"Thanks." McKinnon took the message.

"What is it?" the XO asked.

"Low pressure area moving in fast. We're going to get hammered. They predict winds of fifty-knots, maybe more."

"Great. This ice is moving around enough already. A few knots of wind and we'll have a hard choice to make," the XO sighed.

"I'm going below and talk to doc."

U-761

"Holding steady at fifteen-o-two," Rance shouted into Childers's ear.

Childers looked back at the gauge and gave Rance thumbs up. He walked forward to the motor generator room. Holding the flashlight in his teeth, he traced the maze of wires and cables snaking along the hull. His fingers led him to a large handle shaped switch. He pulled down and the switch locked down with a clank.

Suddenly the diesel chugged like a large truck going uphill. Over the sound of the huffing engine, Childers heard the whine of a generator spinning up. He spotlighted the electrical distribution panel. "Generator is spinning," he shouted. "Still a bit low," He said as he adjusted output. Soon the green ready lights glowed on the panel. When the last one came on, Childers flipped the breaker and the diesel resumed its rough, but steady thumping.

Dim lights spread as if a curtain opened. The lights grew brighter and the interior of the U-boat rose from the shadows.

Childers shielded his eyes since he had not seen light in eighteen hours. He walked forward, ducked his head under the control room hatch. "At least we can see," he smiled at Maurizio and Norse.

Both men removed the tops of the exposure suits as the room warmed.

Norse climbed the ladder to the U-boat's bridge. "Captain?" he said into the radio.

"COB, this is the XO. Captain went below everything okay over there?"

"Yes sir. Childers got the heat and lights on. All we need is cable television and we're set for life," Norse responded.

"Roger that COB."

"Any idea when we can come home?"

"Not yet."

"Wind's picking up," Norse drew the hood back over his head.

"We are expecting bad weather." The exec answered. "You'll be back on board by then."

"Sure hope so."

USS MIAMI

"Try again," McKinnon, barked.

"Yes, sir," answered the radioman.

"Sorry. Not your fault."

"We are lined up with the satellite but everything is coming in garbled. Sometimes it happens this far north," the radioman explained.

"Can we transmit?"

"Yes sir."

"Get this message uploaded and ready to go." McKinnon hand-wrote a message on the back of the recent weather report.

"Aye sir." the radioman took the message.

"When you have it loaded transmit."

"Transmit one properly released outgoing aye sir."

McKinnon stepped out of radio and into control. *Miami* rocked gently. "Captain to the bridge," demanded the 1MC. He pulled himself up the ladder. A howl of wind whooshed down as if to push him back. "Two hours my ass," he hissed as he struggled to the bridge.

"It just started," the XO, shouted over the moaning wind.

"You heard from the COB?" McKinnon shielded his face against stinging bits of ice.

"They have one of the engines running."

"Radio is out," McKinnon shouted. "I've released a message on UHF asking them to not use the satellite."

Another sound came over the dark ice. A crackling noise like broken tree branches falling to the ground.

"Captain," screamed the lookout, "There!"

Off *Miami's* port quarter, fifty-foot jets of exploding ice shot skyward. Like a zipper, the ice was coming apart. McKinnon watched hills of ice crumble and fall into a churning sea.

"We have a problem," shouted the XO. In the stinging ice, he pointed to the ice that held *U-761*.

The pack split at the U-boat's lodged bow. Now broken, the wind pushed on what remained of the three-acre floe. Unable to bear the millions of tons of pressure, the entire ice floe broke away. Now three acres of six-foot thick ice and one German U-boat drifted toward *Miami*.

"Get them back onboard," McKinnon shouted.

"COB, get off now," the executive officer shouted into the radio.

McKinnon looked at the drifting mountain of ice then behind his ship. The space seemed suddenly very small. "Clear the bridge."

U-761

"What is that?" Maurizio shouted as the tearing ice shook the hull. Sheets of frost fell from the overhead, smashing like glass onto the deck. The four men held on as the U-boat lurched and bucked.

"Hang on," Norse shouted. "The ice is breaking up."

His radio crackled, and he realized reception was impossible from inside the U-boat. Norse raced up the ladder. He saw the U-boat drifting toward the *Miami*.

"COB, get off," he heard through the crashing ice and screaming wind. Norse stuck his head down the hatch. "We're leaving."

The remaining three quickly pulled on their exposure suits. *U-761* swayed and rocked as they climbed the narrow ladder.

"Where's the raft?" Rance called over the rushing wind.

"It'd better be there." Norse stepped onto the gun platform. "Stay close, hold on, and keep moving." He crawled through the conning tower railing, when the German submarine lurched to starboard. Norse's feet flew out from under him. He landed hard on the ancient frozen wood.

"COB," Rance called as he reached for Norse. Rance's hand clasped around his, "I got you."

Norse pushed his legs to regain his footing. Childers and Maurizio grabbed Norse under the shoulders. "Get me the hell out of here."

Maurizio reached the lifeline supports and held on as the deck continued to tilt under their feet.

"We gotta speed it up," Norse shouted.

Childers reached the inflatable raft. "Still here," He sat on the sloping deck and dangled his legs over the side of the shuddering U-boat.

The ice shook with the force of an earthquake. The old steel of the German submarine groaned as the force of the insane ice pressed her plates. Explosions of million-year-old ice floes erupted in a thunderous roar.

"Go," Norse, screamed.

Childers pushed off the side. His knees collapsed when his boots hit the tough rubber of the raft's bottom.

"COB you're next," Rance shouted. The U-boat listed further and for once Norse did not argue. He sat down, pushed off, catching the side of the raft. Childers grabbed him before the raft bounced him into the slush and ice.

"We're almost outta time," Rance shouted into Maurizio's ear.

"I know and, I don't want your big ass landing on me, you first."

"You be right behind me," Rance yelled as he too went over the side.

U-761 fell nearly on her side. Maurizio's feet slid down the deck as he landed face first onto the after-casing. His fingers managed to grab the sides. He hung with his legs kicking for support or traction.

"She's going over," Rance screamed from the raft.

Out of instinct, he let go of the line holding the small rubber boat to *U-761's* side. Waves of ice and slush washed around and pushed the raft away from the tipping U-boat.

Norse looked back to see *Miami* growing larger as the giant ice floe moved closer.

Maurizio's left toe found a bit of traction and he pulled himself up to the edge of the deck. The blowing ice stung his eyes and face. With a heavy puff, he launched himself toward the bobbing raft. He misjudged his distance and landed in front of the raft.

An arm came out of the water and Norse grabbed it, then Rance caught the other arm. Both pulled hard. Maurizio's limp body slid out of the icy water his face a mask of terror. They dropped Maurizio in the bottom of the boat. Norse snatched the small oar. "Let's go."

USS MIAMI

"Here they come," the XO shouted above the clamor.

"Chief of the watch, open the vents," McKinnon commanded.

Great plumes of air shot from the *Miami's* ballast tank vents. Almost at once, the submarine settled deeper into the churning sea. McKinnon looked at the oncoming ice. "This is going to be close. Come on COB!"

Ice holding the long trapped U-boat finally surrendered. She fell off to the side sliding along the tipping ice. As the U-boat slid forward, her weight caused the edge of the floe to upend. The jagged edge of the floe opened like a mouth filled with deadly white teeth.

"Look," the XO yelled.

McKinnon turned as the huge mouth opened wider. "XO, get below."

The ice now towered over the bridge.

As air rushed out and ocean rushed in *Miami's* ballast tanks, her bow dipped below the surface.

Twenty feet from the side of the submerging submarine, and near exhaustion, Rance grabbed the line tied to the bow of the raft; balled it, and with his last bit of energy threw the line toward the deck. Caught by the wind it hung like a kite tail for what seemed like days, and finally landed in front of the hatch.

Those in the rubber raft felt a strong tug. Pulled by men on *Miami's* deck the raft slid over the ice.

The raft bumped roughly into the rounded hull of the American submarine.

"Get them on board," a voice shouted.

The rising water lapped at the fairing for the towed array.

His shipmates helped Maurizio to his feet and down the hatch.

As the ocean neared the lip of the escape trunk hatch, the last of the men scurried down the ladder. With a dull thud the heavy hatch sealed as the hull sank. Once in the crew's mess they fell into the vinyl covered, seats drinking in heavy gasps of the warm air.

"Hatch shut," a voice called.

The XO checked the hatch leading to the bridge, "Hatch shut."

The bridge hatch clanged shut. McKinnon appeared out of nowhere, "Depth?"

"Four-eight feet," replied the wide-eyed diving officer of the watch.

"Flood depth control," McKinnon ordered.

At once, the chief of the watch slammed the small control stick forward allowing water to fill the center trim tanks. The submarine descended faster.

"Five-zero feet," called the diving officer, "Downward depth rate increasing. Shut the vents."

"At sixty feet, start pumping as fast as you can. We'll sink like a rock real soon."

A banging grinding noise raked along the hull.

"We're catching some of it. Pushing the sail," McKinnon said calmly.

"Five-four feet, five-six, five-eight," the diving officer called.

The sail slid free of the ice. The submarine rocked gently as she righted herself.

"Status of the engines," McKinnon asked.

"Ready to answer all bells," the OOD reported.

"Good, we're going to need them," McKinnon replied dryly.

"Pumping to sea," the COW reported.

U-761

The U-boat slid back into the water. The sleek hull smashed through the thin ice, sending plumes of mist high over the drifting German submarine. Again, her shark-like bow lifted and fell in the swells. U-761 drifted in the newly created polinya gently bumping against the smooth side of the overturned ice.

The engine still growled as she bobbed in her new home. Moist air warmed by a heat exchanger slowly radiated through the compartments. One-hour later, temperature inside reached thirty-four degrees. Drops of melted ice flowed down the rounded interior of the pressure hull.

21
AWAKENING

"Prepare war, wake up the mighty men."

-Joel, III, 9

Soon after 1000 local, his flight touched down on the rain-soaked runway of Brandenburg International. He collected his small bag and followed other weary passengers off the plane.

"Now what?" he muttered to no one. "I'll get a cab or bus anything with wheels, find a hotel," he mumbled. Blevins followed the signs to Baggage Claim, rounded the corner, and noticed a man holding a handwritten sign; "MR. BLEVINS."

"I'm Blevins," he said quietly.

"Carl Blevins?" the stranger asked cheerfully.

"Yes."

"Sir, I'm Michael Warren." The man shook Carl's hand.

"Good to be on the ground," Carl commented.

"It is a long flight."

"Let's get you to the hotel." He led the way down a small flight of stairs.

"Wait here," Warren smiled and waved. A white van pulled to the curb. Warren slid the door open, helped Carl inside, and climbed in next to the driver. "Well, Mr. Blevins welcome to Germany," he said as the van splashed away from the curb.

"Thanks, but just who are you?" Blevins asked.

"I'm Lieutenant Warren, SEAL Team Six. The driver here is Petty Officer Moody."

"SEALS?" Blevins asked cautiously.

"We're here to show you around and ensure you get what you need," Warren explained. "Don't worry about a thing. Joe and I will take good care of you starting with a little dinner."

U-761

The air warmed slowly but steadily. Bulkheads and stringers creaked and groaned as the warming steel expanded. A thin wisp of steam hissed when droplets hit the top of the hammering diesel engine.

Hotel Das Aldalwine
Berlin, Germany
November 11th

After a quick breakfast, Carl Blevins met up with the two Navy Seals.

"Sleep well?" Warren asked.

"Yes, just not enough," Blevins yawned.

"Where do you need to go?"

"National archives," Blevins answered.

"Big place," Warren remarked.

The white van eased through the sleepy morning. It was a short drive to the National Archives, only a few bicycles wheeled silently through the streets.

The archives building, was a huge structure. Pockmarked with holes, some repaired, some not, it was obvious the building had been here during the war.

They walked toward the huge stone stairs. "God, I am out of shape," Blevins huffed up the last of the steps.

Inside the door, an older man wearing an aged but well maintained suit of dark gray watched them. He lifted his hand and unlocked the top catch to the steel and glass door.

"Guten Morgen," the man said warmly. "Please, come in."

Warren bowed slightly "*Danke. Wie geht es Ihnen?*

The old man smiled. "I am fine, thank you. Come now out of the cold."

The three followed past endless rows of books and cases. The great hall smelled of old paper.

"Come now. It will take you all day to view the material on our *Ubootwaffe*," the old man smiled. He led them down a set of spiral stairs to the main hall with several brightly polished doors, each side-staggered and identified by numbers.

"Here we are," he stopped in front of door 218. "I'll leave the key with you, no one will disturb you. Curious, but which U-boat interests you?"

Blevins studied the small German. "Ah-*U-166*," he lied.

"I remember that one. Lost in the Gulf of Mexico I think."

Blevins's eyebrows rose. "Yes, that is the one. You seem to know a bit about the subject," Blevins commented.

"*Nein*, I watch too much television."

"I will share with you what I find."

"That would be most kind. I will now leave you to your work. If there is any way that I may assist, please call on me."

U-761

Temperatures in the U-boat's compartments reached 67 degrees. Eleven hours after the engine first came to life the crew of the ancient submarine began to stir.

Becker rose slowly. He had to grab an overhead pipe to pull his body upright. "Can anyone hear me?" he rasped.

"Captain?" a weak voice answered.

"Roth?"

"Captain, are you okay?" Roth asked.

"Ja," *U-761*'s commander responded. "How are you?"

"Can't move," the voice whispered.

"Keep trying," Becker urged.

"How long," Roth's weak voice increased in volume.

"I don't know?" Becker reached up to stroke his beard. "Could not have been too long, my beard has not grown much."

"One of the engines is running," Roth noted.

Becker' took another deep gulp of air and slid his body off the bunk. He wobbled a bit then slowly steadied.

USS MIAMI SSN 755

"That ice is making a racket," sonar reported. "We're almost deaf. I can pick up some broadband off the array."

"Okay," McKinnon replied. "I can't go much deeper."

"Roger that."

McKinnon went to the plot. "We've got about ten miles to open water."

The navigator nodded. "At this speed, it'll take us about two more hours."

"Nowhere else to be," McKinnon smiled.

The navigator leaned close. "What did you think?"

"About?"

"The U-boat."

McKinnon shook his head. "Strange things in the ocean—I thought I had seen them all."

Just imagine a piece of history like that right in front of our eyes."

The navigator's brow wrinkled, "What do you think they'll do with her?"

"I don't know. That is going to be a touchy issue. I don't think they'll go public."

"Sad, I sure hope that if I was in that situation I would be able to come home."

"Same thing I was thinking," McKinnon let his pencil fall onto the chart. "I'm sure we'll hear more." He walked forward to his stateroom.

HMS SWIFT
November 12th

"Sir," the radio officer said as he came to attention.

"What is it," the deck officer asked while he scanned the mist and fog.

"We are picking up some garbled transmissions in the two-point-eight megahertz range."

"Fishing boat?"

"Could be, but the location of transmission is twenty-kilometers northeast."

"What?" The deck officer stepped to the chart placed his dividers on *Swift*'s position and traced a light arc. "That puts the transmission inside the ice pack."

"Yes sir it does.

"If it is a fishing boat it's in a very bad situation. Very strange," the deck officer noted. "Could you make out anything?"

"No sir."

"Keep listening I'll inform the captain."

Picking up the bridge phone, the deck officer pushed the buttons for the captain's stateroom. In his ear, he heard the buzzer sounding. He let it buzz three times. "Captain must be doing his workout." He replaced the phone in its cradle. "Quartermaster, enter the radio contact in the log." He then looked at the radar picture. The ice showed as a blue ragged line not two kilometers to the North. "Bloody bad place to be tonight."

22
THE NEW WORLD

"He that shall endure unto the end, the same shall be saved."

-Matthew XXIV, 13

BERLIN, GERMANY
NOVEMBER 13TH

AFTER THREE HOURS, PORING over records Carl Blevins rubbed his eyes. "Warren I'm going to the head.

The bored SEAL gave him a thumb up and went back to his German sports magazine.

Blevins stepped from the room into the musty hall, as he rounded the corner the small German man blocked his way.

"Herr Blevins," the man smiled. "I don't think what you are looking for is here."

"What am I looking for?" Blevins asked. "How would you know?"

The German smiled wider. "No time for that. Here is the man you need. He pushed a folded piece of paper into Blevins's hand. "I must ask you not to mention our little talk." He patted Blevins on the shoulder turned and disappeared into the maze of hallways.

USS MIAMI SSN 755

With pack ice eight miles behind her, *Miami* slid toward the surface of a wind-whipped sea. At fifty-eight feet her communications mast slid up, piercing the angry sea.

"Conn, radio, taking hits on the broadcast," the radio operator reported.

"Radio this is the Captain. We can't get up any further. Would a course change help?" He steadied himself on the still housed attack scope.

"We can try," the radioman responded.

"Okay, we'll come around to the East. I'll put the seas on the beam. Just be quick. Got some sailors are looking a little green."

"Will do, Captain."

Miami's rudder swung ten degrees to starboard. Her blunt nose turned, bucking and twisting as the ocean slapped at her.

"You okay diving officer?" McKinnon watched the gyro slowly turn to the East.

"I have a ten pucker factor right now sir. Watch the angle," he blurted at the planesmen.

The rolling doubled when her bow lined up with the waves. "Steady on course two-two-zero," the helm reported.

"Okay radio we're steady," said McKinnon.

"We have acquired the satellite," the radio operator reported. "In receipt of flash traffic, buffer printing."

"Subject line?" McKinnon asked.

"Operational orders," radio reported.

U-761

Edel trudged along the steel deck, his footsteps heavy and unsure. "Captain," he said softly.

Becker turned his head slowly, "Everything operating?"

"Yes but how?"

"I don't know. Who started the diesels?"

Edel shrugged his shoulders. "Any luck with the radio?"

"None," Becker answered. "Gerlach?" he whispered."

"He's awake but weak."

Becker rubbed his chin. "What now?" he asked mostly to himself.

Edel rubbed the thick stubble of his own chin, "Home?"

"When can we dive?"

"An hour more on the batteries," Edel responded.

Roth stepped through the control room hatch. "Captain, *Sturmbannführerr* Gerlach asked for you."

Becker looked at Edel. Again, their bond needed no words.

"Tell him I'm coming."

"Yes sir." Roth ducked under the after control room hatch.

"I wonder how long we slept," Edel commented.

"I don't know." Their eyes met. "I do know we are alive."

Becker went to the SS officer, and knelt next to him.

"So it seems your experiment worked."

"I don't know if it was all we had hoped for. How long?" asked Gerlach.

Becker rubbed his head. "I don't know. The ice has changed. It seems everything has changed."

"What now?"

Becker stood. "We go home."

"If there is a home to go to," Gerlach managed, as his voice grew even weaker.

"There is always home, always. Get some rest." Becker stopped and chuckled. "I don't think we need more rest but still…"

Gerlach's lips arced in a slight smile. "No, we don't."

Berdy managed a quick meal of canned potato soup and sardines. The men did not understand why they were so famished.

Becker entered the zentrale where Edel watched the helmsman test the rudder control. "Chief, are we ready?"

Edel turned. "Yes sir," he said quietly.

"Diving stations," Becker ordered. "Volker, are you sure of our course?" Becker asked.

"Course is set, captain. I estimate thirty-kilometers to open water."

"Up scope," Becker ordered.

With a hiss, the silver tube lifted itself from the hull. The optics came up, stopping just under Becker's eyes. He snapped the handles down and peered out. "No contacts, down scope." Becker slapped the handle of the periscope against the optics. The silver dripping tube receded smoothly into the U-boat's hull.

"Let's go home," Becker smiled. "Chief dive the boat."

Edel nodded. "Open the main vents."

At the ballast control, the Kingston valves opened with a rush of escaping air. Water surged into the ballast tanks.

"Five meters," Edel called. "Boat is heavy. Pump out six thousand liters."

"Ahead standard," Becker ordered.

Edel looked at the engine order telegraph then back to the depth gauge, "Hurry."

The dull bronze propellers bit into the ocean, *U-761* shuddered. Her nose dropped ten degrees. "Stern up ten," the chief ordered.

"Rudder answers," the helmsman called. "Speed two knots."

"Bow up five," Edel said softly, "Twenty-five meters."

Water slowly flowed over the control surfaces. The U-boat responded as if drunk. Her hull rolled gently and the bow staggered to level. She lightened herself as water streamed from her trim tanks.

"Boat is stable, trim good." Edel exhaled.

"Let's go home." Becker smiled.

HMS SWIFT

The seas calmed some, still the wind whistled through the gray sky. She sailed west, skirting the edge of the ice. Her radar probed with its invisible fingers for signs of a rouge whale ship.

Her crew recovered quickly from the storm and heavy seas Old sailors found new ammunition with which to tease and torment younger members of the mess. Tonight the "Blue Nose" ceremony would take place to initiate those who have never crossed the Arctic Circle, afterwards they planned movie marathon.

After eight bells, Arctic fog rolled in a thick heavy mist covering *Swift* as though a heavy blanket descended over the entire ship. Order went out to station extra lookouts and operate the auxiliary radar. She slowed to eight knots and turned 11 degrees south. On this course, she opened the distance with the ice by three miles. The mist caused ice to form on her upper-works. If too much was allowed to accumulate, the small ship could become unstable. Armed with brooms and shovels the off watch cleared the rapidly developing frost. A few less lucky ratings climbed the swaying mast and knocked heavy ice accumulations from the thin wire of the radio aerials.

Rumors spread throughout the ship that tonight would be last night hunting the phantom whale ship. Tomorrow *HMS Swift* would turn her fantail to the desolate ice and start the trek to somewhat warmer Scotland and home.

THE AUTOBAHN
NOVEMBER 13TH

"Warren signaled and pushed the silver BMW into the passing lane. A flat-nosed semi-truck flashed by in a blur. "What do you know about this man?"

"Nothing really," Blevins sighed.

Sliding back to the travel lane Warren only smiled.

"How long till we arrive," Blevins asked.

"An hour at this speed but I can speed up if you like."

"Hell no, an hour is just fine." Blevins shrank in the seat when Warren again passed a long line of slow moving tanker trucks. "That sign said Goslar, eighty-kilometers," Blevins said as he craned his neck.

"Like I said, less than an hour," Warren nodded.

Forty-five minutes later Warren pulled in front of the hotel. "Let's get checked in," he urged and popped open the trunk. "Remember, we're here doing research for a book on ancient Germanic symbols." Warren took out a rather beat-up suitcase.

Blevins put his backpack under his arm.

"This meeting has to be hush-hush. This guy is, well shall we say, a person of interest to one of our allies."

"You mean Israel?"

"What a beautiful old house," Blevins commented to change the subject.

They walked up a narrow stone path to the rustic looking inn. Warm light glowed from the windows. The entrance like out of a fairy tale had a huge oak door arched at the top with heavy iron hinges holding it to the ancient stonework. Warren tapped lightly on the inch thick wood.

U-761

Becker opened the war log. He studied the pages and let his fingers rub the paper. The edges crumbled between his fingers He picked up the fountain pen he always used to make an entry in the log. He pressed the pen lightly to the paper but it made no mark. He shook the pen to get the ink to the nib. Again, he tried and again the same result. Becker twisted the top of the pen off and turned the pen upside down. He placed a small scrap of paper down to catch the ink but it did not spill out. Becker tapped the pen lightly with his hand. A black powder rained over the small bit of paper.

Roth stepped through the hatch. "Captain?" the Radioman asked. "How have you felt since …?"

His eyes rose to Roth. "Sore, I guess you might say. Why do you ask?"

"Most of the crew has the same soreness and fatigue. I don't know sir maybe it's nothing, but our bodies are not the same."

"Frimunt?"

"No change. The *Sturmbannführerr* is another story."

"What do you mean?"

"His throat is healing but he gets weaker." Roth rubbed the back of his neck.

"And you, Roth, how are you?"

"My bones hurt."

"Could be from the cold," Becker offered.

"I don't think so."

"Keep watching; report only to me."

Edel ducked his head around the corner and interrupted. "Captain we need you in control," the Chief said nervously.

Becker walked as fast as his aching legs would allow.

"The sound room," Edel pointed.

"A contact?" asked Becker.

"I don't know what it is," Veldmon answered, "listen."

He handed the earphones to Becker. "All stop," he shouted. He rushed for the search scope. "Up scope," he ordered. "Chief, get us to eighty-meters—now."

"Both planes down fifteen," Edel barked.

As the scope rose from its well, Becker grabbed the handles. He lowered his body and peered into the sea while the scope finished its upward movement.

Becker spun the scope trying to focus in the eerie, dark blue. Emerging from the gloom a massive wall of ice hung like and upside down mountain. In fewer than two minutes, the U-boat would collide with that mountain.

Becker swung the scope from port to starboard. "Chief, increase the angle, both engines ahead full. Report speed," he shouted.

"Six knots," the helm responded.

The U-boat dove deeper. The water grew darker the image of the ice faded into blackness.

"Deeper chief deeper," Becker urged.

"Depth seventy meters," Edel wiped condensation from his nose, "Flood negative tanks."

The crew braced themselves when the U-boat's nose dipped at a twenty-degree angle. Along the entire submarine items fell to the deck. The crew held on not daring to attempt a passage along the wet slippery deck. Her hull creaked as the sea pressed on her old steel.

Becker wrapped his arms around the scope to keep himself from sliding forward. The wall of ice moved faster in the optics and grew closer. Suddenly the wall of white evaporated. "Clear water," Becker shouted. "Level off!"

"Both planes to zero," The Engineer barked. "Depth one-hundred-twenty meters."

"Lower the scope—be quick," ordered Becker.

The sound of the tormented and surging mountain of ice came through the hull. A grinding terrible noise grew as *U-761* passed under.

"Battery?" asked Becker.

Edel looked at the meter mounted above the helm station. "Thirty percent," he said softly.

"We're not out yet. Both motors slow ahead," Becker ordered. The crackle and grind of ice grew louder.

"Estimate three kilometers to open water," Volker shouted over the noise.

Suddenly *U-761* rocked from a blow worse than any depth charge. She fell over to port, but quickly righted herself.

"Taking water from the torpedo loading hatch," a voice screamed over the snap and popping ice.

"We must have been hit by a chunk," Edel yelled. "Boat is getting heavy in the bow."

A shower of sparks flew across the zentrale and the lights went out. Soon the red emergency lights flickered to life.

"Salt water shorted the circuit," the electrician called.

"Bow planes up ten," Edel ordered. The nervous operators tried to focus on their gauges.

"What is happening up there?" demanded Becker.

"Thirty percent left on the battery," warned Edel. "We need to pump out the torpedo room."

Becker went to the intercom. "I need answers," he yelled. "Volker, how far to open water?"

"Maybe a kilometer," Volker answered.

"Chief, get our nose up," Becker said calmly.

A voice crackled over the intercom. "Leak secured."

"Pump bilges," Becker ordered, "Ahead standard."

"Battery is at twenty-percent," Edel said.

23
CONTACT

"He smote them hip and thigh."

-Judges, XV,8

"Contact bearing one-nine-five," the radar operator reported. "Designate this contact as Romero-one."

The combat watch officer stepped to the console. "What do you have?"

"A contact appeared out of nowhere, just the other side of that berg." The operator pointed to his screen. "There it is again."

"Right, switch to high PRF," the officer ordered.

The radar pulse increased allowing a better picture to develop.

"Bridge combat," the officer said into his headset microphone, "Romeo contact, bearing one-nine five; range two thousand meters. Contact course is one-zero-two."

Swift's commander answered when the stateroom phone buzzed. "Yes?" He listened intently, and a smile crossed his lips. "Good. Sound action stations."

The veteran Royal Naval commander opened the stateroom door when the alarm sounded. "This bloody fog," he huffed as he reached the bridge, "Situation?"

"Surface radar contact sir no visual yet. Contact bears two-two-zero: speed four knots. Range to target—one-eight-hundred meters. Angle on the bow is starboard zero-eight-zero. Ship is at action stations.

"Send a signal in the clear for any ship in sight to turn on lights and heave to."

Within seconds, transmission began. "Unidentified ship, unidentified ship, this is Royal Navy warship *HMS Swift*. We hold you on radar. Turn on required navigational lights and stop your engines. Prepare to be boarded."

"Signals report no response."

"Bloody obstinate whalers," he hissed. "Helm, come to new course zero-seven-two."

"Hold visual contact," the port bridge wing lookout shouted, "Came out of the fog." "What is it?"

"Not sure sir. It was long and low to the water. I did see a bow wave though."

"That does not sound like a whale ship."

"I intend to put a shot across her bow," *Swift's* commander announced. "Quartermaster, run up the Ensign. Gun director place a shot fifty meters ahead of the contact's last radar bearing."

In less than five seconds, the unmanned turret swung *Swift's* 76mm Melara cannon over the patrol ship's side. The battle flag of the Royal Navy slid quickly up the yardarm. The gusty wind caused the flag to whip and snap while it climbed to the peak of the mast.

"Ready to fire," the gunnery officer reported.

"Commence firing," Kirby ordered.

The compact, but powerful gun erupted. The muzzle flash lit the surrounding gloom with a momentary burst of bright orange.

U-761

The surfaced U-boat made little more than a ripple as she slid along the surface. On the bridge, Becker wiped drops of freezing water from his face. The diesels chugged to life their shafts turning the generator, feeding the power-starved batteries.

"Helm left three degrees. New course zero-eight-nine," Becker ordered softly.

Out of the gloom the rough texture of another large iceberg appeared. Almost invisible in the heavy fog the berg sat like a hill in the ocean.

U-761 answered her rudder and her bow swung away from the jagged ice.

"This will be good cover till the batteries are full," Becker said barely audible. The lookouts took their positions.

"Destroyer," the starboard lookout screamed. A loud boom echoed across the water and the sky lit up in a bright flash. The high explosive round impacted the ice shelf thirty meters in front of *U-761's* bow. Chunks of blasted ice rained over the submarine.

"Alarm," Becker cried.

The lookouts scrambled down the hatch.

Becker dropped down the ladder and spun the hatch wheel shut. "Twenty meters," he snapped. "Be quick."

"Herr Kaleu, the batteries are almost empty." His eyes wild, "We can't stay down."

"I know. Helm right hard rudder," he ordered. "Action stations flood tubes one through four."

"Propeller noises," Veldmon called. "Bearing zero-three-zero—closing."

Becker looked up. "He's coming after us."

"Tubes one-through-four flooded, Herr Kaleu," Hamlin reported.

"We'll get one shot," Becker noted loudly. "Helm steer new course, two-six-eight. Chief, take her to one-hundred meters."

"Contact is slowing," Veldmon said in almost a whisper.

"He can't risk slamming his nose in the ice." Becker climbed the ladder to the attack center. "Raise the attack scope."

HMS SWIFT

"Contact is gone, sir," the puzzled radar operator reported.

"What?

"Lost it, sir."

"Bloody hell."

"Combat reports loss of contact, captain," the bridge phone talker reported.

"Lost?" You think we hit it?"

"We would have seen a hit on thermal imaging," the first officer responded. "Radar and gunnery track don't match either. The round went fifty meters ahead of target."

"Dead slow ahead," the commander ordered. "Signals send a contact report to Fleet."

U-761

U-761 slipped through the inky sea her propellers turning slowly as her motors ate the remaining battery power.

"We have to come up now," Edel warned.

"Switch lighting to lanterns," Becker ordered from his perch in the conning tower. "Veldmon, what is the contact doing?"

"Slowing, propellers sound muffled."

"Keep listening," Becker whispered. "Helm, come to course one-eight-zero."

"Herr Kaleu, that takes us under the berg," Volker said astonished.

"I know, lieutenant."

U-761 slipped under the floating berg. The tip of the periscope coming meters from the bottom.

With one eye tight against the periscope, Becker peered into the gloom of the Arctic Ocean. Becker noticed the darkness grow a bit lighter. "We're clear, Periscope depth now chief."

The propellers stopped. "Battery is gone."

"Use air but get me up," Becker shouted.

"Switching torpedo control to manual," *Oberbootsmann* Hamlin said calmly.

"What is he doing?" Becker asked. The gloom grew lighter.

"Very faint almost stopped," Veldmon cupped his hand around his earphones.

"Careful chief we're coming up fast," Becker warned.

The U-boat barely moved when the scope popped over the surface. Becker moved the cross hairs a few meters and a gray shape filled his view. "There she is. Range eight-hundred meters. Angle on the bow—port zero-eight zero. Bearing zero-two zero."

"Match," Hamlin shouted. The manual computer indicated the correct interception course.

"Tubes one and three, one degree spread," Becker ordered.

"Set," Hamlin called. "Ready."

"Tube one—los," Becker called out.

The U-boat shuddered slightly as the torpedo left the tube.

"Torpedo running," Veldmon announced."

Becker paid no attention, "Tube three—los."

Again the submarine trembled as the twenty-three foot torpedo sped away.

"Surface the boat."

HMS SWIFT

"Contact," the radar operator shouted. A blue blip appeared on his screen. "Regain of Romeo-one."

The information digitally linked to the fire-control computer on the bridge. "She bears two-six-zero?

How the devil did she do that?" the commander asked aloud.

On the Swift's stern, Midshipman Royce Hill stood at his station, shivering in the angry stinging mist. "This God-awful cold," he shivered. "I spent my first three days throwing up now this," he chattered to a reservist able seaman

Hill's eyes followed the small swells that rolled gently off the side of the iceberg and into the blue-gray ocean. He glanced over the side to find the horizon when a shape rose from the sea. "What do you make of that?"

The older man stopped, squinted then his mouth fell open. "It's a bloody damned submarine." He moved carefully but quickly to the Boat Deck phone. "Submarine off the starboard side," he shouted.

"What is that in front of it?"

The Able Seaman looked over the side. Two small mounds of frothing water snaked toward his ship.

U-761

The U-boat rolled slightly as she heaved herself up from the ocean. Water poured from her tower and deck.

Becker had the hatch open before the hull cleared the icy water. "Keep the watch below," he shouted down the voice pipe.

HMS SWIFT

Her commander could not see the contact. He glanced at the radar repeater screen and confirmed something sat in the ocean.

"Submarine off the starboard side," a voice crackled over the bridge intercom. All eyes on *Swift's* bridge scanned for a shape.

At the stern, Midshipman Hill was mesmerized by the small mounds of foam, churning toward him."

The older sailor's eyes went wide and his free hand clamped on the extra cloth of the Midshipman's coat. "Run," he screamed, shoving the young man. His fingers stabbed at the bridge intercom button, "Torpedoes!"

"Ahead flank," *Swift's* commander screamed.

The helmsman shoved the throttle forward, fuel poured into the cylinders and the twin Crossley diesels roared. Her three-bladed screws sawed at the water sending a plume of water behind her.

The small patrol ship reached 5 knots when the first torpedo struck. Moving at forty knots, it smashed into the hull one meter below the water line, forward the funnel. The detonator pistol felt the collision and released a firing pin. The warhead exploded sending expanded gases through *Swift's* thin hull plates.

The shock wave pushed the welded plates inward until they could stretch no more, at which point they tore. The full force of the warhead entered the ship. The wave of air and water moved at just over the speed of sound. Its sheer velocity caused the surrounding air to ignite.

Not yet weakened the pressure again stressed the already rending metal until it like the impact point stretched and tore loose. Two seconds later, the second torpedo found its mark just under the bridge window.

Royce Hill stumbled after the first torpedo exploded. His world went into slow motion. He saw a plume of water shoot five times higher than the mainmast. He saw the angry blast of red and orange shoot from the inside that terrible column of water. The deck jumped slamming him to the deck his knees. His mind cleared quickly. The stern disappeared to the rear of the funnel. He tried to stand, but waves of pain from his damaged knees glued him to the deck. He reached out. The ship seemed to fall on her side, then a sudden silence. He felt light as if floating in air, the pain gone. He looked down on his ship and saw it explode into a fireball. Strange, he thought. How did I get up here? Then his eyes caught sight of a headless body in the air next to him its arms and left leg missing "That's my coat." He knew nothing more.

24
THE GAMBLE

"If you want to avoid collision, you had better abandon the ocean."

Henry Clay:
To the House of Representatives,
22 January 1800

FIVE MEN LIE DEAD and one nuclear warhead was gone. The five-ton truck, whose best days passed some twenty years ago lumbered down the small foothill. Covered in sheets of ugly brown and black ice, the pitiful rutted excuse for a road tested the strength of the tired wheels. Lieutenant Cheslav fought the steering wheel as the truck slid over a hill and skidded around a corner.

"You can slow down," the colonel grumbled.

The gears of the truck ground and clanked as the wheels struggled to find traction.

"We need to get our package ready to mail soon." Cheslav grunted. "I give us 12 hours. If we are not at sea by then…"

"This whole thing is really starting to freak me out." Blevins walked to the edge of a wooded ravine.

"Yeah, I don't like it much either, but this is where the man wants us to meet him," Warren's trained eyes scanned the area for even the smallest hint of danger.

Tires crunched along on the gravel road.

"That him?" asked Blevins nervously.

"Don't know," Warren responded. "Get back in the trees. We'll check it out before we expose ourselves."

Obediently the onetime submariner moved behind a thin row of bushes covered by straight tall pines.

A black armored sedan rolled slowly up the small hill. The car came to halt just short of the two Americans. It remained motionless for a half minute.

The driver's door opened. A small man, well dressed in a black tweed suit and tie, stood. He looked around and unbuttoned his jacket. Satisfied with the surroundings the man stepped to the rear door and gave the window two gentle raps with his knuckles.

The rear door popped open and a shoe found its way to the pavement. An older man of perhaps eighty emerged from the dark interior. His eyes steel blue, nose chiseled thin and like the driver, his suit hand tailored with a perfect fit for his muscular frame. The older man straightened his jacket while the driver scanned the area.

"Herr Warren?" the driver called.

The SEAL leader stood up from the brush. "Hallo," he said in his best German.

In a flash the driver's hand, held a dull silver automatic pistol.

"Easy," Warren shouted.

"Walk toward me Herr Warren," the driver ordered in a monotone voice, "The other man?"

"He's here," Warren said cautiously.

The driver motioned with the pistol. "Have him show himself."

"No deal." Warren approached the driver. "Put the gun away and we'll talk."

The older man placed his hand on the driver's forearm pushing the automatic's muzzle toward the dirt and stone. They exchanged a glance; the driver placed the weapon into a holster under his jacket.

"Okay Chief," Warren called over his shoulder.

Blevins stood and cautiously walked toward the men.

The older man extended his hand and smiled warmly. "Forgive me for the measures I must take," he said bowing slightly.

Blevins took the old man's hand, "Yeah no problem."

"One more thing I must ask of you gentlemen," He crooked a finger. "Please, remove your jackets and roll up your shirt sleeves."

"Why?" Warren asked irritably.

"Members of Mosad have tattoos," the old man answered. "The *all seeing eye of justice* they call it."

"You think we work for the Israelis?"

"I must be cautious at all times."

Warren peeled the windbreaker from his body, unbuttoned the sleeves, and rolled the material past his elbows.

"Slowly turn your arms over if you please." the old man scanned Warren's arms.

"Thank you and now for you."

Carl Blevins did as told and exposed his arms to the old man, "Thank you gentlemen."

Blevins and Warren retrieved their jackets.

"You are Carl Blevins?" the old man asked.

"Yes."

"Then it is you who needs information. Please, let us walk."

Blevins looked at Warren.

Warren nodded, "Its okay."

The two ambled down the path with the bodyguards not far behind.

"Because I know any information I give you will be subject to authentication, I will tell you something of myself," the old man said. "But that is all you will know of me and please ask no more. I have a few years left and want to enjoy them in peace."

"Of course," Blevins agreed.

"During the war I was a young but highly placed member of the SS. I was what you in the United States call a 'paper pusher.' I in charge of filing and storing documentation for activities related to the research branch of the SS. When the war ended, I found myself in a situation that most men never face. In May 1945, I was to destroy files and documents relating to our special projects. But I thought I could use this information as shall we say a life insurance plan."

"So you hid everything?" Blevins asked.

"Yes and so far the insurance plan has paid great dividends."

"I bet," Blevins said coldly.

"I know the information you seek. That file was not supposed to be made however somehow it was."

"How could you know what I'm after?"

The old man laughed. "Our networks are vast."

"You know what I need?"

"Yes, and it is a file I myself have not looked at."

Blevins stopped walking. "Why not," he asked.

"Herr Blevins if I see a book of matches, I don't have to open them or light them to know they can burn down my house. Herr Blevins," the old man smiled. "Our business is done here." The old man reached in his coat and pulled out a CD. "Take this. What you look for is here."

Blevins took the CD in his hand.

"Oh, and please, Mr. Blevins, forget we ever met. It could be as dangerous for you as for me."

"How do you mean?"

"Ah, I almost forgot." He once again reached in his pocket. "Here this is for you also." He held out a small brown paper wrapper.

"What is this?"

"A treat for your dog Ping," the old man smiled.

"How do you know about my dog?"

"Like I told you, Herr Blevins, our network is vast."

USS MIAMI SSN 755

"Yes skipper I'm sure. Nothing makes a noise like that," the senior chief explained. "The only contact we had was that *Brit* warship two days ago. I used it for training my narrowband operators."

"Think we need to sneak back up and take a look?" The executive officer asked.

"First we need to know more." McKinnon rubbed the back of his neck. "You have the whole event on tape?"

"Yes sir."

"Good, make a copy."

"What do you think, XO?" McKinnon asked.

"Right now all I have are the facts. One, we passed a small British warship a day or so ago. Two, the sonar gang used the ship for training and followed it. Three, last night we heard it blow up. That's all I know."

"You think we missed a Russian boat?"

"It is a very big ocean out there."

"Let's get to PD and see what's going on."

"Yes sir. Next scheduled PD trip is in about two hours."

U-761

Becker cruised among what remained of *HMS Swift*. The explosions left little, just bits of smoking wreckage bobbing in the ice-chocked sea. A large Royal Navy ensign its edge charred floated lazily in the gray-green water.

Hamlin wanted to retrieve the waterlogged flag, but Becker left the flag to drift over the sailors it recently led into battle.

Three hours later Becker guided his U-boat to shelter offered by a large berg. *U-761* lay motionless.

U-761's commander stuck his head into the tiny radio room.

Roth slowly adjusted the radio frequency dial and his ears cocked to the side to pick even the smallest whisper of the world.

"Anything?" asked Becker as he sat down on the small folding stool next to Roth.

"Just static, Herr Kaleu. It's like the whole world just turned off." Roth removed the headset, and rested his elbows on the tiny table. "Even in Mid-Atlantic we could get some information, some news, anything."

As he picked up the headset, the static broke. A voice fought through the static. Roth slammed the headset to his ear.

"This is the BBC World News Update," the faint female voice announced in English.

Becker and Roth looked at one another.

"Today's top story is the ongoing war on terror. Protests across the country and continent continue for the third day. An anti-war rally in Berlin turned violent, as police with dogs and water cannons broke up a demonstration in the civic center."

"What?" Roth asked.

"Quiet," Becker barked.

The rather pleasant voice continued, *"Protests began last week when the Prime Minister announced six-thousand more troops would be sent to the fighting. Germany announced it would add two-thousand additional troops wherever needed.*

"Another suicide bomber claimed the lives of seventy-five Israeli troops at a check point in the disputed Gaza strip.

"Stay tuned here for the latest in weather and sports," the voice urged just as static once again overwhelmed the signal.

"The war is still going on?" Roth hissed.

Becker tried to decipher the news. He understood English but the words didn't make sense. "I need to talk to Gerlach."

25
THE WAGE OF SIN (I)

*"Power is not revealed by striking hard
or often but by striking true."*

-Balzac, 1799–1850

U-761

SNOW BEGAN AT NOON. By 1400, it came down in sheets of blinding white driven by vicious gusts of wind. Sheltered in the lee of the giant berg, the German U-boat bobbed gently.

Becker sat at the tiny wardroom table with Gerlach across from him.

"Are you sure that is what you heard?" the *Sturmbannführer*r rasped.

"Yes," Becker confirmed. "My English is not great, but I did understand."

Gerlach stared at the pipes and wires hanging over him, "The war continues."

"What about Israeli troops?"

"That is most interesting. The Jews have long wanted Palestine. Perhaps Hitler made a deal."

"There is the possibility Germany has lost."

Gerlach rolled his head slowly toward Becker. "I don't think so. How could a defeated nation send troops?"

THE PENTAGON

"Gentlemen lets find out what is going on," Malroy huffed.

"We need to get the facts here." Royal Naval Captain James Brewster began. "What we know is *HMS Swift's* last communiqué was a request for information of submarine activity in her operating area at 1545. At 1610, a signal picked up from an emergency life raft faded. We have been contact *Swift* since then. It is Her Majesties government's assumption the ship was torpedoed."

"We share in the grief at the loss of *Swift* and her crew," Admiral Malroy said. "However we cannot assume anything. We must have facts. What facts do you have?"

"At present we have only the request for activity in her operating area but we also have a recording taken from our Homeland Defense Acoustic Warning System. I have the recording and will now play it for you."

The captain punched the buttons on his rather large state-of-the art laptop. They heard the faint hum of a ship's propulsion. Brewster narrated, "This is *Swift* operating normally. Then she slows. If you listen, you can hear another set of propellers. Our lads in Faslane determined these noises to be two three-bladed screws."

The CNO spoke, "I don't know of many countries whose boats still have three bladed screws."

"Neither do we admiral," Brewster explained. "Listen further." A faint but distinct crack similar to snapping mousetrap was heard. "That's the ship's main gun. As you will note the two three-bladed screws disappear."

"Disappear?" asked Malroy.

"There is a brief pause, where you can hear only *Swift*. At one point her screws almost stop."

"If your ship tangled with a submarine why in the name of God would she slow down?" Malroy asked.

"We don't know," Brewster confessed. "She was in rather heavy ice. Perhaps that played a part."

"Excuse me Captain," Malroy raised his hand, "You and I go way back. So please understand what I am about to say."

"Go on, Admiral."

"It sounds like you fired the first shot. Trust me submarines do not react well to that."

"No warship of the Royal Navy would engage a vessel without the highest authority or unless she herself were attacked."

"Captain," the CNO said, "If you can, please tell us what operation did the *Swift* conduct?"

Brewster walked around the large table to find the right words. Our ship operated under a UN charter to protect whales."

"Whales," Malroy asked.

"Yes, a Norwegian whaler threatened a pod of endangered whales. Her mission was to intercept the whaler and safeguard the whale's passage south."

"So maybe this submarine business is bullshit," the CNO blurted.

Brewster's eyes narrowed. "No, admiral we checked and found the whale ship in question still tied to her pier in Tromso Norway."

"Could your ship have run into a berg? Malroy asked.

"No. I have another recording if I may?" Brewster asked.

"Please go ahead."

Brewster again keyed his computer. "This is about five minutes after the two threes faded.

They listened to the whirring sound of precision balanced screws of the British warship, then a mechanical clank.

"I'll be damned," Malroy exclaimed. "Tube doors opening."

"Yes," Brewster said. "But there is more."

Again, the room went silent as *Swift's* last moments played. A distant whooshing noise followed by the rapid grinding noise of high-speed propellers.

"Launch transient," the CNO admitted.

"Followed by another," Brewster added.

"Who would be taking pot shots at ships?" The CNO asked, "Especially warships?"

"Maybe someone with nothing to lose," Malroy offered.

Captain Brewster cleared his throat. "Admiral Malroy as you said, you and I have a long history. I consider you one of the finest officers I know, as well as my dear friend. What I must ask is not easy for me, but it is my duty. Does the United States have any submarines operating in the area?"

"You think we did this," the CNO blurted.

"Easy," Malroy cautioned. "Captain Brewster I understand your concern in wanting to get the facts. Although we are the best of allies you know I cannot discuss operations that are not being conducted in cooperation with the Royal Navy," Malroy said in his best official tone.

"Please advise your president, Her Majesties government *will not stand aside* for this unprovoked attack. The defense minister is even now discussing our options to safeguard the sea lanes."

"Captain I'm from Texas, so let me be sure what you are saying here." Malroy sat upright in his oversize chair.

Captain Brewster beat Malroy to the punch. "I am saying is that the agreed pull-back of forces seems to have been violated. That puts Russia in default…"

"Wait a minute," Malroy interrupted. "Are you saying you'll pick a fight with Russia? I understand the loss of a ship. Look at our own losses of late. Any action taken by your government in retaliation will have to be without the consent of the United States."

Brewster slapped the table. "I will also remind you of the NATO charter!"

"Captain an action I understand, but one that can lead to nothing other than total war, no. I am willing to put whatever assets in place to find the truth. But I must insist that Great Britain respect the agreement as it stands until all the facts are known."

UNITED STATES FLAGGED
CONTAINER SHIP SS MINGO
66,000 TONS

"Anything else on that rescue beacon," *Mingo's* master asked.

The first officer looked at the radio log sheet. "Nothing more, it just faded."

"We're near the area of the transmission. We'll slow and take a look." The captain leaned over the greenish-blue radar screen. "Post extra lookouts in the bow."

"Sir," the navigator interrupted. "Slowing will put us behind schedule."

"It's the law, you know that. We have to investigate any emergency beacon. Besides, if it were me sitting there freezing my ass off on some damned iceberg I'd sure hope someone would come looking for me."

"Yes sir," the navigator agreed. "Still, I am required to inform you."

"Duly noted," the Master nodded. "Ring up dead slow."

U-761

The reloading of the two torpedoes went well. The short day ebbed as the unseen sun slid over the ice.

U-761 moved from her place next to the large berg to hug the edge of the ice pack until Becker found a safe place to make a break for the open ocean. The diesels purred while the U-boat's sleek bow sliced into the sea.

Cheerful as ever his pot and its lid clanking Berdy came through the after hatch. He steadied himself against the gentle roll of the surfaced U-boat. "Herr Kaleu," the cook smiled, "I made sweet rolls. Would you care for some?"

Becker sat up. "You always take such good care of us." He took one of the sticky warm rolls. "Thank you Berdy."

About to ask how the stores of food held up when something seemed different. "Berdy, how old are you?"

The cook looked surprised. "Herr Kaleu, I'm twenty-six. You do not remember. We had a cake three days after we left port."

Becker tried to hide his forgetfulness. "Of course ... it's just that-around your eyes-there are wrinkles."

The cook reached up and felt the corners. "Just a little tired." His face once again broke into his ever-present smile. "Keeping this crew fed and happy is a hard job."

"Have you been feeling well?" Becker asked.

"Captain, do not worry about me. It is you, I'm worried about."

"Me?" Becker asked.

"Oh yes, captain. Have you looked? Your beard has sprinkles of gray and so does your hair."

Becker's hand tugged at his beard. "You think feeding these guys is a job? You should be in my shoes," Becker grinned.

"No, I'll stick to my pots and pans," he laughed. "If you will excuse me, I want to get these to the bridge before they get cold."

Becker bit into the warm roll.

CONTAINER SHIP SS MINGO

"Radar contact, bearing zero-one zero, range two-thousand meters, and closing," the radar operator reported. "Small contact on the right drawing left."

"Lifeboat?" the first officer asked.

"Can't tell," the operator responded. The radar's invisible beam swept the area again. "Contact fades in and out. It must be low to the water or else this mist is causing ghosts."

"Slow to three knots."

The foaming wave at Mingo's bow dropped off.

"Firming up that bearing now," the radar operator reported. "Bearing now is two-seven-seven."

U-761

"Contact off the starboard bow." The lookout cried.

Hamlin had the watch on the bridge. He raised his binoculars. "What is it?"

"Looks like a warship, cruiser size."

The outline of a large ship emerged from the gray. "Damn, heading for us." The bulk of the ship loomed closer. He could see no upper works, no weapons. Only one type of ship fit that description. "Alarm," he called down the hatch.

The lookouts slid down the hatch in seconds. Hamlin looked again. The giant ship pointed its huge curving bow directly for them. He cast a last look and dropped down the hatch, landing roughly on the steel deck of the conning tower deck. He could hear the water race over the deck. He reached the thick rope of the hatch and pulled hard. The hatch clanged shut and he spun the dogging wheel as the ocean closed over the conning tower.

By the time he climbed down the ladder, Edel was already at his station. Becker came through the hatch. "What is it," he demanded.

"Close," Hamlin panted.

Becker dashed up the ladder to the attack center. "Chief, hold us at periscope depth."

Hamlin regained some strength and followed Becker up the ladder, "Sir, very large ship, believed to be a carrier."

Becker's eyes narrowed, "A carrier?"

"Yes sir," Hamlin confirmed.

"Up scope," Becker ordered. The steel tube hissed as it slid from the top of the U-boat. Becker grabbed the handles and shoved his eye to the monocular sight. Green water splashed in front of his eyes as the scope continued upward. Three seconds later the water fell away. Becker stared into a horizon of ice. He pushed a small button with his left thumb. With a soft hum, the periscope spun slowly around. He took his eye from the scope long enough to look at the course gyro repeater. When he placed his eye back to the optic window, it filled with the steel sides of a massive a ship. Becker gasped at the size of the beast looming over him.

His sailor instinct took over. "Right hard rudder," he shouted. The seemingly endless wall of curved steel drew closer.

Volker stuck his head through the hatch. "That is toward the ice."

"I know," Becker responded.

Volker looked back into the control room and nodded. "Hydrophone reports the contact is slowing."

"Damn," Becker cursed.

"Captain they're trying to drive us under the ice. Drive us under and drown us."

"Two kilometers to the ice, Herr Kaleu," Volker warned quietly.

"Action stations," Becker ordered. "Range eight-hundred, bow angle thirty starboard."

Hamlin stood behind him and fed information into the torpedo data computer. "Gyro angle is one-four-three."

"Helm left ten degrees rudder. Ease me over. Hydrophone?"

"Screw still turning slow."

"Good," Becker grinned."

"Gyro angle now zero-eight-seven," Hamlin called out in a low tone.

"Keep coming around," Becker said softly. "Open bow caps on tubes one through four. Set up tubes one, two, and three."

"Tubes one, two, and three are set. Gyro angle now zero seven zero."

"Set a six degree spread," Becker ordered. "Torpedo speed thirty. Set running depth at two meters."

"Spread set, depth set. Gyro angle now zero four-eight."

Becker looked again at the U-boat's gyro repeater, "Helm rudder amid ships." Becker peered into the tiny window of the periscope. His target grew larger. He waited until the angle decreased so the weapons would not have to turn, increasing the chance of them running true.

"Rudder zero," the helm announced.

Becker hesitated. "Something just doesn't fit."

"Captain," Hamlin called softly, "Bearings are matched. We are at the firing point."

Becker placed his eye back to the scope. The light faded and seconds ticked off. "Stand by, tube one."

"Tube one ready," Hamlin answered.

Becker bit into his lower lip, "Tube one—los."

The German sub bucked as the weapon entered the sea.

Becker panned down and saw the wake of the torpedo, speeding toward the target. Five seconds went by, "Tube two—los."

Becker peered at the surface of the ocean. Suddenly his mouth dropped open. The second torpedo skipped along the top of the water like a stone thrown by a child.

There was no time now the firing solution was fading. He launched the third weapon, "Tube three—los."

"Weapons away," Hamlin announced as he shut off power to the torpedo data computer.

Becker saw the wake of the third weapon running true. He moved the scope around looking for the errant torpedo when his eyes caught a glimmer on the sea. He froze. The second weapon glanced off a floating chunk of ice, turned toward his periscope.

"Chief, get us down fast, both motors ahead full." Becker shouted.

Becker felt the nose of his U-boat dip. The entire boat vibrated while the screws chopped at the water. The whining of the torpedo's motor grew louder. "Faster chief," he said through clenched teeth.

Becker took a last look as waves closed over the scope. Becker caught a glimpse of the torpedo closing in on the U-boat. "Hang on," he screamed. "The torpedo is coming back."

As the damaged weapon closed, its gyro ordered the rudders to turn. The gimbals that held the spinning gyro in place cracked, which threw the rotation off balance and another signal told the rudders to hold the torpedo on a straight course unknowingly and uncaringly aimed for *U-761*. The gimbals frame stressed by centrifugal force broke in half. The rudders locked.

Becker closed his eyes. The noise seemed as if the torpedo would punch through the U-boat's side at any second.

The whirring of the torpedoes engines suddenly faded. He opened his eyes and a rush of air came out in relief.

"Unterwasserhorche?" he asked quietly.

"Torpedo fading astern," Veldmon sighed.

"Get us back up." Becker leaned over the conning tower hatch.

"Veldmon, can you hear the other torpedoes?" he asked as again the periscope slid up.

"Five seconds," Volker shouted up the hatch.

Becker grabbed the handles and flung them down as the scope lifted from its well.

"Now," Volker shouted.

Becker saw a plume of white boiling water shoot up from the center of the unknown ship. An angry puff of black emerged from the base of the still growing plume of water. "Hit," the Becker shouted.

"Four seconds on number three," Volker shouted. The rumble of the torpedo's detonation filled the dripping interior of *U-761*.

The plume of water fell. A jagged hole of rent steel showed itself. The ship seemed to turn slightly away from the incoming torpedo.

The second weapon reached the steel hull. This time there was no plume of water, no rumble. A blinding bright white flash erupted from the doomed ship.

Becker's mouth dropped open as the flash of intense light changed to a new shade of yellow orange. The fireball grew larger, expanding outward and upward. A wave of overpressure tore the white tops off the small waves.

The wave of supersonic air rushed past the U-boat's periscope and Becker saw the large ship's bow dip into the water. The area of the ship where the explosion occurred lifted clear of the water. "She broke her back," Becker yelled and jammed his eye back to the scope. He peered into the fading light and into the dying ship.

"She's breaking up," Veldmon yelled.

Another series of fainter explosions erupted.

"Going down," Veldmon said in a soft almost sad voice.

Becker swung the scope back to his victim just as the sea closed over the flag flying at her stern. Torn and mangled by the explosion, the flag waved proudly its bars of red and white. In the corner, a field of blue covered with stars. "American," he said to no one.

Hamlin turned his head. "What?"

"She was American," he said softly. "Chief, surface the boat."

26

THE WAGES OF SIN (II)

*…this war of grouping and drowning, of ambuscade
and stratagem, of science and seamanship…*

-Winston S. Churchill

"*BARSUK—BARSUK,* THIS IS HARBOR control. Do you read?" a static filled voice asked.

"Harbor control this is *Barsuk*—go ahead." Captain Rurik answered calmly.

"*Barsuk*, you are ordered to return to port," The monotone voice stated with no more inflection than a Kiev taxi driver." You have no orders and no piloting plan."

Rurik put the radio's microphone to his mouth. "Harbor control, this is *Barsuk*. Contact us on the frequency to strategic defense command. Give them your name and rank so they will know who delayed a mission vital to the defense of the motherland."

Cheslav laughed aloud in the tiny wheelhouse of the aged Russian patrol ship.

"Now a little something extra, just for good measure," Rurik said. "Harbor control, this is *Barsuk*. Have you made the connection yet? I have the commanding officer of strategic rocket command onboard waiting."

A blast of static came from the small radio speaker welded to the plotting table. "*Barsuk*, this is harbor control. A technical error on our part ...uh... continue with your mission."

"Thank you harbor control, *Barsuk* out."

"Well done," Cheslav laughed. "That should buy some time."

"Speaking of time lieutenant, don't you have something to take care of?"

Cheslav looked into Rurik's cold eyes, "Now?"

Rurik shrugged. "This is as good as a time as any."

"It should be taken care of before he is noticed."

Cheslav looked out the pilothouse window. "It is getting dark. Captain, with your permission, I would like to show our guest around the ship."

"By all means," Rurik answered coldly.

GOSLAR, GERMANY

"Man, was that the definition of weird," Carl Blevins sighed.

"I don't want or need to know anything." Warren closed the door on the silver BMW.

Aren't you the least bit curious?" Blevins asked.

The young SEAL leader cranked the high performance engine and backed up. "No."

Blevins scratched his neck. "Okay, fine. Tell me something?"

"Sure," Warren floored the gas pedal. "First, are you trying to give me a heart attack?" Blevins grabbed the dash for support. "Second, is there an interpreter we can trust?"

"I don't know. If you need one, I can see what the boss says."

U-761
NOVEMBER 15TH

Sleep came hard for Becker. Although near exhaustion, his eyes refused to close. He looked at Ada's picture. He ran his fingers over the frame and across her face. He smiled and gently returned the picture to the wall.

Anton Kruger walked silently past. "Kruger," Becker called from his bunk.

The large torpedo mechanic stopped and ducked his head just short of the hatch. "Herr Kaleu?"

"Your boys did a great job yesterday," Becker smiled.

"Thank you," Kruger grinned.

"How is the torpedo gang?"

Kruger lifted his plate-sized hand to his scraggly beard. "We are well, sir."

"Have you noticed anything strange on this boat?"

"Strange?" Kruger asked.

"The crew seems depressed."

"Oh no, sir," Kruger said shaking his head. "I know what you mean though. The men talk more of home than usual, but depressed, no."

And you, Kruger?" Becker asked.

"I never really had a home." The giant torpedo man admitted.

I envy you," Becker smiled. "You are a truly free man. No one to answer to, no worries about family."

"Don't envy me." Anton Kruger said in a low voice. "I want a family and someone to worry about. It's all about dying."

"What?" Becker asked.

"It is strange I know, if I die out here so what? Who will remember me? Who will care?" His usually intense blue eyes softened. "No one," Kruger shrugged his bulging shoulders. "So, did I really ever exist?"

"You're a deep thinker Kruger."

"I just want it all to mean something."

"Keep close watch on your boys, we still have a long way to go."

Iranian Cargo Ship KANGAN
Four Hundred Twenty Five Nautical Miles
North West of Norway

Captain Nasim shivered in the arctic air, while his 300 foot converted water tanker plowed through the swells. He paced between the wings of the bridge and the out-of-date radar system. He jumped when the rusted door to the bridge wrenched open with a squeal.

A large dark figure loomed inside from the pale blue light of the *Kangan's* bridge.

"Good morning, General Shatrevor." Nasim looked up from the glowing radar screen.

Shatrevor, the most wanted terrorist in the world moved closer his soft-soled shoes making not a sound. "It seems night never ends in this part of the world." His dark Arab eyes glowed in the pale light. His narrow eyes gave his entire face a serious, frightening look.

"Are we on schedule for our rendezvous?"

"Yes general. The sea is building, but we will reach the designated point in time," Nasim assured.

"Is the welcome ready?"

"We are prepared as you directed." *Kangan's* captain said proudly. "All we have left is to receive the blessings of Allah."

"That my dear captain we already have."

USS MIAMI

At four hundred feet, *Miami* was an invisible part of the sea. She followed a box-shaped course slowly cruising through the cold deep water. At her stern, the pencil thick wires of her towed array sampled the ocean for any noise or frequency. In her bow, the powerful passive sonar sniffed the water for a hint of anything manmade.

All was quiet in the silently prowling American submarine, except for the conversation in the wardroom.

"You're sure?" the XO asked.

"Yes sir," the sonar officer nodded. "Look again."

The XO flipped through the sheets of sonar screen printouts. "Here we pick up this merchant."

"Correct."

"Big son of a bitch on one five-bladed screw turning thirty-five RPM, that would make her speed about six knots.

"Okay, I see that," the exec nodded.

"Now once again, here is the overlay from the sounds we heard the other day." The sonar officer flipped through the papers again. "This tiny trace here," He stabbed the faint yellow line. "That is something with two three-bladed screws."

"I agree." the XO moved his chair closer.

"Then the rest of the story you know. Suddenly these two screws start giving off a harmonic. Now the only way for that to happen would be for it to be submerged. Look at this line. This is a classic diesel engine line. The screws stay, but the line for the engines goes away and we get a harmonic from the same screws."

"But there is nothing in class?"

"No, but this is a submarine. If it walks like a duck..."

"What about yesterday?" the XO asked.

"Here again the big merchant plods up along this point. What do we have? Those diesel lines again. The big guy slows and the diesel line goes away."

"I will grant you this is all based on bottom bounce still this is gospel."

The XO scratched his head

"Now here you go with two high bearing rate traces that lead right up the big merchant's ass and then BLAMO!"

"We have to find a hole in this thing."

The young officer lowered his head. "Don't know who or why, but what I do know for a fact that we're sitting on our hands while some jackass tries to start World War Three."

"Nothing on class, I don't understand," the XO said in a whisper. "Why?"

"I don't know either, but there is a diesel submarine somewhere up there."

"I'll wake the skipper and show him what you have."

The Pentagon
Office of the Chairman of the Joint Chiefs of Staff

Commander Enright came into the office with a red folder held between the fingers of his right hand.

Malroy looked up. "What's up Tim?"

"Sir, we have another incident." Enright handed the folder to his boss.

"What now?" Malroy took the folder.

Mingo, an US flagged container ship out of New Orleans, exploded not far from *HMS Swift's* last position."

"We have any conformation on this?" Malroy rubbed his eyes.

"One of our Key Hole satellites caught it on thermal. We traced positions of all ships in the area. *Mingo* is the only match."

"What was her cargo?"

"One hundred and sixty container boxes with everything from Corvettes to furniture, oh and twenty three-thousand gallons of a new type of jet fuel."

"New jet fuel?"

"Yes sir, I don't know much about it. Supposedly more environmentally friendly, whatever that means."

"How old is this data?"

"Three hours," Commander Enright responded.

RUSSIAN PATROL SHIP BARSUK
84-MILES NORTHWEST OF THE KOLA INLET

"Damn pig," Cheslav cursed. He tore off his hat and jacket, went to his tiny washbasin, and filled it with warm water. He saw his face splattered with thick dots of blood in the mirror. In the warm air of the stateroom, the blood ran down his cheek and over his nose. He heard the flimsy door open behind him. "Who is it?" he called.

"Just me," Rurik answered. "Did you give the colonel a good send-off?"

Cheslav turned back to the basin and dipped his hands in the water. "That fat ass bled all over me."

Cheslav threw handfuls of water on his face. "I must have shot him too close."

"He is gone through?" Rurik asked in the dim light.

"Fell over the side," Cheslav answered as he scooped another handful of red water up to his face.

"How close were you?"

"I had the gun right at the base of his fat head." Cheslav rubbed at the blood on his face.

"Yes, that was too close," agreed Rurik. "A meter is best."

Cheslav smiled into the mirror. "How would you know?"

"Oh I don't, but I will see."

"What?" Cheslav reached for his towel. Rurik brought a pistol from behind his back, centered the front sight on the young lieutenant's nose, and gave the trigger a slight squeeze. A small hole appeared dead center. His head jerked back as a gush of blood and brain spattered the mirror behind him. His legs crumpled and his body dropped to the steel deck. He twitched and squirmed, but finally stilled.

Rurik stepped closer careful to avoid the quickly expanding pool of blood that flowed and sloshed with the movement of the ship. "Yes," Rurik said coldly and kicked Cheslav's feet inside the tiny washroom. "A meter is just about right."

Goslar, Germany

Blevins set up his laptop computer. The translation program loaded quickly, as the retired CPO poured a tumbler of brandy.

He slipped the CD into the drive and sat back.

On his screen, a series of files opened. The scanned images were perfect in every detail. Blevins tapped the mouse button until another program opened inside the files. "Okay," he sighed. "Hope this translation program is worth the money I spent." One by one, he highlighted the files and moved them into the electronic brain of the translator program.

Blevins's mouth fell open when he reached page ten.

27

CONFUSION

'The well-spring of war is the human heart."

-Stephen B. Luce, 1827–1917

STRATEGIC MISSILE ASSEMBLY AND STORAGE
AREA NUMBER 3
PECHENGA, RUSSIA
NOVEMBER 15TH

IT WAS MORNING WHEN the new watch officer entered the compound. Five minutes later, an alarm sounded that would be heard around the world.

GOSLAR, GERMANY

Retired Chief Machinist Mate Carl Blevins checked again. What appeared like formulas made no sense to him and the medical terms, he didn't understand, but if these documents told the truth, even a half-truth, Carl Blevins looked into the window of eternal life.

Blevins ejected the CD and carefully placed in its case. He stood and walked quickly to the door and out into the narrow hall.

"Mike," Blevins tapped on the door. "Mike, come on man."

"Okay... okay," came a voice through the door.

Blevins heard the lock turn and pushed the door open, nearly knocking Warren off his feet.

"Mike, we need to get back to Berlin now."

Warren stumbled back a few steps before finding his footing. "Slow down. What's wrong?"

"Wrong? Nothing's wrong," Blevins huffed. He moved closer to Warren, and pulled the CD from his pocket. "Mike, this is the biggest thing since... since... well I don't know, but we gotta get this to Malroy."

"What is it?"

"You really want to know?"

Warren shook his head. "Yes, but I can't."

"Well it sure sucks to be you," Blevins smiled. "Get your ass in gear lieutenant."

"I'll be down in five," Warren threw on the shirt he had worn the day before.

Blevins grabbed the keys to the silver BMW. "I'll drive."

"Hey Carl," Warren called as the door clanked shut. "Carl?" Warren shoved on his other shoe and followed Blevins out the door.

THE KREMLIN

The encrypted message from Strategic Missile Assembly and Storage Area Number 3, flashed from its transmitter to a secure satellite directly to the newly appointed Director of Strategic Forces.

In the style of the old Soviet Union, the message itself started an automatic chain of events. For three minutes, confusion reared its ugly head. The watch officer, a young captain from Tbilisi read the code assigned to the plain language message, matching the letters with prearranged meanings in an old dust covered binder. The codes matched a vital war warning, or the compromise of a nuclear weapon. Unsure what the message really meant. The young officer panicked and managed to upload the wrong preset orders. Not understanding his error, he tapped the send button. Instantly another Russian satellite received and as programmed issued orders to all Russian forces.

The twenty-year old plan failed to prepare for events happing now. Most of the Russian military set in motion. However, those in charge had no way of knowing fleets were moving, aircraft were lifting off, and the entire world was again near the brink.

A separate automated alert in code transmitted from the missile site. This simple message stated only that a warhead was missing.

Within minutes, Vitenka had the message about the missing warhead in his hands. A dozen phone calls, and two hours later the ad hoc heads of the respective services filed into his office. However, he had no idea the bulk of Russian naval power was beginning to deploy.

He removed his glasses, folded them carefully, and laid them on top of the message.

"What else do we know?" Vitenka asked calmly.

Admiral Ryshenko, Director of Fleet Operations spoke first, "We believe the missing warhead to be on the patrol ship *Barsuk*."

Vitenka nodded. "Where would they take the warhead?"

Silence … Vitenka paced. "That is a question we must answer. Is there a foreign influence? Is this an act of theft—an act of terrorism—or is this revenge?"

Ryshenko lifted his head. "I take full responsibility for this."

"That is admirable," Vitenka said. "However, it does not help in the least. We are not here to assign blame. We need to prevent a nuclear exchange. The stakes are far above one man's career or life. We are all to blame for this. We need to solve the problem or at least contain it."

"We must destroy the ship," Air Force General Norslav hissed. "It is always the navy causing problems."

Ryshenko's eyes narrowed and his fists clenched.

Vitenka could see the storm coming and like the hand of God halted it. "This is not the time," He shouted. His sudden anger startled those around his desk. "I need answers not bickering."

Norslav seemed stunned. "Yes, sir," he answered meekly. "I can have a strike force over the ship in fewer than thirty minutes."

"What of our agreement with the Americans," asked commander of the army.

"Ah." Vitenka raised his finger in the air. "Another item we must throw into the equation."

"We must tell them."

"No" countered Norslav. "That would cause a panic. NATO would over-react."

"We must then be covert," the army commander cautioned.

Vitenka's brows rose. "You have an idea, general?"

"The warhead is from one of our SS-N-20 missiles. An explosion aboard *Barsuk* should not cause a nuclear yield. It would merely sink to the bottom,"

"*Should not?*" Norslav huffed.

"What about another ship or submarine on a rescue mission?"

"The story of a search and rescue mission would not hold up if we send a submarine," Vitenka pointed out. "But a warship could work."

"It would have to be a fast ship—well armed."

"The captain must also have a good head on his shoulders," Air Force General Norslav said.

"The destroyer *Strogiy* can put to sea in two hours," Ryshenko declared.

All eyes looked at the admiral, "*Strogiy?*"

"A Kashin class guided missile destroyer. She is both fast well-armed and guard ship of the Northern Fleet this week. Her crew is ready."

"And the captain," Trofinoff asked.

"He is my son," Ryshenko said proudly.

"What if we fail?"

A hush surrounded the men in the office.

Vitenka broke the silence, "We cannot win this situation. We have to plan for the best way to lose. Either way men will die."

"We have to act now," Norslav declared. "That ship must be stopped or put on the bottom."

Major General Trofinoff spoke next. "It would be criminal to not inform the Americans if we do not catch or kill this pirate. They will forgive us for many things, but not something like this. We can fool ourselves and each other, but we all know where a nuclear warhead will be used and by whom."

Vitenka nodded his agreement. "Then it is settled. Admiral Ryshenko, get *Strogiy* to sea. Talk to your son personally. This may be the most vital mission a Russian warship has ever undertaken."

U-761

Edel found the Becker at the plot table. "Captain, we need to talk, *quietly.*"

Becker pulled the brown jacket off his shoulders, and lifted his chin toward an empty area near the ballast control valves. "Over there."

In the somewhat secluded space Edel turned. "There is a problem."

"Oh good, another we can add to the list," Becker sighed.

"Our food," Edel took his greasy cap from his head.

"What?"

"I just talked with Berdy. The smoked meats are decaying by the hour."

"Decaying?" Becker asked as he pushed his cap back on his head.

"Not so much decaying, but crumbling." Edel lifted the cap from his matted thin hair. "That's not all. The canned and jarred foods are turning to powder."

"How much do we have left?"

Edel drew in a deep breath of the stale submarine air, "Another week at the most."

"Talk to Berdy, have him stretch what we have."

Edel nodded and moved off aft toward the small galley.

Becker made his way forward to the wardroom. Volker sat at the small table across from Gerlach. Volker had the master sight for the bridge taken apart. He cleaned the precision ground optics. "Volker, can you excuse us," Becker sat at the head of the small table.

"Of course, Captain," Volker gathered the delicate parts in his hands.

"What is it, Captain?" Gerlach asked curiously.

Becker waited until Volker moved out of earshot. He leaned forward, "How long?"

"I don't know," the Gerlach rasped.

"I think you do," Becker hissed. "I think you're still running your experiment."

"No." Gerlach sat back. "I have what I need."

"Tell me what you know."

"I know what you know." Gerlach smiled slightly. "I know that we are alive. The Forever Project was a success. But I wonder how successful."

"Go on," Becker urged, his voice just short of threatening.

"I think we slept for a number of years."

"How many," Becker asked.

"I estimate twenty—maybe thirty, maybe more. Time seems to be catching up though."

"What will happen?" Becker asked.

"I don't know. Maybe it will stabilize. Of course, it could continue at a faster rate, each man ages faster each day. It could depend on the man, his health. I just don't know."

"What about our food?"

Gerlach raised his tired yellowing eyes. "I wondered about that myself. Anything organic or natural might age at an accelerated rate."

"What about you?"

Gerlach smiled. "I'm giving myself morphine injections twice a day. It takes the edge off." Gerlach lifted his hand. "My disease was also asleep, but now it too is alive and well. There is good news though. Frimunt is doing well. The accelerated aging has also accelerated his healing."

Becker did not care for Gerlach as a man, but as a person, he did not like to see him suffer. Though he had seen death many times, he forced himself to ask the next question. "How long do you think you have?"

"Another question I cannot answer. A few weeks—less, who knows?"

"What can I do for you?" Becker asked kindly.

Gerlach chuckled. "No captain, I hope I see this to the end. This is like a novel you just can't stop reading. You have to know how it ends." Gerlach shivered then pulled the dirty gray blanket up to his chest.

Headquarters of the Russian Northern Fleet
Polyarnyy, Russia
November 16th

The sortie message flashed via satellite. According to procedure, the order went to Northern Fleet Deputy of Communications where it again was misunderstood as a fleet action. Even with the Soviet Union a memory, doctrines, and procedures remained. The Soviets knew if hostilities broke out their bases came up on the A list of NATO targets. All combat ships put to sea.

The rotting piers vibrated when the long still warships moved to a pre-determined hold point and awaited orders. Even the massive and beautiful battle cruiser *Peter the Great*, cast her mooring, and slid into the channel.

Within thirty minutes of the order, thirteen Russian warships set course north-northwest. Sixteen more got underway within the next two hours. Luckily, the order addressed the surface fleet. Sailor on the submarines berthed nearby watched in amazement.

The Autobahn, Germany

The BMW flew down the pavement as if the laws of nature and man were but suggestions. Warren cowered in the passenger's seat his fists clenched. "Carl, for God's sake ease off."

"Come on lieutenant, I can do this with one hand; see," Blevins held one hand up.

Warren went white. "Damn it, Carl."

"Relax, Mike. I got this under control. I'm in a foreign country. I'm doing—let's see—one-hundred and thirty miles an hour. It's dark and I'm half-drunk. What could go wrong?"

Warren reached for the glove compartment. In the dark of the car, he felt around.

Carl looked over to see this tough SEAL clutching a rosary.

"Mom told me these would come in handy." His fingers ran over the beads.

"Can you call ahead and get me a secure line to Malroy?" Blevins asked.

"Sure thing, I'll also have a pair of clean boxers waiting on me." Warren whined.

Carl glanced at his passenger, "Wimp."

28

DUTY

*"Blessed be the Lord my strength, which teacheth
my hands to war and my finger to fight."*

-Psalm CXXXXIV

CHAIRMAN OF THE JOINT Chiefs of Staff was in his office forty-five minutes after the orbiting surveillance bird code named Key Hole snapped images of Russian warships sailing for open water.

Malroy's mood matched the November morning-dark and threatening. "Where the hell are the others?" he demanded.

"On the way," the on-duty watch officer answered nervously.

"The secretary?" grumbled Malroy.

"ETA is about ten minutes."

"Damned politicians," Malroy gulped his first cup of coffee. "Get me a line right to Vitenka's office."

"Already taken care of," the watch officer announced.

"The president," Malroy huffed.

The watch officer a newly promoted Navy captain shrugged his shoulders. "I don't know. I believe he's on Air Force One."

"That figures," Malroy huffed. "We have comms?"

"God I hope so," the captain sighed.

Russian Patrol Ship Barsuk
60 Miles from the Edge of the Ice Pack

"Captain what our orders are?" The navigator asked. "We are due for communication with Fleet."

"We will maintain radio silence," Rurik hissed.

"This is highly unusual."

"What is unusual is your attitude," Rurik barked. "Never question me."

"Yes, sir," He said and returned to the navigation charts.

"Maintain this course and speed for another hour then slow to five knots," Rurik ordered.

Iranian Cargo Ship Kangan
25 Miles from Barsuk

Shatrevor entered the shabby rusted pilothouse. He placed his rough olive hand on the captain's shoulder. "Today we become heroes. Today is a final step to ending the blight on our people."

"Everything is ready, general."

"Good. You have done well captain."

"Allah has smiled on us."

Shatrevor nodded. "That he has. I am going to look below."

"The rendezvous will be in two hours," Nasim added.

Shatrevor nodded and stepped down the ladder. On the main deck, he strolled to a hatchway. Years of corrosion made him strain, but the hatch creaked open. He pushed until a latch caught and held the steel door open. Shatrevor braced himself against the slight roll of the converted water tanker then climbed carefully down the next set of steps.

The lower deck, a dark cave-like hold reeked of bilge water, diesel, and human sweat. The only light came from a string of tired looking bulbs. Shatrevor moved carefully aft. He heard muffled voices and the whir of machinery as he neared the main cargo area.

The light grew brighter and the voices became more distinct. He came to the main cargo deck. Chained to eyebolts along the deck, nine T-72 main battle tanks awaited their mission. The squat menacing looking tanks wore paint matching the dull green of *Kangan's* side.

The tank crews checked, tested, cleaned, and repaired.

As Shatrevor emerged from the dim light, the tank crews came to attention. A sergeant rushed forward and gave a stiff salute. "General, we are ready for action."

Shatrevor returned the salute. "Today you become instruments of Allah. Your aim will be true, and your hearts will show no mercy."

The sergeant dropped the salute. "We have rehearsed many times. My men are ready."

"Show me."

"Certainly general," The sergeant trotted to his tank. "Again men," He called with his hands cupped around his mouth.

Men ran to their tanks. Turrets hummed, and traversed to assigned sectors.

Shatrevor walked to the sergeant's tank. "All angles are covered?"

"Yes sir. The ship's crew will be there," the sergeant pointed to the five sailors standing along the bare steel. "When you give the command they will use sledge hammers to knock out the pins you see holding the false bulkhead. The bulkheads will fall and my tanks will open fire."

Shatrevor shook his head. "Impressive."

The sergeant continued, "Each tank has an assigned target. Tank 1 and 3 will target the weapon system. Tanks 4 and 5 will engage the bridge and radio. Tank 2 and 6 will use sabot rounds to punch through the hull."

The general looked puzzled. "What of the other tanks?"

The sergeant smiled. "Those gun tubes are loaded with canister shot."

Shatrevor tilted his head, "Canister?"

"Yes sir. Like a huge shot gun. Each round contains five-hundred steel pellets. These rounds will sweep the decks."

Shatrevor gasped, "We are a battleship!"

U-761
15 Miles from Barsuk

Becker stood over his shoulder while Hamlin plotted the course south. "No contacts the past eleven hours," the *Oberbootsmann* reported. "I think we're safe for now."

Becker sighed, "We'll see."

"Do we use radar?" Hamlin asked.

"I don't want any transmissions leaving the boat."

The Pentagon

"Who can give me a guess as to what is going on?" Malroy asked.

The CIA liaison spoke first, "All we have are pictures. Nothing even hinted at this."

"Okay, since we don't know anything, let's see what we do know," Malroy sighed.

"We know the bulk of the Russian surface fleet sailed last night," the CNO answered.

"Where are they going?" Malroy asked.

"We did get a request for the Russians to conduct a search and rescue mission," answered the deputy under secretary for readiness.

"What rescue?" Malroy sat up in his chair.

"They claim one of their fisheries ships, caught fire, and is sinking off Murmansk."

"The story checks out?" Malroy asked.

"We didn't check, sir."

"Makes not one bit of sense," Malroy grumbled.

"I hate to throw a wrench in an already broken machine," The Chief of Naval Operations interrupted.

"What now?" Malroy asked.

"We've tracked an Iranian tanker for the last week. As of last night she was positioned seventy-five miles from the ice pack."

"What is it doing that far north?"

"It's not uncommon for Iranians to move up and down the coast. They do trade with the Russians, the French, and even the Germans," CIA explained. "I'll grant you a tanker that far out of the shipping lanes is interesting."

"Come on people. Let's get this puzzle worked out," Malroy boomed. "CNO put the fleet in motion. I'll brief the secretary and the president."

The intercom buzzed. "What?" Malroy snapped.

"Sir," answered a business like female voice. "There is a call over the secure line."

"Unless it's the President of the United States or Russia, I'm busy," Malroy shouted at the phone.

"Sir," the voice responded calmly. "It's a Chief Blevins calling from Berlin. He says it is most urgent."

"I am busy now. I'll get back to him." Malroy pushed the button severing the intercom. "Get the fleet to sea. I want a quiet deployment."

RUSSIAN BATTLE CRUISER
PETER THE GREAT
25 MILES OFF LISTA LANKA ISLAND

On the bridge, her commanding officer enjoyed the feel of the icy sea breeze. "Air is always fresher at sea," he called to the shivering miserable bridge watch. He chuckled at the sight of the helmsman and lookouts. "First time at sea?" he asked.

The seasick watches could only nod.

"You'll get your sea legs. How long have you been aboard?" He asked one of the lookouts.

"Two years," the young sailor answered.

"Two years, and you have never been to sea?"

"No, sir," The lookout managed before his breakfast rushed back up his throat.

"Has it been that long since we've put to sea?"

Those on the bridge were not the only miserable souls. Wallowing about in the machinery spaces, the engineers were both seasick and leaderless. Most senior sailors and key officers had not made it to the ship in time for the emergency sailing. The young ratings did their best, but a lack of training and maintenance showed.

The main lube oil pump for the port shaft lost pressure. For a trained and well-led crew this would be nothing more than a minor inconvenience. The roving on watch engineer would have bypassed the pump allowing the identical pump take over the duty. He would have removed and cleaned the oil filter strainer, put it back in and close the pump-housing lid. A total of three minutes was all that was required. However, these watches were unsure and fearful, so they did nothing.

Since there was less oil to remove heat from the center bearings, temperatures built. An alarm sounded in the maneuvering room as the bearing began to smolder. The junior officer in charge decided the sensor must be bad and twice silenced the alarm. Vanes in the lube oil, ground by the same contamination that blocked the filter strainer shattered. Large chunks of broken steel and gasket material blocked oil flow to each shaft bearings. The blockages also traveled to the pump on the opposite side of the engines. Without lubricant, each of the ship's two propeller shafts rated at 75,000 horsepower labored under the added strain and resistance. Within three minutes the raw power on the now oil starved shaft bearings caused them to turn red hot. Steam and smoke filled the shaft space as the spinning shaft generated enormous friction. The surrounding steel burst into a blowtorch of flame. At two thousand degrees, the nickel-carbon shaft softened. Centrifugal force caused the shaft to bow and a wobble developed. The wobble transmitted its force through the hull and the entire 24,000-ton ship shook. At three-thousand degrees, the shaft melted in a flash of super-heated plasma. The air ignited in a thunderous explosion.

On the bridge, the captain felt the rumble an instant before a blast erupted from the stern. A plume of water shot high above the tripod-like superstructure. The ship lurched to port. "We've been torpedoed," he shouted as a wall of seawater rained down on the armored command bridge. "Signal Fleet," he screamed over the roar of escaping steam. Smoke billowed from the stern. "Shut flood control doors," he ordered. *Peter the Great* listed to port and settled slightly at her stern. Damage and casualties reports came in. Then there was silence as the power failed. Both reactors had scrammed. In such situations, diesels started in automatic and turned a set of auxiliary generators. The ship sailed with three of the four generators out of order. The fourth came to life, but shut down when it was hopelessly overloaded.

Most of the great cruiser's escort ships heard her broken communications about a torpedo. Passing the foundering battle cruiser at flank speed two Udaloy class destroyers turned and pounded the water with active Horse Jaw sonar.

The destroyer *Simiferopol* suddenly slowed. In a flash of light and smoke, she fired her anti-submarine rockets.

The rockets arched high above the ship before they nosed over and fell. Unlike depth charges, RBU warheads would only detonate if they struck the hull of a submarine.

In a well-defined chevron pattern the warheads fell. Three struck underwater rocks at fifty-meters and exploded. Geysers of furious water bubbled to the surface. The rest sank harmlessly into the mud.

THE KREMLIN

Admiral Vitenka tried to make sense of the reports as they came in. "Who ordered the fleet to sail?"

"The signal was misunderstood," the deputy communications minister shouted above other equally loud voices.

"It is not important why the fleet sailed," Ryshenko fumed. "We have been attacked."

"If that is so by whom were we attacked?"

"Admiral, are you already such a politician that you do not see the obvious?" Ryshenko blurted, "The Americans."

"What proof do you have?" Vitenka hissed.

"I have a sinking cruiser and five-hundred dead Russian sailors."

"Why would the Americans suddenly attack our ships?" Army General Trofinoff asked.

"Why is not important," Air Force General Norslav shouted. "We have done everything the Americans wanted. We always have and each time we lose ships and men."

Vitenka shouted back. "Would you have us take a path of no return only to find out later it was a mistake? As a Russian you can think with your heart, but as a general, you must think with your head."

"We still must be on guard," Trofinoff observed.

"I will grant you that," Vitenka nodded. "We will maintain our fleet at their present location. Order the alert levels raised to level three."

"What of our missile submarines?" Ryshenko asked.

Vitenka thought a moment. "No those we keep in port. The Americans will surely see them as they pass to their dive points. That could lead to a further escalation."

"What does this new president plan to do?" Norslav asked.

"Hopefully exactly what I tell him to."

ABOARD THE RUSSIAN DESTROYER STROGIY

Her raked bow sliced through the rolling sea sending up clouds of spray. The ship rocked and shuddered as she smashed into the oncoming waves.

"Captain, we received orders on fleet emergency frequency," The communications officer announced as he stumbled onto the bridge.

"Well, read it," The captain urged.

"Missile cruiser, *Peter the Great*, has been torpedoed by unknown submarine. Alert level is now level three. All units are to defend themselves as deemed necessary."

"Is that all?"

"Yes, sir," The officer wiped the water from his face on his sleeve.

"Very well, I..."

"We have gained a new contact," reported the radar compartment. "Contact bears zero-two-zero. Course is three-five-eight. Range to contact is twenty-five thousand meters."

The captain walked to the plotting table. "Quartermaster, bring the ship to action stations."

29
THE DAY OF DYING

A Pale horse: and him that sat on him was Death.

-Revelation, IV,8

U-761

NOVEMBER 16TH

BECKER EMERGED OUT OF the bridge hatch.

"The sky is clearing," Volker said.

"It seems so. Get the flak guns manned."

"Aye sir," Volker stepped to the voice pipe at the front of the bridge.

U-761's commander walked aft to the flak deck. He looked astern, squinting in the haze. Becker could still see the ribbon-like line of ice. A half hour later clouds of fog and mist evaporated.

Edel came topside. "Captain the batteries will no longer hold a full charge. The plates corrode faster than I have ever seen. We need to change the electrolyte."

"How long will it take?"

"Four hours minimum, but that's not what worries me."

"The batteries will take most of our fresh water."

"Yes," Edel shivered.

"Find Baldric, have the torpedo gang load our acoustic torpedo."

"Can I ask why?"

Becker pulled Edel close. "I don't think it is 1944. I do not know what year it is. For all we know it may be 1965. We need every trick we have to get home. I don't know if we have a home."

"I've noticed things," Edel noted. "The air seems different the sea has changed. Nothing makes sense."

"How's the crew?" Becker asked.

"They've changed somehow, matured maybe?"

BARSUK

"Radar holds a new contact, bearing is three-four-eight," the combat officer reported.

"Three-four-eight," Rurik asked. "Are you sure?"

"Yes, target bears three-four-eight."

"Wrong direction," Rurik mumbled to himself.

"Is this part of an exercise we're conducting?" the navigator asked.

"When I tell you, you'll know," Rurik snapped. "Helm come left."

"We have another radar contact. This contact bears one-seven-eight. Moving slow and closing our position."

"There you are," Rurik smiled. "Helm, zero the rudder. Engine room make turns for three knots."

The communications officer appeared on the bridge. "Captain, we received some strange messages from Fleet, and from the destroyer *Strogiy*."

"Of course you did," Rurik yelled. "We're playing the role of the terrorist ship."

"This is all an exercise?" the communicator asked suspiciously.

"Why else would Fleet use this bucket of rust?" Rurik lied.

"What role does the *Peter the Great* play?"

Rurik looked puzzled. "What do you mean?"

"This message," the communicator said as he read the message, "*Peter the Great has been torpedoed and is in sinking condition.*"

"*Strogiy* has ordered us to stop or they will open fire."

"Visual contact," The bridge lookout yelled, "Large freighter off the port quarter."

"Officer of the deck close on that ship," Rurik ordered.

"Is this also part of the exercise?" The communicator asked.

Before Rurik could answer, another report came in. "Bridge, this is electronic surveillance we are being illuminated by targeting radar."

"Seems the good guys have caught us," Rurik smiled. All stop," He ordered. "What about the contact to the north?"

There was a pause. "Captain, contact has faded."

"Faded?" Rurik asked.

"Aye sir, faded."

"What was the last range?" Rurik asked somewhat alarmed.

"Range at time of loss was two-five hundred meters."

"A contact cannot just fade unless.... Distance to the freighter?"

"Two-thousand meters," Radar reported.

"We've been found by a submarine. Man, action stations."

"What of the exercise?" The communications officer asked.

"A submarine is not part of the drill. Now get to your station."

IRANIAN CARGO SHIP KANGAN

"There she is," General Shatrevor smiled. "Bring us alongside."

"Certainly general, I will have the deck crew make ready to receive our package."

Shatrevor nodded his approval.

U-761

"It appeared out of nowhere." Volker said between deep breaths.

"What was it?" Becker asked.

"Small warship-maybe a frigate, never seen a ship like it," Volker stammered.

"Boat is steady at three-zero meters," Edel reported.

Becker stepped behind Edel, "The batteries?"

Edel looked over his shoulder at Becker, "Forty-percent and dropping fast. We can't be down long."

"Herr Kaleu, I have picked up another ship," The hydrophone operator reported. "Sounds like a freighter, two four-bladed screws, closing."

"Man, battle stations. Chief, bring us up to periscope depth."

"Periscope depth, aye," Edel answered. "Five rise on both planes."

Russian Destroyer Strogiy

"Target is stopped," Combat reported. "The merchant continues to close."

"Report the status of our missile battery."

Missiles are still being fueled."

"What is taking so long?"

"We sailed before the weapons technicians came aboard," the weapons officer reported.

"Get people on the fueling detail now," The captain bellowed. "Take the sonar operators."

Barsuk

"Action stations are manned," the watch officer reported.

Rurik did not reply. "Distance to the freighter?"

"Five hundred meters," Answered the navigator. "Shouldn't we maneuver?"

"New visual contact, Its *Strogiy*," The look out announced.

Now Rurik paid attention. "Damn."

"Periscope off the starboard bow," Another lookout yelled wildly.

"Get me a firing solution now," Rurik screeched. He looked aft. The Iranian ship was painfully slow. "Rig the hoist over the hold."

"What?" the watch officer yelled.

"You heard me! Get it done."

"Captain this is not an exercise is it?" The navigator snarled. "What are you up to?"

"Solution set," a voice came over the intercom.

The navigator moved toward Rurik. In a flash, Rurik's pistol came up and fired. The navigator let out his last breath as the bullet dug into his chest. He fell slowly to his knees then forward.

"Captain," the helm screamed.

Rurik spun to face him and squeezed the trigger. The helmsman's neck spurted a thick red stream of blood. The dying man crumpled.

Another bullet found its mark just above the sternum of the weapons officer.

The quartermaster stepped toward the bridge door, the pistol cracked again. The back of his head came apart under the impact.

The freighter moved closer, Rurik could see men on the deck ready with lines. He saw one of the davits move over the side, a heavy canvas sling dangled from a hook.

IRANIAN CARGO SHIP KANGAN

"Another warship on the starboard beam," Nasim cried out.

The smile left Shatrevor's face. "What?"

"She is making speed this way," A voice called out.

Shatrevor picked up his two-way radio. "Sergeant, are you ready?"

"We are ready."

"We now have two warships to deal with. Can you handle it?"

"Allah will guide us."

U-761

"Another warship-high speed, closing," Veldmon whispered.

Becker swung the periscope to the left. "I need a bearing."

"Bearing is two-seven-eight moving left."

Becker moved the scope to the bearing as the Russian destroyer topped the horizon.

"I estimate new contact making thirty-knots," Volker reported.

"She must be re-supplying from that freighter," he said calmly. "Volker set up a solution for the first and second ships with tubes one-two and three. Set up tubes four-five-six for the new warship. We'll launch the forward tubes turn and shoot from the stern." Becker took his eye off the scope and wiped sweat from his brow. "Set stern torpedoes for magnetic detonation."

BARSUK

Rurik leapt from the bridge wing to the main deck. The sides of the Iranian ship loomed closer. He trotted aft to the main loading hatch. Three sailors cranked the winch that opened the steel door. "Move your asses," he screamed.

The sight of the pistol encouraged the sailors to double their efforts. They looked up just as the freighter ground against their ship.

With the sling over the hatch, Rurik motioned for the davit operator to lower the cable and sling into the hold.

"Secure the box in that sling," Rurik shouted.

"Captain, what is happening?" One of the sailors shouted over the sound of grinding steel.

His answer came in the form of a bullet in the center of his chest.

Rurik looked at the other sailor. "Do you have any questions?"

The sailor jumped into the hold, wrapped the heavy sling around the box fastened the clips and secured the box he then stepped back under the cover of the deck.

Rurik waved his arms and the box lifted slowly from the hold. Again, he turned and looked at the Iranian ship's bridge, and saw a dark bearded man. He smiled and waved. The man returned his smile. Rurik cupped his hands around his mouth. "I am ready to come aboard."

The bearded man laughed and shrugged his shoulders while the freighter's blunt bow turned and opened the distance from the bobbing patrol ship. As Rurik watched, the box swung onto the deck of the freighter. With the warhead safe on deck, the Iranian tanker increased speed away from Barsuk.

Rurik trembled with rage. He lifted the pistol and emptied the remainder of the magazine at the freighter. Drool ran down his chin as he headed for the bridge. In the wheelhouse, he punched the buttons for the remote operated 76mm cannon.

U-761

"Weapons set, ship is ready," Volker announced.

"Commence firing," Becker ordered.

At Volker's direction, the torpedoes launched. Volker held the chronometer in front of his face watching the seconds tick awaiting the next launch. Eighteen seconds later tube four sent its torpedo into the sea. "Tube four away."

"Helm, left hard rudder, both motors ahead flank," Becker barked as he swung the scope toward the onrushing warship. "Come on turn," he urged. The compass slowly swung to the new heading.

"Bearings for tubes five and six matched," Volker announced.

"Tube five-los," Becker ordered.

"Weapon away," Volker said as he penciled another tick mark on the chronometer's face. "Three seconds."

"Tube six—los," he ordered.

Again, the U-boat shuddered. Becker snapped the periscope handle up. "Fifty meters fast."

IRANIAN SHIP KANGAN

"This is better than I could have planned," Shatrevor shouted. "The problem is out of our hands. Let the Russians deal with their traitor. Who cannot say Allah is not at work here?"

Captain Nasim did not seem to share the joy. "Do you think they know?"

"What does it matter? We are a poor merchant ship sailing the ocean. They would not board us. We are more or less, allied with *Big Brother Russia*. Is that not true?"

"Yes, but if they know we have the weapon; I imagine they will attempt to get it back," Nasim said quietly.

"Don't lose your nerve. Allah provided for every circumstance. Remember you have a belly full of tanks just waiting my word. This will be a great day."

The smiling stopped when the first of *Strogiy's* main gun rounds landed fifty meters ahead of *Kangan's* bow.

"They mean to stop us," Nasim said nervously.

The smile on the general's face faded. His eyes narrowed and his lip curled exposing his yellow teeth. "Then we will stop," he hissed. He picked up his radio. "Sergeant, the time is now. Aim true."

The entire ship vibrated when the false steel sides fell with a splash. Instantly the tank turrets traversed to their assigned positions.

Tank two's gunner thumbed his range finding laser and in half of a second, his gun tube belched out its first high explosive round.

BARSUK

Frantic, Rurik jabbed at the switches and buttons for *Barsuk's* gun control. Nothing worked. Before dying the weapons officer had tripped the power control breaker for the gun aiming system.

He screamed when the first of *U-761's* torpedoes exploded against his hull.

The explosion vaporized the center of the ship. The light steel plating crumpled and tore as if made of paper. An immediate secondary explosion followed from *Barsuk's* s fuel bunkers. On the bridge, the overpressure of the explosion pulled Rurik's body apart before he also added fuel to the blast.

STROGIY

The Iranian tanker aimed true. A 120mm high explosive shell bored into *Strogiy's* bridge before detonating. Fragments of the shell and pieces of the deck smashed into every living soul on the bridge. Torn bodies spewed blood and gore. They collapsed where they stood.

The second tank round, this time an armor-piercing sabot, punched into the forward 76mm turret. The impact lifted the turret from its mount. The pressure of suddenly superheated air destroyed everything and everyone inside. The forward end of the ship erupted in a geyser of fire. The ship ripped apart when her own ammunition added to the destruction.

KANGAN

"Still worried, captain?" Shatrevor yelled.

Nasim didn't hear him. Flaming wreckage from *Barsuk* rained on his ship. A dozen small fires erupted while his crew tried desperately to put them out.

Nasim picked up the microphone for the engine room when he looked out the bridge window. "General," he said quietly. "Allah has abandoned us." Nasim pointed to the two thin trails of frothing water heading for the ship. "Torpedoes," He announced as if he ordered a glass of water.

"Do something," Shatrevor screamed.

"I will." He fell on the deck and prayed.

The first warhead smashed into the aged ship's rounded underside. A nine-meter hole opened allowing water of the Arctic Ocean free access to the interior. The ship fell on her side. Seconds later the next weapon bore in. Striking five meters forward of the bridge, almost lifting the old tanker out of the water. The list increased. Unable to bear the weight the chains holding the tanks snapped. The T-72 tanks slid on the deck, crushing anything and anyone in the way. The weight of the sliding tanks and the inrush of water caused the old tanker to roll over. In a boiling ocean of water and fire, her bow dipped under. For a few seconds she bobbed in the water, her screws still turning lazily. Then as if the sea were tired of toying with her, she went down.

STROGIY

The destroyer sailed on as she burned. A firefighting team from the repair party tried in vain to fight the magazine fire that raged three decks below the flaming turret.

The emergency steering compartment controlled the ship, but no one gave orders. Those fighting the flames topside had seen the flashes of light and heard the rolling explosions while their intended targets evaporated.

A shout rang out over the screaming alarms. A slender wake swam toward their ship. Shipmate trampled shipmate in a struggle to get away from the impending explosion. Ten seconds later the torpedo swam under the hull.

A magnetic field surrounded the weapon's nose. As it passed under *Strogiy's* hull, the field suddenly altered. A trip lever moved up and the primer detonated. The shock of this small explosion set off the main warhead.

The sea around *Strogiy* turned a brilliant white as a bubble of super-heated gas and steam blew the water from under the ship. The same bubble shot upward tearing into the thin underside. The center of the ship lifted and the sea rushed in at the speed of sound to fill the void left by the explosion. It bent the ship up and down, snapping her into two pieces. Bow and stern floated apart for some fifty meters before they sank in a surging whirlpool.

30
THE BRINK

"The circumstances of war are sensed ratherthan explained."

-Maurice de Saxe: 1696—
1750, Letters and Memoirs,
IV

U-761
NOVEMBER 16TH

"LESS THAN TWENTY MINUTES left on the battery," Edel warned.

Becker looked to the hydrophone operator, "Anything?"

Veldmon slowly rotated the hydrophone wheel, his head cocked while he listened. "Clear, Herr Kaleu."

"Helm, come to course north. Surface the boat," Becker ordered.

"We sank them all," Volker announced.

"We've made how many patrols together?" Becker removed the dingy cap from his head.

"This is six," Volker replied.

"We've seen it all. So tell me, what is different?"

"The enemy seems... well, sloppy," Volker shrugged.

Becker nodded his agreement. "Have you ever known the English or the Americans to be sloppy?"

"Perhaps we have been lucky," Volker offered.

Becker sighed. "Luck maybe, but it's like they had no idea we were even here. Does that sound insane?"

"They misjudged us before. Maybe the ice interfered with their radar or ASDIC."

"You said you have never seen a warship like that." Becker probed. "What did you mean?"

Volker slowly shook his head. "I don't know."

UNITED STATES EMBASSY
BERLIN, GERMANY

"Carl, I don't think you'll get through," Warren sighed. I just came down from communications.

"What do you mean?" Blevins asked.

Warren shook his head. "Intel has it that three Russian ships were sunk by a submarine. A few days ago a Brit destroyer got deep six'd, and a day after that, a cargo ship blew up."

Blevin's did not look surprised "Where?"

Up north around the ice pack," Warren drained the last of his coffee.

"Do they know what's going on?" His voice cracked.

"Carl, you okay?"

"Do they know who's doing the shooting?" Blevins drew in gulps of air and staggered forward.

"Hey, come on sit down," Warren reached for the Blevins.

Do they know?"

"No, no one knows anything." The SEAL said gently. "Carl, what's wrong?"

"They don't know," Blevins reached into his jacket and pulled out the CD. "But I do."

THE KREMLIN

"This is either an overt act of war or they have a madman in one of their boats," Admiral Ryshenko yelled. Tears streamed down his face.

Defense Minister Vitenka stood and walked around his desk in front of Ryshenko. He placed his hand on the weeping man's shoulder. "Arman," he said softly, "we will find the truth. I promise you and I promise your son. But you understand what I must do?"

Ryshenko looked up. "What?"

"I cannot let the situation get worse till we know answers. I must relieve you of your command."

"No," Ryshenko screamed. "I will avenge my son. I will kill them all."

"Please, my friend, do not make this any harder than it already is," Vitenka said soothingly. "We must show restraint. Now go. Your deputy will assume your post."

"You cannot," Ryshenko blubbered.

Vitenka nodded toward the door. Two uniformed Army officers entered. "Take him to his quarters," he said softly. "Have his wife brought to him. You will use every courtesy."

"Yes sir," the senior of the two responded.

Vitenka returned to his desk. The minister of defense sat again at his desk, and turned his eyes to the officers around him. "What happened?"

Ryshenko's Deputy, Captain, First Rank Pupynin opened a folder. "Sir, we have lost two ships-both sunk. Missile cruiser *Peter the Great* is severely damaged. Fleet salvage and tugs are enroute to her now. It is not known if she will remain afloat."

"Casualties," Vitenka asked.

Pupynin flipped the page. "Count is now at seven-hundred dead. The number of wounded is not yet reported."

"What of survivors?" Vitenka asked sadly.

"There are only a dozen from *Strogiy*; no officers are among them," Pupynin read. "Patrol ship *Barsuk* exploded and sank after being ordered to stop, no survivors. In addition, an Iranian tanker suffered an explosion after which she capsized and sank no survivors."

"And our response," Vitenka crossed his arms over his chest.

Pupynin flipped to the next page. "The destroyer *Simferopol* engaged a submerged contact near the area where *Peter the Great* was attacked. Her commander reports three hits with RBU weapons."

Vitenka listened emotionless. "Who would do this?"

"It was a deliberate act of war," Air Force General Norslav shouted. "Can you not see that? Two attacks—hundreds of miles apart. Not the actions of one man."

"But why," Vitenka asked, his voice cool and quiet.

"The West sees a weakness. We are poor in almost everything except the one thing the West needs."

"Oil, Oil is the reason," Norslav yelled.

An officer rushed into the meeting. He bent down and whispered in Vitenka's ear.

Vitenka's eyes flared. "Who ordered our rocket forces to full alert?"

"I did," Norslav hissed. "I have also put up fighters around our bases and Moscow."

"On whose authority," Vitenka screamed.

"On my authority," Norslav shouted back. "I will not sit here and contemplate the reason. My duty is to defend the Motherland. You seem to have forgotten that."

"General, you are a fool. What do you think the Americans will do now?"

"Let them come."

"You have brought us to the edge."

"All part of their plan."

"I should have you arrested," Vitenka hissed.

"You are most welcome to try, but I warn you, my feelings in this matter are not mine alone," Norslav said defiantly.

Vitenka's eyes narrowed. "What are you saying?"

"You and your puppet president are inviting attacks. You sit here and do nothing while Russians die."

"You will kill all of Russia," Vitenka shot back.

"Better to be dead than conquered. You forget your history Vitenka."

"What about you?" the defense minister asked.

"Sir, I must side with Norslav. Our country is under attack. We must defend ourselves. To back down now would be a further sign of weakness."

"I do agree. We cannot back down now, but not for the reason you give. If we back down, the West will wonder who is in control. Right now that is also a question I would like answered." Vitenka shut his eyes.

The door opened again, and the same officer came to Vitenka's side. Vitenka listened, and nodded. "The seeds you planted are taking root," Vitenka said with an icy stare. "Three American Battle

Groups have left station and are transiting the North Sea. You can be assured their strategic missile submarines are deployed."

"It is not war I want," Norslav said quietly. "We have for too long been against the wall, we must stand up. It is the Russian way."

"What has the Russian way gotten us for the past hundred years? It is time we did things the human way," Vitenka clipped.

"We don't have time to play word games. We are all reasonable men, men of honor. I'll give you this-forty-eight hours-two days-to tell us who is behind these attacks."

"If I do not," Vitenka growled.

"Then you will be removed. The stakes here are too high. Force must be met with force."

Vitenka glared. "You'll destroy us all."

THE WHITE HOUSE

"Sir, I don't think the British would go this alone," Malroy sighed.

"If not the British, who?" the president asked.

Secretary of Defense Martin Samuals shook his head. "We don't know."

"Just for the sake of argument let's say the Brits are not behind these attacks. Could it be the Russians?"

"We can account for all Russian submarines except for one," Malroy announced.

"Only one?" the president tapped his finger on the desk.

"A Kilo class," Samuals explained.

"Gentlemen, I was Air Force-what the hell is a Kilo?"

"It's a small diesel-electric submarine, very quiet," answered Malroy.

"Could that be the submarine causing this mess?"

"Best guess—yes," Malroy, answered.

"Are the Russians in control or do we have some AWOL sub-skipper out there?"

"Mr. President, I can't answer that," Malroy sighed.

Samuals moved to the chair in front of the president's desk. "Whoever's doing this, threatens world shipping lanes. What if this jackass decides to hit a few oil tankers?"

"We have bigger problems," Malroy interrupted.

"A bigger problem?" asked the president.

"Your predecessor cut a lot of funding for security. Charleston, Savannah, New York, Boston-hell, any port is wide open. You start sinking ships here and the panic will be unimaginable."

"That'll kill the economy," the president observed.

"That's the good news. A Kilo is capable of launching cruise missiles."

The president leaned forward. "Martin, put us at DEFCON 2. I can't take a chance, not until we know what we're dealing with."

"Mr. President what about the obvious?" the SECDEV asked.

The president's brows arched, "The obvious?"

"What if this is an attack by the Russians?"

"Why, why would they do that? It makes no sense," the president said as he shook his head.

"None of this makes sense," Malroy muttered.

"Should we bring this to the UN?"

"No," Samuals answered. "If we do that, sides will form. We could push the Russians into a corner."

"I thought we trusted Atopov and that admiral friend of yours?"

"I don't really any Russian. We acted on a request before the whole world went to hell."

"Martin, I need answers. How are we going to get ourselves out of this one?"

"Going to the DEFCON-2 might cause them to rethink their plans," Samuals shrugged.

Malroy shook his head. "Or it might provoke them into doing something stupid."

"Whatever happens, I want to be ready," the President whispered. "Go to DEFCON-2."

Malroy placed his hands on the president's desk. "Let me talk to Vitenka."

U-761

I hope this works." Edel stepped along a thin plank. Thankfully, the U-boat rose and fell gently in the light chop. Once across the plank he tested his footing on the iceberg. "Send me the torch," He called.

A line was tossed. Edel pulled the hose and cutting head for the torch onto the iceberg. "Now send the hose and pan."

"Okay chief," Hamlin called. "Haul away."

One of Berdy's large pans had a hole cut in the bottom. A spare valve was welded in the hole and a thumb thick hose attached with a threaded coupling. Edel set the pan and hose to the side and took a small hand pick from his waist belt. He hammered at the ice until he dug a meter wide hole in the ice. He scooped up the chunks of ice, and placed them into the pan and continued until it could hold no more. Huffing from his effort Edel dropped the pick and lit the torch. "Ready in cell three?" He called across the ice.

"Ready chief," a voice called back.

Edel placed the flame next to the pan. Steam rose, the ice cracked and hissed. Within minutes fresh water flowed from the hose into the starved batteries. "It's working," Edel called to the U-boat's bridge.

31
HARD TRUTHS

"If ye go to war ... ye shall blow an alarm with the trumpet."

-Numbers, X, 9

THE PENTAGON
NOVEMBER 18TH

"EVERYONE, KEEP YOUR MOUTHS shut," Malroy warned. "I'll do the talking. One wrong word and this could be the last day for a lot of people."

Those around the table nodded.

"Okay then." Malroy punched the button to activate the intercom.

"Central communications," A pleasant voice announced.

"This is Admiral Malroy, Chairman of the Joint Chiefs of Staff. Do you have a connection with the minister of defense?"

"Yes sir, Defense Minister Vitenka is standing by," the voice answered.

"Very well, put me on line."

"Connection is complete, sir," the voice said as the intercom switched off.

Malroy pressed the red flashing button on the communications panel. "Minister Vitenka, this is Admiral Malroy. Can you hear me sir?"

A slight pause..., I can hear you," Vitenka answered.

"Mr. Defense Minister, I need not tell you of the recent events in the area of the Arctic Ocean," Malroy said.

"On the contrary you do need to tell me about these events."

"Is it your country's position the United States is to blame for the loss of your naval units?" Malroy asked.

"There are those who believe this to be the case," Vitenka answered.

"Mr. Minister the Royal Navy has lost a warship and the United States a cargo ship. Can you give any reasons for these attacks?"

Pause... "Admiral Malroy I can assure you no Russian ship or submarine fired on any vessels. Can you answer the same question?"

"You know the United States would never commit an overt action at sea."

"And how would I know that?" Vitenka asked.

"We're not stupid. When in our history have we been the aggressors?"

Vitenka sighed. "We are not getting to the point."

"You're right. Why did your country deploy its fleet? We had an agreement."

"Admiral what I tell you now is truth. The signal was a mistake."

Malroy cleared his throat. "Am I to believe that an entire combat arm of the Russian military was deployed due to a mistake? If that is so, is it possible one of your commanders made a mistake?"

"I pose the same question to you admiral."

"Mr. Minister, this is not getting us anywhere. We know one of your submarines a Project 877 class is missing."

"Admiral, that ship was destroyed during the coup."

"I see. And you have confirmed that?"

"Unfortunately yes," Vitenka said sadly. "Admiral, listen to me please. One ship had orders to conduct a special operation. I can assure you the operation had nothing to do with the security of the United States or NATO."

"If that is so, Mr. Minister, why has your country increased its readiness?"

"Perhaps you already have that answer."

"I can assure you we have abided by the agreement you and I made."

"Perhaps you have a rogue?"

"No Mr. Minister we have control of our forces."

"So, we both are ignorant or liars," Vitenka sighed. "Admiral like you I need answers quickly before events get-how do you say-out of hand."

"Is that a threat of military actions?" Malroy snapped.

"No," Vitenka retorted. "A statement of fact, some events are beyond my control at this time."

"Mr. Minister, I have been ordered to bring the armed forces of my country to full alert."

"I have issued the same order," Vitenka answered.

"Okay, let's cut the polite crap. If you think we sank Russian ships, you are wrong. Now I ask you to back down before this thing does get out of hand."

"I cannot do that, my country has been attacked by someone. What would you have me do? What would you do?"

"I'll give you that, Mr. Minister, but you must pull back."

"That is not an option right now. Your forces are closing on our waters as we speak. Will you have them stop their advance?"

"Stalemate," Malroy sighed.

"It appears so," Vitenka said coolly.

"Let's agree to keep this line open, sailor-to-sailor."

Another long pause hung in the air.

"I agree to that, but I must impress on you time is not with me. Do you understand?"

"I understand."

"Good, admiral, I will be waiting to hear from you," Vitenka said. The line went dead.

The chairman of the Joint Chiefs of Staff blew out a low whistle, and placed his hands behind his head.

"He's in trouble."

"You mean he doesn't have control?" asked the CNO.

"I think he's been threatened. Vitenka is a tough old bird, a cool player. He tried to tell me something. He kept mentioning time."

The telephone in front of the CNO buzzed. "Yes?—All right, get me more information." He replaced the receiver.

"Something new?" asked Malroy.

"Our Key Hole satellite detected hot spots on the hulls of docked Russian missile boats."

"They're getting the boomers to sea."

"CNO get some assets to sit on those missile boats. Pass the word personally. No one is to cause an incident. I want those boats trailed, but in a nice way. Do I make myself clear?"

"Yes sir."

"What else?" Malroy asked.

Before anyone could answer, the buzzer in front of Malroy sounded. He punched the button on the intercom. "Go ahead."

"Sir, a Carl Blevins is calling on the secure line from the embassy in Berlin."

"Damn it," Malroy shouted. "I'm busy. Tell Chief Blevins his assignment is over and get his ass on the next flight back to Groton."

"Uh... sir," the voice said nervously.

"What is it?" Malroy bellowed.

"Chief Blevins said, well he said …"

"What did he say?" Malroy yelled at the unseen voice.

The voice cleared its throat. "Chief Blevins said, 'If that fat son-of-bitch doesn't talk to me now he's going to fly over here and chicken-choke you till your eyes roll out your ass."

The room went silent. Malroy stared at the communications panel. "Must be important, put him through." Malroy punched the button.

"Chief Blevins I'm a little busy for a report about that damned U-boat. I guess you might have heard we're about a gnat's ass away from the third world war?"

"I know, and if you'll shut up and listen, I have the answer. I found out what *U-761* was doing in the ice. You'd better sit down for this one."

U-761

"Two cells are beyond repair," Edel panted as he emerged from the battery space under the E-motor room. "The plates are eaten away. Nothing I can do."

"How much power will we have?" Becker handed the chief a filthy rag.

"Good news is the other cells are about eighty-percent functional."

Edel took the rag and wiped the grime from his face and arms. "We'll have about seventy-five percent total capacities."

"Only seventy-five," Becker asked.

"Be grateful for that Herr Kaleu."

"I am," Becker smiled. "When will the cells be refilled?"

"About four hours. Then three hours to recharge."

"You look like hell. Get some rest." Becker said quietly.

THE WHITE HOUSE

"Admiral, if I didn't know you personally, I'd say you've lost your mind," the president said quietly.

"I agree this is the strangest thing I've ever heard, but it makes some sense," Malroy answered.

"Just to re-cap, I'm supposed to believe a Nazi World War II U-boat is alive and well and blowing the hell out of everything in the Atlantic?"

Secretary of Defense Martin Samuals sat silently his eyes wide and his hands busy buttoning and un-buttoning his blazer. "If this is true why didn't they just give up when they came out of the ice?" he asked weakly.

"I don't know," answered Malroy. "How would they know the war was over? Remember when those Japanese troops came out of the jungle a few years back. They didn't know the war was over."

"Let's say this is real," the president said, raising his hands. "What's this guy doing?"

"He has to be low on fuel or food. God only knows what mental or physical shape they're in," Malroy offered.

"That's not an answer," the president shot back.

"If it were me, I'd try to get home."

"What do we know about the skipper?"

"Manfred Becker. I have our people checking him out. What I know so far is that he was one of their best."

"Seems like it," the president responded. "I just can't believe this."

"Sure would make a great movie," Samuals said.

"Who would believe it?" Malroy shrugged.

"How do we sink the son-of-a-bitch?" the president asked.

"Why sink it?" Malroy blurted out. "Two big reasons I think

that would be a bad idea. First, this is a German submarine. We're not at war with Germany."

"Not good enough," The president countered.

"The second reason; this guy wants to get home. Wouldn't you?" Malroy clasped his hands in front of him. "Mr. President it would be murder. Don't forget one important thing. So far, he's bagged a modern British frigate and possibly three front line Russian warships. If he gets lucky and we lose a ship or two you'll have to answer a lot of very hard questions."

"Why don't we tell the Germans?" Samuals asked. "It's their submarine."

"God no," the president shot back. "Our relations with Chancellor Niestle are bad enough. They stay out of the picture until we absolutely have to tell them."

"I agree," Malroy nodded.

"What about the Russians?" Samuals asked. "They're itching to kill something."

"Oh sure," the president mocked. "I'll just call ole Atopov and tell him, 'Hey listen, we managed to resurrect a Nazi submarine that is sinking your ships would you mind going out and killing that for us?'"

Samuals bowed his head. "You have any better ideas Mr. President?"

"No but I ..."

Malroy cut him off, "Just a minute-wait one minute."

"Yes?" the president asked.

"What if we worked together?"

"Who?"

"Us and the Russians," Malroy thought aloud.

"I think you need to take some leave Sailor," the president sighed. "I don't believe this, why would they?"

"It doesn't matter if you, I, or the Russians believe it. It is a way we can both agree to a pull back. It will buy time," Malroy explained.

"We send a submarine and they send a submarine and everything else goes back to the barn."

"A bit risky," Samuals pointed out.

"A lot less risky than where we are now."

"What makes you think the Russians will play fair?" the president asked.

"Unless they've all lost their minds over there, I think they need an excuse to back down."

"I don't like it," Samuals grumbled. "But I like a nuclear war even less."

"What happens if you find the U-boat?" the president asked. "How do you communicate with it?"

Malroy looked perplexed for a moment. "We'll try the WQC-2 underwater telephone. If they have a hydrophone they should be able to pick it up."

"What will you say? Do they speak English?" Samuals asked.

"Mr. President, give me the go ahead. I will get the details worked out. We don't have a lot of time."

"If this goes south, we'll all be looking for jobs," he said quietly.

"If this goes south, there might not be any jobs," Malroy answered.

Office of Naval Intelligence

The on duty technicians were used to strange research requests but the one that just came from the Joint Chiefs was so far the strangest yet.

It took three hours but they found information on a long dead U-boat commander missing since 1944. What they found caused both seasoned researchers to gasp.

The information bypassed the usual protocol and went directly to Malroy's office.

The Pentagon
November 19th

"Admiral, how did you get this number?" a surprised Vitenka asked.

"Now is not the time," Malroy said into his cell phone. "Are you alone?"

"For now," Vitenka replied.

"You will hear a faint buzz as we talk. It's a device that prevents interception of our call."

"Listen to me carefully," Malroy, said slowly. "I lied to you earlier."

"I am listening," Vitenka replied.

"We had information that one of your missile boats was hiding under the ice and …"

Vitenka cut him off, "Where did you get such information?"

"I don't think that's important now, I …"

"I think it is very important," The Russian interrupted.

"We need to trust one another. We have a satellite that found a shape under the ice. We thought it was a Russian missile boat. So we sent an attack boat to check it out."

"You violated our agreement," Vitenka replied… "I would have done the same.

But your submarine did not find a Russian did it?"

"No."

"Then why tell me these things?" Vitenka asked.

"Because," Malroy paused, "our submarine found a German U-boat."

"Why would the Germans go into the ice? Their submarines are coastal boats."

"Mr. Minister you don't understand. It was not a modern U-boat."

"You mean a Nazi U-boat?"

Malroy flipped through his note pad. "Yes a *Type IXC*."

"You must forgive me. I do not understand what this has to do with our situation. It will be great historical artifact, but I …"

"Wait just…"

Ten minutes later, Malroy finished the whole story.

"I don't think anyone could concoct such a tale." Vitenka observed.

"I have worked out …"

Vitenka cut in, "However you and I have a trust. I believe this story. Unfortunately, those around me will not."

"You have to make them believe."

"That I cannot do, there is a great supply of confusion and fear. Why would they trust me? They need proof."

"Is it that bad?" Malroy asked.

"It is. I have little time to produce answers."

Malroy sighed. "I don't know how …" Malroy stopped in mid-sentence. "Will you and the ministers be open to an expert?" Malroy asked hopefully.

"I don't know about the others, but I am," Vitenka responded. "I will get him here and let him make his case. But I must tell you, time is against us."

32

RIVALS

"Our swords shall play the orators for us."

Christopher Marlowe:
Tamburlaine, I, 1587

"I'M GOING WHERE?" CARL Blevins asked astonished.

"Yep, Moscow," Lieutenant Warren said as he lifted hefted a small knapsack to his shoulders.

"Wait … Its damn cold there and all I have is this," Blevins protested holding the bottom of his blue windbreaker.

"Oh, that does suck," Warren shrugged. "You ready?"

"Why are we going to Moscow?"

"I don't know, and don't want to know," Warren smiled. "Here, this is for you." The SEAL reached inside his shirt and pulled out a large envelope from his waistband. "Don't open it till we're in the air."

U-761

"What's happening to him?" Becker asked.

Roth shook his head. "He's dying. His condition deteriorates by the minute. He cannot eat. There's nothing I can do for him."

"Can he speak?"

"He's in and out, but you can try."

Gerlach's face turned a sickly yellow. His once piercing black eyes were now lifeless dull gray. Gerlach's breath labored.

"Gerlach?"

The dying man's eyes slowly fluttered open. Gerlach turned his head toward Becker.

"Can you hear me?" Becker asked.

"Yes," Gerlach's voice a hushed whisper.

"Are you in pain?"

Gerlach forced his lips to move, "Doesn't matter."

"Is there anything I can do for you?"

"Destroy the gas; the canisters-all has to be destroyed."

"Why?"

"It worked." His shrunken eyes glazed, his mouth parted, and his breath rattled from his lungs.

"What haven't you told me?"

Roth looked into Gerlach's eyes. He felt for a pulse. "It's over, sir. He is gone …

Herr Kaleu?" Roth asked quietly. "What are your orders?"

"He saved us you know," Becker said.

Roth pulled the wool blanket over Gerlach's head. "Yes," he said softly.

United States Ballistic Missile Submarine USS WEST VIRGINIA SSBN 735 Classified Location

"This makes not one bit of sense." The captain stared at the message. "Cancel alert status? This location, can we go there?

The XO shrugged. "I don't know but the orders are authentic."

The captain folded the message and tucked it in his breast pocket. "I hope someone knows what they're doing," he sighed. "All right XO secure alert status." He reached under his left leg and lifted the phone. He pushed the button for the conn.

"Conn, officer of the deck," a voice answered.

"Officer of the deck, this is the captain. Proceed to four-hundred feet. Make turns for ten knots. Come to new course zero-five-zero. Have the navigator come to my stateroom."

THE KREMLIN

Their footsteps echoed through the ancient halls of marble and once finely painted wood. Here and there, a bullet hole allowed the cold November chill through panes of broken glass. Blevins and Warren walked between two not exactly friendly guards.

"Wow, do I feel out of place," Blevins struggled to keep pace with the men at his side. "Looks like this place took a beating."

"Quiet," Warren whispered.

"This sure ain't the White House."

"Carl, please."

"You think these guys are Spetsnaz?"

"I don't know, but I bet they speak perfect English."

"We do," one of the escorts, answered.

"Oh sorry," Blevins replied.

"No problem."

"Anything else you'd like to ask Mr. Jackass?" Warren chuckled.

The four ascended a set of wide winding stairs. At the top, a guard motioned for them to turn left. The hallway narrowed, plaster blasted to powder by gunfire lay smudged and trampled.

At the end of the hall, large oak doors blocked the way. Another set of guards armed with AK-47s, stood stone-faced.

The two escorts stopped. "This is as far as you go."

Warren nodded.

"The ministers are waiting Mr. Blevins," The other said emotionlessly.

"Carl, get in there and get your stuff done."

"But …"

"Get your ass in there chief."

U-761
NOVEMBER 20TH

While Roth sewed the body in a blanket, Edel placed a scrap angle iron at the feet to ensure the body sank.

As gently as the confined space within the U-boat allowed Gerlach was carried topside and lain along the deck's edge.

"Put him over," Becker said softly.

Two diesel mechanics lifted the body over the side.

"Hamlin," Becker called. "The canisters, throw them over."

THE KREMLIN

"Mr. Blevins," Air Force General Norslav smiled, "That was very compelling and it does explain much. However I must ask you one question."

"Yes sir?" Blevins responded.

"Do you believe it?"

Blevins cleared his throat. "General this world is full of crazy sh… I mean unusual things. I am like you. I have to see to believe."

"A good answer, but not for the question I asked," Norslav snapped.

"First off it's Chief Blevins, and yes, I believe it. We have the chance to prove it. I also have the feeling that you would rather blow up the world than give us the chance to find this U-boat."

Army General Trofinoff interjected, "Chief Blevins what are your—how do you say—credentials?"

Blevins scratched his head and sighed, "I'm a retired chief petty officer."

"Retired?" Norslav sat back and folded his hands in his lap.

"I retired last year."

"You were assigned to submarines?" Vitenka asked.

"Yes," Blevins said proudly.

"Do you hold degrees from universities in America?" Trofinoff asked.

"No."

"What makes you an expert?" Norslav asked sarcastically.

Blevins cleared his throat, "I build models."

"You build models?" Vitenka sat up in his chair.

"Yes, model submarines." Blevin's face reddened.

"You mean to tell me we are supposed to trust the fate of Russia on an American who plays with toy boats?" Norslav laughed. "My time is wasted here." the general stood to walk out.

Carl Blevins dressed in old jeans and a sweater and still wearing the thin blue windbreaker, stepped to the right blocking the general's path. "Sit down, dude," Blevins yelled.

Norslav's eyes widened and his chubby cheeks quivered in total surprise.

"You heard me. Park it and let me talk."

Norslav's head swung to Vitenka.

"Sit," Vitenka, said softly.

Rash-like redness spread across Norslav's face. "My men would never talk to me this way," he hissed.

"I'm not one of your men," Blevins quipped.

"Please go on Chief Blevins," Vitenka urged.

"I'm no diplomat and God knows I'm no officer. I am a guy, who has done a lot of research. Hell, I don't think I would swallow it myself. It is up to you. Don't forget one important thing. If it is true and we find *U-761* the gas they used is like—like well it means we might live forever. Or, you can listen to the *chunky monkey* over there, and blow the whole world to hell."

Vitenka glanced at the other ministers. Trofinoff nodded as did the director of strategic missiles indicating their agreement. Captain Pupynin also nodded. Then Vitenka turned to Norslav. "General?"

Norslav gave a slow nod.

"It is settled then," Vitenka said. "Chief Blevins we will work with the American Navy and find this German submarine. Let me say this for the record. Should this prove to be some sort of trick or an attempt to gain advantage, I will have no recourse but to take military actions to protect the Russian people."

"Sounds fair to me," Blevins nodded.

"Chief, are you ready to go?" Vitenka asked.

"Go?"

"Yes. You are the expert on this matter and I have none. You will accompany our submarine in the search."

"Wait one minute," Blevins, protested. "You mean me on a Russian submarine?"

"That is what I mean," Vitenka answered.

The two escorts reappeared and each took a place next to the retired chief. Vitenka spoke Russian to the two men. Both nodded and turned. The taller of the two motioned for Blevins to precede him. The huge doors swung open and Carl found himself again in the hall.

Warren rose from a rickety chair and came to Blevin's side. "How did it go?"

"Oh just fine, and by the way I just joined the Russian Navy."
Warren's mouth fell open, "You what?"

USS MIAMI

With only her number two scope and number one BRA-34 receiving antenna raised, the American submarine remained hidden in a vast empty ocean. She ducked twice when trawlers had come too close for comfort.

In his stateroom, Grant McKinnon sat at his small but efficient desk. The exec and the navigator stood next to him. "Looks like they've agreed," McKinnon announced.

"We're about to re-write naval history," the navigator observed.

"Or end it," The XO whispered.

McKinnon touched the neatly folded chart on his desk. "Work with sonar and build us a search plan."

The XO shook his head, "Aye, sir."

"What do we do when we find it?" The navigator asked.

"We're supposed to get her to surface and give up."

"How will we do that?"

"We are downloading pre-recorded sound bites in German. When we get close we play the tapes over the WQC."

The XO slowly shook his head. "At least they can't shoot at us."

"Remember the funny looking torpedo our guys found? That is the Great Grandfather of our own ADCAP."

"You mean to tell me there is a pissed off Nazi running around with a homing torpedo and we're going to play tapes for him?" The navigator asked.

McKinnon smiled, "Strange world, huh?"

"What about the Russians?"

"You can guess their feelings on this. They're pretty trigger-happy anyway."

"What boat are they going to send?"

"If it were me, you know who I would send," McKinnon answered.

"You think it'll be *Vepr*?" The exec asked quietly.

"Like I said, that's what I'd do," McKinnon answered.

"The pissed off Nazi doesn't seem so bad."

"Rules of engagement," The XO asked.

"Against the Russians we can protect ourselves. You know as well as I that getting a shot at *Vepr* will be a ten on the next-to-impossible list. As for the German we cannot engage."

Miami's Navigator winced, "Why not?"

"Here's another part of the puzzle," McKinnon handed the XO a message marked *'For COs Eyes Only.'*

The XO took the message and read it silently. "Talk about a small world. You think he knows?"

"I don't know but we might need his help." McKinnon shrugged. "You know who I wished we had onboard?"

"Who," The XO asked.

"That chief who retired last year... You remember he builds those models?"

"Oh yeah," the nav smiled. "Ole Carl Blevins, he would love this stuff."

33

TO SEA

"…Over the wine dark sea."

Homer: The Iliad, c. 1000 B.C.

THE SMALL ROOM WAS warm, the lights dim. Wind blowing from the mountains whined as it flowed past the windows and doors. What sun there was, made its brief appearance then sank into the ocean.

With the last of the dinner dishes dried and put away, Evelina walked to the small living room. Her usual smile seemed muted, her mood somber. She slid closer to Danyankov. "This frightens me."

Danyankov wrapped his arm around her slender shoulders drawing her head to his chest. "This is nothing new. You have seen worse with your father. "Danyankov said softly.

"No Valerik this is different."

The commander of the most feared Russian submarine on the sea looked puzzled. "How is it different?"

"Because it's you," She cooed her voice just above a whisper.

"Don't worry," he blurted.

"But I do." A tear rolled down her smooth face. "I don't think I could stand losing you."

"You won't lose me."

"I have heard the fleet is forbidden to sail. So why must you go. Can you tell me?"

"You know I can't."

She pulled back. "Father told me not to fall in love with a sailor," She said with a slight grin. "Now look at me."

"I am and you're beautiful."

"Why do you have to go?"

"I'm so afraid."

Danyankov took his arm from around her shoulders. "I am willing to prove to you that I will come back." He fumbled through his pocket, fished out a small box, and nervously opened it.

Evelina Vitenka gasped.

"This is how." He removed the small diamond ring from its red felt-covered box.

"Valerik," She shouted. "Are you asking me...?"

Danyankov's large hands trembled and placed the ring on her slender delicate finger. "I am... if you will have me."

She admired the ring. Her body trembled. "Of course I will." She threw her arms around his neck. "You will come back?"

"I have to now, that ring cost me two month's pay," He smiled.

Now she had a smile that seemed to brighten the room. He nudged her close, held her tight.

"My father-has he talked to you? He has not called in days." She nuzzled his neck. "I want to tell him of our engagement," She cooed.

"He is a busy man."

"You men are always too busy."

"Maybe he will call tomorrow."

"I don't want to think about tomorrow," She complained. "All this is new to me."

"To me also," Danyankov whispered.

"Is everything going to be all right?" she asked.

"I hope so."

USS MIAMI

With a small swish, the periscope vanished from the ocean's surface. *Miami* descended to the darkness and turned east.

McKinnon drained the last bit of coffee from his cup. Setting the cup on the wardroom table, he glanced at the weapon's officer. "The search plans ready?"

"We have a plan for the Akula, she's no problem. The U-boat though, we have no idea how she would sound. I figured on two-three blades she would sound like the thousand or so other trawlers."

McKinnon rubbed his chin. "What about submerged?

"Submerged it might sound like a distant trawler. We'd be on top of her before we knew it."

Lapadnaya Lista
November 21st

The sun managed to achieve only a dull cold ribbon of orange. Snow spit from the dead sky adding to the dirty brown slush that covered everything. Carl Blevins was up and dressed well before the pitiable sun. He repacked his small backpack and waited. A heavy rap at the flimsy door startled him. "Da?" he answered in his best Russian.

"Mr. Blevins?" a voice in perfect English asked from the other side. "It is time to go."

Blevins picked up his backpack, went to door.

"Good morning. Mr. Blevins I'm Lieutenant Shurgatov."

Blevins shivered in the cold. He extended his hand to the Russian, "Nice to meet you."

"Mr. Blevins, you …"

Blevins held up his hand. "Please call me Carl."

The smiling Shurgatov nodded, "Carl then. The ship will sail within the hour. I must apologize for your quarters, but they are the best we have."

"I understand," Blevins lied.

"If I may say, you don't seem dressed for sea duty."

"I know," Blevins replied.

"Not to worry. My quarters are on the way. We'll stop and get you some proper clothes."

"Thanks."

"Come, we must be fast. Captain Danyankov gets very upset if he has to wait."

Blevins stepped into the thick snow covered slush. "Danyankov?" he asked.

"Yes. You've heard him?"

Blevins shivered again, but not from the cold.

USS MIAMI

Chief of the boat and the navigator sat with McKinnon in the wardroom.

"Nav, where are we?"

"About ten hours away," the navigator said quietly.

McKinnon looked at the chart. "The ice will raise hell this time of year," he mumbled.

"If we come shallow we'll have to watch it. Last satellite image showed some major bergs in our op area."

"You have them plotted?"

"Yes but the current is a good five knots, so the damn things are miles from the last known location."

"Nav I want to enter the rendezvous area from the Southeast. Remember we have to look like we just arrived."

"What about depth separation between us and the Akula?"

"We're the deep boat." McKinnon studied the chart then turned to Danny Norse.

"COB, this is the game plan. Have the tracking party manned in six hours. Battle stations an hour after that. I want a meal served early. Get the cooks on it. Have the attack center and torpedo room do a check on our weapons. Everyone else I want in the bunks. Who knows when they'll get another chance for some rack time."

"Will do," Norse nodded.

"COB," McKinnon stopped him, "What do you think?"

Danny Norse turned back toward McKinnon. He looked down at the white tiled deck of the wardroom floor. "What I saw on that boat... I cannot even put into words. Those guys didn't look dead," Norse observed. "They had pictures of their families and girls on the bulkheads. It's strange how submariners are all the same."

"Is there anything at all you can think of that might persuade this guy to give up without a fight?"

"Would you?" Norse asked bluntly.

K-157 VEPR

"Please we must hurry," Shurgatov urged.

They trudged through a mix of new snow and thick frozen mud. The cold air hung heavy with the smell of rotted wood, and burning coal spewing from the antique power plant. The two men rushed along a row of squat gray buildings whose once white paint had long since peeled away. At the end of the buildings, an archway of crumbling brick connected yet another stretch of dilapidated structures. With Blevins a few paces behind, Shurgatov entered the archway. Blevins caught up by the time they reached the narrow waterfront.

A small brick guardhouse stood at the head of the second pier. Shurgatov gave the guard a wave and rushed past. The guard yawned and raised his arm in a half-hearted salute. A narrow path clear of ice and snow snaked awkwardly down the center of the rusted rotting pier. Lieutenant Shurgatov took the lead and they trotted toward the waiting submarine. Blevins gasped when he caught site of the Akula.

Blevins felt a tug on his sleeve. "Please come now. No time to sightsee," Shurgatov pleaded.

"Sorry," Blevins responded. Clumsily he slapped the oversized fur hat back on his head and trotted toward the gangway.

Shurgatov strode up the inclined wooden planks of the gangway. Standing on the deck, he stopped and turned to Blevins. "We made it," the young Russian smiled.

Suddenly those on deck went rigid. Blevins stumbled when his foot hit the deck, not noticing everyone else at attention. Again the hat slid sown his forehead and over his eyes.

Then a hand pushed it back further up his forehead. With the hat back where it belonged, Carl Blevins found himself staring into the most unfriendly face he had ever seen. The piercing eyes shot through him, the lips turned down at the corners as if made of clay. Even the air around the face seemed menacing.

Shurgatov stepped up, gave a snappy textbook salute. He spoke in Russian to the statue-like man. Shurgatov finished and turned to Blevins. "Chief Carl Blevins this is Captain First Rank Valerik Danyankov."

Blevins's left eye twitched, his mouth opened, but no words

came out. He blinked and cleared his throat. "Captain, it is good to meet you," He stammered and extended his hand.

Danyankov looked at the hand and then back to Blevins's face. Without turning, he spoke again in Russian to the stone-faced Shurgatov.

"He says your uniform is a poor fit," The lieutenant translated.

Blevins decided to match stares with this legend of the Russian and indeed NATO navies. He narrowed his eyes and contorted his features into his best war face. It might have worked had the fur hat not again fallen over his face. He pushed the hat up and looked at Shurgatov.

Danyankov spun on his heels. The blast of Russian coming from the captain's mouth echoed off the submarine's hull. Danyankov ranted for what seemed minutes then stomped down the hatch in the leading edge of *Vepr's* sail.

When he had gone, the men moved like stunned survivors of an earthquake or hurricane. Shurgatov took a deep breath. "That is our captain."

"Wow, I thought I had some bad ones," Blevins breathed. "What was he so pissed about?"

"He's in a very good mood today."

Blevin's mouth fell open.

"It is his way."

"So what did he say?" Blevins asked.

"He wanted me to welcome you aboard and tell you what an honor it is to be working with a member of the United States Navy."

"Bullshit. Now what did that dick with ears say?"

Shurgatov sighed, "He said that you are to be with me at all times and no questions about his ship will be answered. He is not happy having you on his boat. You will eat after the crew and that I am responsible for you. I am to keep you on a leash."

"Is that all?"

"Not exactly," the young Russian confessed.

"What else?" Blevins asked.

"If you get in his way or cause any problem he will unscrew my head and poop down my neck."

Blevins burst into laughter. "I'm glad he's in a good mood."

Shurgatov chuckled, "Let's get you below."

U-761

Near exhaustion, Edel slumped over the rail to the port diesel. The battery was charged although three cells were corroded beyond repair. In the torpedo room, the brace near the hatch went in with little trouble. There was still the leak in the air compressor.

"How bad is it?" Becker asked.

Edel rubbed at his bloodshot eyes. "We'll need that air. The banks are slowly draining I think the check valves are leaking."

"What do you need?" Becker asked.

"Time," Edel Shrugged.

Becker sighed, "How much?"

"Give me another hour."

VEPR

The nearly frozen water of the harbor parted grudgingly as *Vepr* slid down the channel. A flight of gulls flew escort a short distance, their white wings standing in sharp contrast to the dark sky.

Vepr rounded the towering rock formations that marked the passage to the open sea. Water flowed over the rounded bow, and splashed against the bottom of the sail. The ship pounded her way forward into the growing darkness and the unknown.

34
RENDEZVOUS

"In confidence and quietness shall be your strength."

-Isaiah, XXX, 15

U-761
November 22nd

BECKER AWOKE SLOWLY. A wonderful aroma wafted under his nose. He sat up testing the air. Looking toward the radio room Becker saw Roth smiling back at him. "What is that?" Becker asked.

"The off watch did some fishing. Berdy is frying the catch now."

"I never realized how hungry I am."

"I know Herr Kaleu. It seems years since we had a real meal." Roth laughed.

Less than an hour later, the fish were mere piles of bones on the wardroom table. Edel leaned back from the table. "What is your plan?"

"Not much of a plan." Becker took a deep breath. "We'll run as far as we can on the surface. We alter course every ten kilometers or so. Stay down during the day and run surfaced at night.

Edel smiled, "Home."

"A long way to get there," Becker sighed.

"We can leave when you say." Edel tucked his head next to the thin cushion that lined the back of the seat.

"We'll give your black gang a few hours' sleep."

USS MIAMI

"This is the last trip up until we make contact with the Akula," McKinnon said as he briefed his control room watch standers. "You know what's riding on this. Any questions, ask. Something breaks fix it." McKinnon studied the faces that stared back at him. "All right let's do it." McKinnon clapped his hands like a football coach.

VEPR

Seventy meters beneath the surface, *Vepr* passed the north tip of Norway. Beneath her, the ocean floor fell away until the bottom lay fifteen hundred meters below.

In the command center, Danyankov studied the chart. "What is best speed to the meeting area?"

"Fifteen knots."

"Make turns for twenty knots. Get me down to three hundred meters. And do it smartly."

"Maintain this course depth and speed," Danyankov ordered. "Watch officer find Shurgatov and bring the American to my cabin."

The VM-5 reactor purred silently while *Vepr* slid through the sea. Her systems ran at peak performance. All seven million parts of this lethal warship operated as designed, except for a key item.

At the touch of salt water the dissimilar metals in the port stern plane connecting pintle began to disintegrate Heat from welding forced contaminates into the material causing microscopic pores to open after the new pintle submerged. Water slowly but steadily entered these pores and caused an electro-chemical reaction. As the port plane cycled the reaction found greater surface area to attack. The pores opened further allowing more conductive seawater to surround the pintle.

By the time, *Vepr* reached her cruising depth, fingernail size flakes of metal peeled away. Like tiny snowflakes, they swirled into the slipstream where they dissolved into the salt of the ocean.

"Downlink complete," The radioman called over the 27MC.

"Very well," the OOD responded. "All stations going deep."

At her present six knots, she seemed no more than a hole in the water.

"Dive get a good one-third trim. I want watch to watch compensations," McKinnon ordered. "I don't know when we'll get the chance again."

"Aye sir," the chief in the dive seat answered.

"Conn radio, any new traffic?" asked McKinnon.

"Radio, Conn, negative."

"We're on our own," The XO whispered.

"Conn, Sonar," a voice came over the combat circuit, "Sonar holds ice noises bearing two-six-eight all the way to course north."

"Very well sonar," McKinnon replied, "Looks like we've arrived."

"You figure out what we're listening for?" the XO asked.

"Not a clue," McKinnon sighed. "I've got a pissed off German and a cocky Russian out there somewhere." McKinnon shrugged. "We're gonna earn the paycheck this month."

VEPR

"He has ordered me to leave the cabin," Shurgatov said apologetically.

"I'll be fine." Blevins replied.

With the door shut, Valerik Danyankov's eyes remained fixed on Blevins.

"You do speak English?" asked Blevins.

"Mr...."

"It's chief," Blevins interrupted.

Danyankov's eyes narrowed.

Blevins narrowed his.

"Very well, *Chief Blevins* we are at the meeting area. You will tell me what you know about this U-boat."

"You've read the report I sent," Blevins said in his best hard-ass voice. A voice he perfected and often used when getting things done with his A-gang, or getting what he needed from a supply officer or even a squadron commander or two.

"Yes I have been briefed. What I want to know where the American submarine will enter the search area? What depth will they be at?"

"Captain," Blevins folded his arms over his chest. "First of all I was a machinist mate. The only time I went to control was to stand my watch and grease the periscope. Second, I wouldn't tell you if Jesus Christ ordered me too."

Valerik Danyankov leaned back in his seat. "Good."

"What?" Blevins asked.

"You are a loyal man. I can trust you."

"Trust me with what?"

Danyankov leaned forward, "The truth."

"What truth?"

"You know of me?"

Blevins frowned. "Yes I do. Most of the American Navy knows about you."

"Is it true what they call me?" Danyankov asked. "Am I 'The Prince of Darkness'?"

"There are other names, but yes."

Danyankov laughed. "Good, good."

"Listen is there any point to this?"

"What do you think of my boat?"

Blevins shook his head. "What are you talking about?"

"My boat, Tell me what do you think of her?"

"She's beautiful."

"My crew what do you think of them?"

"They seem top shelf. Well trained seem to know their stuff."

"You saw the condition of the base-no?" Danyankov asked.

"Yeah," Blevins forgot all formality. "It's pretty much a shit hole."

Danyankov grinned. "This is true."

"However, my ship is the best submarine in the Russian Navy."

"That's great."

Danyankov leaned closer. "Chief Blevins I am hard because I have to be. My men need to fear me. They do not desert as so many have. They perform their duties to the utmost. They do not steal from the ship or from each other. They keep this submarine from becoming one of those rusting hulks you saw along the waterfront. They make do with what they have."

"If that works for you fine, but why are you telling me?"

"I need you to understand, and I need your help."

"What do you need from me?" Blevins asked. "This mission this search could mean the difference. My country and yours are once again ready to wipe each other from the planet." Danyankov's voice lowered. "A month ago, I would have welcomed war with America. Now I have no desire to see it. What I ask of you is simple-give me the truth."

"I will," replied a stunned Blevins.

"I am not sure I believe a submarine from so long ago can come back, but I know the American submarine out there is very real. Should this all be true, I need you to not be fear giving me the truth."

"You can count on me, skipper," Blevins stood and took hold of the brightly polished doorknob.

"Don't call me that," Danyankov sneered. "There is more I need of you."

Blevins returned and sat down. "Yes, skipper?"

"This is a personal matter," Danyankov said almost sheepishly.

"What can I do?"

"I am getting married soon and I..."

Blevins smiled. "You need a best man? I'll check my schedule."

Danyankov's face broke into a wide grin. "No, you ass, I need some information on Las Vegas."

"Is that before or after the wedding?"

Danyankov flushed "After of course."

"Just checking," Blevins, grinned. "If we get out of this alive I'll get you a great room on the strip."

Danyankov nodded. "Good. This conversation must be kept Between you and me-yes?"

"Of course," Blevins smiled.

"Forgive me for what I must do now. Please stand up."

"What?"

"Trust me," Danyankov whispered.

Blevins stood and as he did, Danyankov screamed in Russian. The door flew open and Shurgatov stood with a look of horror.

Still screaming Danyankov gave Blevins a forceful shove that sent the American skidding into the wide-eyed lieutenant.

Thanks to Shurgatov's quick reflexes, Blevins managed not to tumble into the narrow passageway. Danyankov slammed the door so hard the steel frame seemed to vibrate.

"I see you made a friend," Shurgatov said sarcastically.

"What's that guy's problem?" Blevins panted. "What the hell was he saying to you?"

"It seems Captain Danyankov has questions about your parents being married when you were born," Shurgatov answered quietly.

"That son of a bitch," Blevins hissed, as he stepped toward the door.

The lieutenant grabbed Blevins's shirtsleeve just in time. "No. Please remember what he said he would do after he unscrewed my head?"

U-761

Those on the U-boat's bridge were silent. Becker stood at the front, to the side of the surface's aiming device mount (UZO). Although the wind ebbed, the chill of the Arctic remained. Becker shivered as he tightened the fleece jacket around his neck.

Edel stuck his head from the bridge hatch. "She's ready Herr Kaleu."

Becker smiled back. "Good work." He turned to Volker. "Number-one, start both engines and steer for home."

Volker's cold reddened face broke into a wide grin, "Aye captain."

Becker leaned over the cone-shaped voice pipe that led to the zentrale below. "Pass the word to all hands we are making for Germany. We will man actions stations on the surface. We have many miles between us and home."

VEPR

The sleek blue gray hull flowed like a part of the sea. The seven blades of the scimitar-like screw turned lazily when she slowed to the best listening speed.

In her rounded almost bulbous bow, the powerful MGK-540

sonar system probed the audible and ultrasonic frequencies for anything manmade.

Vepr entered the meeting area at sixty-meters. A thermal layer stretching from ninety-meters to two-hundred and forty meters would make finding the *Miami* difficult. He slowed to allow his array to droop below the layer.

The commander prepared his weapon systems and ordered the battery of ten 553mm torpedo tubes loaded and ready.

The weapons operators double-checked the status of both the weapon and launching tubes. As *Vepr* started her hunt, the weapon's operators ran one last series of checks. Every torpedo gave the electronic equivalent of thumbs up. As was standard procedure, another set of tests were run using *Emergency Firing Computer*. The ten waiting torpedoes signified by a steady green light, happy and ready to serve the Motherland. Tube #4 refused to switch back to the normal command center computer.

The warrant officer in charge noted the fault and logged it. "Another relay gone out," he sighed.

One of the torpedoman nodded his head. "That happened last month. Would you like to take the tube from service?"

"No, leave it as is for now. You know what will happen if I tell the captain. Go draw the relay from supply."

"I think if we ever needed all ten tubes our asses would be hanging by a string."

The warrant laughed. "And the same would hold true if the captain found out about this."

At the stern, the pintle holding the port stern plane to the stabilizer began to crack. The protective coating applied in the shipyard was gone, washed into the sea. *Vepr's* slow pace decreased stress on the pintle. A half-moon-shaped chunk of failed material fell out, which left one-third the diameter of the original pintle.

USS MIAMI

"Conn sonar," called the sonar supervisor over the 27MC. "Sonar holds new contact, designate sierra two-three. Contact has two-three blades at eight-zero RPM. Contact just started."

"Very well sonar. Designate contact as master-one. Attention in the attack center," he called out so all could hear. "Designate master-one as contact of interest, tracking party, track master-one."

"Conn-sonar, be advised master-one is intermittent due to ice noise.

"Hold that contact," McKinnon urged as he watched the waterfall display mounted above the periscope stand. "Sonar I am maneuvering to put the array on it."

VEPR

"Sonar holds new contact. Initial classification is merchant, based on noise."

Danyankov moved slowly to the plot. His fingers traced over the chart. "Bearing to contact?" He asked.

"Contacts bear three-four-zero degrees," sonar reported.

"Track that target."

With a push of the button, the highly automated sonar system of the Akula analyzed the sound pressure bouncing off its transducers. The information flashed by optic cable to the computers, converted to a display the slow human mind could observe, then fed into the waiting torpedoes.

"Captain, hold new contact, possible submerged. Bearing is one-nine-four. It appears to be blade tip cavitation."

"Diving control come left to new course two-zero-zero," Danyankov directed. "I found you first," he whispered to himself. "Sonar go active."

USS MIAMI

"Contact is in and out," sonar reported. "We're getting more noises from the ice. Believe contact is maneuvering around bergs."

"Very well sonar. Keep me outta' trouble," McKinnon called.

"Master one is making eight knots, course zero-eight-four," reported the plot coordinator.

"We're almost steady on course."

An excited voice shouted a warning, "Conn, sonar gained a seventy-two hertz tonal on the array, submerged contact bearing one-nine-zero!"

The interior of the *Miami* suddenly filled with the resonance of energy from a Russian active pulse. The WLR-9 early warning system chirped as the sound wave enveloped the hull.

McKinnon had been sloppy. The distraction was total and complete. The Akula found his ship and slipped into a perfect firing position. If this had this been a shooting war the next sound *Miami's* sonar would have detected would have been a salvo of incoming Russian 53CM-K homing torpedoes.

"Conn, sonar receiving active from *shark-gill* sonar carried on late model Russian type 2–3 submarine. One-hundred percent probability of detection," he added with a sigh.

"Sonar conn aye. Line up to go active. Go active when ready."

"This guy is the best," the XO whispered.

"Sonar I need underwater comms set up in control."

VEPR

"Captain received an active transmission from the contact."

"Scared the hell of him I think," Danyankov smiled.

"In receipt of underwater communication," sonar reported.

"Bring the at sea telephone on line," Danyankov ordered.

"Captain you are ready to transmit," the sonar officer reported.

Danyankov held the handset to his ear and pressed the talk button. "Yankee-1, Yankee-1, this is Gray Ghost do you copy?"

"Gray Ghost, Gray Ghost this is Yankee-1. I read."

35
VOICES

"The sword itself often incites a man to fight."

-Homer, Odyssey, XVI,c. 1000 B.C.

THE ARCTIC OCEAN

"YES, WE HOLD THE same contact." Danyankov reported.

"Recommend you proceed to periscope depth to investigate," McKinnon responded over the underwater intercom.

"I concur," Danyankov replied. "Yankee-1, this is Gray Ghost have you received instructions for stopping this U-boat?"

"Gray Ghost, Gray Ghost, this is Yankee-1. We have recordings to play for contact. How copy?"

"Yankee-1, Yankee-1, this is Gray Ghost. I do not think contact can hear while surfaced. I have a U-boat expert on board who says contact must be submerged—over."

"Gray Ghost, Gray Ghost, this is Yankee-1 understand contact must be submerged—break—any ideas?"

"Affirmative Yankee 1—break. We will proceed to periscope depth—break. Be ready with your recordings, Gray Ghost out."

"Diving command," Danyankov bellowed. "Proceed to antenna depth. Plot, bring the ship to one-thousand meters ahead of contact."

Vepr angled toward the surface.

"Report contact," he ordered.

"Contact by plot bears one-nine-three. Range one-two-hundred meters."

"Up scope," Danyankov barked. "Stand by for periscope observation." Danyankov lowered the handles of the scope. "It is true." His words came out a bit shaky. "Stand by for observation on surfaced U-boat."

Blevins arrived in seconds shepherded by Shurgatov.

"You need something?" Blevins asked gruffly.

"Take a look," Danyankov nodded.

Blevins placed his eye to the scope. His mouth dropped open. Only a gasp escaped his lips.

"Is that a U-boat?" Danyankov asked.

Blevins remained silent.

"Is that the U-boat?" Danyankov demanded.

A smile formed his Blevins's lips though his eyes remained hidden by the periscope. "Sure is, and she is a beauty."

"How do we get it to surrender?" Danyankov asked quietly. "Can we use radio?"

"My guess is she's not been able to contact anyone. Worth a try though." Blevins again pressed his eye to the scope.

"Raise the radio mast," Danyankov ordered.

"Hang on there cowboy." Blevins moved his eye from the scope. "These guys have very good optics and very good lookouts. I would be careful sticking too much out of the water. You spook this guy and he'll head right back for the ice."

"Stop the mast at the periscope window," Danyankov ordered.

"I'll give your radio room the frequencies." Blevins stepped away from the scope.

"The hell you will," Danyankov roared. "I will not allow an American in my radio room."

"Calm down. I will write them down. Blevins looked around the command center, "Who speaks German?"

"I had not thought of that," Danyankov admitted. "Still, I will not allow you in the radio."

"Your boat," Blevins shrugged.

"Could we use a flare to get him under water?" Danyankov asked.

Blevins shrugged. "It will get their attention."

"Launch signal flare," he ordered.

"You might consider sticking your sail out of the water," Blevins added.

"But what about spooking him?"

"This whole thing is a crap shoot."

U-761

The U-boat swayed gently with the long rolling swells. Both diesels hummed, sending a slight vibration through the steel hull. At her stern, the mist of her exhaust formed a cloud that faded into the cold air.

In the dim light of the Arctic noon, *U-761* sailed into an empty horizon. Volker had taken the watch when the U-boat departed from her bunker-like iceberg. He set his binoculars between the voice pipes and rubbed his eyes.

Suddenly the sea ahead of the U-boat erupted in a greenish orange flame. An object with a sizzling tail of fire shot from the water. Light from the comet-like object illuminated the U-boat in an eerie orange glow.

Fifty-meters high the projectile exploded in a puff of angry black smoke that changed to an intense glowing ball of burning gas.

"Star shell," one of the lookouts called.

Volker scanned the sea and sky in a quick, but practiced turn of his neck. "From where?" he shouted.

As the object fell closer, the sea ahead of the U-boat boiled. Volker heard it before he saw it. His neck turned just as a massive hump emerged in *U-761's* path.

The men gasped as the shape reared up.

"Alarm," Volker screamed, "Left hard rudder!"

VEPR

"She's diving." Danyankov yelled, "Right full rudder, new depth seven-zero meters."

Defying her usual grace, the 12,770-ton Russian submarine slipped awkwardly under the waves.

"Contact," Danyankov demanded.

"Lost in surface noise," sonar reported.

"Find it," Danyankov bellowed.

"Regain contact," sonar reported.

"Bearing?"

"Bearing three-five-zero, I am isolating the sound now."

"Ahead slow. Center the rudder," Danyankov ordered. He pivoted to the left, his hand reached for the underwater communication handset. "Yankee-1, Yankee-1, this is Gray Ghost, contact is submerged. Contact bears three-five-zero."

"Confirm regain of contact. Two three-blades, making five-zero RPM," sonar reported.

McKinnon's voice came through the speaker. "Gray Ghost, this is Yankee-1...understand all—break. We are beginning audio playback, now—now—now."

As if the sea were haunted, a voice floated up from the dark, a voice strange to those listening on the two nuclear submarines and stranger still to those for whom the message was intended.

U-761

"Hold us here," Becker snapped. "Tell me again."

Volker peeled off the heavy oilskin coat. "I don't know what it was, something like a whale. It has to be a submarine."

"Holding depth at twenty-meters," Edel announced.

"We're heading for the ice," Hamlin said softly.

Becker nodded. "Both motors ahead, dead slow." He looked over to the sound room, "Anything?"

At his hydrophone station Veldmon, turned the steering wheel sized hydrophone control. "Nothing sir," he whispered. Just the..." Veldmon's mouth dropped open. His lips moved, but nothing came out.

"What is it?" Becker hissed."

His eyes shot toward Becker's, "Voices."

"What?" Becker stepped to the tiny sound room.

The hydrophone operator turned his head. "They know your name," he managed. Without looking Veldmon reached above his head, and toggled a switch. A small, but powerful speaker crackled. The sound came into the control room, faint at first. Veldmon adjusted the radio gain. He moved the hydrophone wheel to the left. The voice came in not perfect, but understandable.

A voice from the ocean flowed into his ears. The voice was in perfect German, with a slight hint of being from the Alsberg region.

"Kapitanleutnaunt Becker and the crew of the German submarine U-761. The war ended. Repeat. The war is over. This is United States submarine, USS MIAMI. We are operating below your vessel.

Miami is in coordination with Russian submarine Vepr. You are to cease all hostile action and surface your ship. Repeat; cease all hostile action and surface.

No harm will come to you or your crew. If you refuse to surface or are perceived to make an attack, we have orders to destroy your vessel."

There was a pause before the message began again.

Becker looked around the control room at the expressions on his men's faces. He saw a few with a gleam of hope in their eyes though most of the eyes peering at him contained only fear.

"A trick?" asked Hamlin.

"I don't know."

"It's not a trick. They knew where to find us. They could have easily torpedoed us on the surface. Maybe the war is over Herr Kaleu," Hamlin argued.

"Maybe they couldn't get a good bearing on us." Edel remarked as he nervously stroked the stubble at his chin.

"Or maybe they want us alive," Hamlin countered.

"Captain?" asked Volker.

Becker turned. "Left full rudder," he ordered. He picked up the microphone for the ship's address system. "Baldric load tube two with the *Leche*."

Edel's head snapped around. "You're attacking?"

Becker remained silent.

Edel had been in the German navy long enough to understand the meaning of that silence.

USS MIAMI

"Contact has changed bearing rate," sonar reported. "Master one is turning on a reciprocal bearing. Wait... uh-oh."

"What is it?" McKinnon asked.

"Looks like there might be a layer, I'm betting its fresh water from the bergs."

"Conn, aye," the officer of the deck, replied.

"Sonar, conn, I'm going to maneuver to the east," McKinnon announced.

"Conn sonar, I can hold master one on the array."

"Then, what is the problem?"

"Captain we're receiving transits from master one, sounds like they're doing something with the tubes."

"Launch transits?" McKinnon asked nervously.

"Negative, sounds like the may be tube loading or unloading."

"You think *Vepr* can hear?"

"I don't know. We hold an intermittent seventy-two hertz tonal on her last good bearing. *Vepr* is on the right drawing right."

The XO moved beside the captain. "You think they're loading that acoustic weapon?"

"I would," McKinnon replied quietly. "If this guy thinks he's cornered, he'll take a shot."

"It'll have to be a lucky one. I mean, how good can that weapon be?"

"He's been real lucky so far," McKinnon, sighed.

"What if he does shoot?"

"I'm not worried about us. What will that Russian do?"

VEPR

The Akula maneuvered to keep contact with the turning U-boat. The crack on the stern plane pintle opened wider. Water rushing by caused a small vibration. As both sides reverberated, a harmonic began. The ultrasonic sound started in the low Db range, but grew quickly when *Vepr* increased speed.

In the torpedo room the warrant officer with the torpedoman, were ready to repair number 4 torpedo tube.

"We'll have to make this fast," the warrant officer warned.

"I've done this three times before."

"Just be sure the master circuit is bypassed when you replace the relay. There is a live weapon loaded," the warrant warned.

"Don't be such an old woman." The torpedoman fished in his pocket and found his flat head screwdriver. He quickly removed four screws holding the maintenance cover on the Emergency Firing Control.

In the command center, Danyankov paced. He looked toward Blevins. "What do you think he'll do?"

"If I have done my homework correctly, and I have, this guy is no fanatic. He wants this thing to be over just as much as we do. So, if no one does anything stupid…"

"Exactly what does that mean?" Danyankov asked.

"I think he'll give it up and go home."

Danyankov continued to pace.

U-761

"Steady new course," the helmsman reported.

"Do you hear anything?" Becker asked.

The hydrophone operator shook his head. "No, Herr Kaleu, just ice."

"It could be below us," Hamlin offered.

Baldric's voice crackled over the intercom. "Captain, *Leche* torpedo is loaded."

"Periscope depth," Becker ordered.

The tension in the U-boat hung heavier than the stale air.

The lights went out then came back as sickly dull red.

"Bow planes up ten, stern up fifteen," Edel ordered.

36

DELIVERANCE

"They that go down to the sea in ships, and occupy their business in great waters: these men see the works of the Lord and his wonders in the deep."

-Psalm CVII

USS MIAMI

"BEARING SHIFT ON MASTER-ONE," sonar announced. "Wait, master one is going to the roof. I hold hull pops."

The XO shrugged. "Think he's giving up?

"I hope so. Sonar, do we still hold master-two?" McKinnon asked of the Akula.

"Sonar holds the Akula on passive narrow band. Weak seventy-two and a fifty-eight hertz tonal on …"

"Conn, sonar," McKinnon asked.

"Loud metallic transient from master-two," sonar barked.

"Launch transients?"

The pause seemed hours. "Negative the Akula just broke something in a big way."

"A collision?"

"I don't think so. It sounds like a major part of her hull. Master-two is in trouble, transients louder now. Oh my God…."

VEPR

Danyankov had also heard the U-boat rising. The plot showed *Vepr* nine-hundred meters from the U-boat. On his present course, Danyankov would pass the German at a range of only two-hundred meters. That is if the U-boat did not maneuver. Too, close even for Valerik Danyankov. He ordered a twenty-five degree rudder shift.

When the rudder went over the Russian submarine's blunt bow dropped eight degrees. The planes operator countered the rise by applying a ten-degree rise angle.

At her port stern plane the harmonic rose in decibels. The frequency of the remaining metal reached the frequency of the harmonic. The crack in the pintle spread like a spider web until chunks of steel and contaminated fill-material exploded. With the rudder turned water pressure over the loose control surface doubled. Gravity pulled the stern plane downward wrenching the remaining inboard support shaft. The shaft held, but stretched. As it elongated the moving water forced the jammed stern plane aft toward the spinning nickel bronze screw.

The hydraulic system sensed this problem and attempted to realign the control surfaces. The shaft and yoke, which connected the two stern planes was now under the force of the rushing ocean and the ship's own five thousand pound per square inch hydraulic system. The yoke snapped at its midpoint. The undamaged starboard stern plane locked in the dive position. The nose of the Akula dropped as if she had fallen off a cliff.

The hydraulic servo sent a last signal to the command center. Next to the operator, an alarm shrieked.

In the torpedo room, the technician had only to swivel the contact pins of the new relay in place until plastic latches captured the inexpensive part. When the nose dropped, he lost his footing. Out of instinct, he tried to withdraw his hand. The relay lodged the pins into the incorrect alignment. As his sweaty fingers retracted, the nearness of his skin to the live common wire caused a ninety-volt arc from the power transfer bus into the control relays for tube-four.

Outdated and far too complicated the Emergency Firing Computer made events automatic and unstoppable. The ninety volts energized the tube control system, which sent signals to control valves. Torpedo tube 4 flooded and equalized with sea pressure.

A small part of the ninety volts isolated another set of relay switches from the command center. No further information flowed from the targeting computers. The voltage continued as a step-down transformer and another relay shut allowing a lower voltage to energize a memory drive. This drive sent last known targeting information to a flash memory. The memory detected the information and sent its own signal to another relay. A quarter second after it shut power flowed into the waiting torpedo.

Instantly the torpedoes acoustic nose activated. Gyros spun as the torpedo became aware of where it was. The torpedoes on board computer did a second long self-check. It noted the downward angle of the submarine, but the preset parameters were within tolerance. Satisfied the torpedo signal demanded target information.

Back in the Emergency Firing Computer, the flash memory heard the signal. A burst of information flooded the torpedo. It took a quarter second for the computer to understand the inrush of information. The torpedo was happy enough to signal the submarine herself.

Vepr took control. Tube four's outer door swung open. As the tube opened a switch on the door's outer edge closed. A millisecond later, satisfied it had obeyed its human masters the torpedo tube ordered valves atop three high-pressure air flasks to open. This air acted on the firing plunger. The plunger moved aft driving a column of water into the tube behind the weapon. Blocked by the torpedo water pressure built rapidly until a sensor was satisfied. A lug set into the top of the torpedo held it in place until it rolled out of the way. Water pressure behind the torpedo pushed the weapon at almost four-Gs, into the sea.

The engine started when the torpedo left the tube. As programmed, the torpedo turned to the set gyro angle. It banked to starboard then slowed as its computer recalled the search speed of twenty-eight knots.

USS MIAMI

McKinnon looked at the waterfall display above his head. "What's going on?" he asked as calmly as he could.

"Conn sonar, the Russian has suffered some a casualty—wait—

wait." Raw nerves tensed. Then a near panicked voice echoed through the speaker. "Conn-sonar, torpedo in the water!"

"Where is it sonar?" McKinnon yelled.

"Torpedo bears zero-four-zero," sonar alerted. "Conn-sonar, it's a Russian weapon by nature of sound."

McKinnon opened his mouth to order a flank bell when the sonar supervisor broke in, "Conn, sonar, master-two has launched against master-one."

McKinnon watched the waterfall display. The electronic image of the torpedo a bright green line traveled across the screen.

"Not a thing we can do," McKinnon whispered.

U-761

Veldmon heard the sudden grinding wrenching noise. To his ear, it sounded like someone slowly crushing tin can. He turned his head to report, when another sound emerged from the grinding noise. He pressed the headset to his ear. The sound was a strange yet familiar whirring sound. He listened for only a second before his mind comprehended. "Torpedo!"

Becker did not let surprise delay him, "A homing torpedo?"

Veldmon answered his question a half second later. "The-the weapon has asdic!"

"Ahead flank," Becker screamed. "How far to the ice?"

Hamlin did a quick guess, "Berg is three hundred meters bearing three-four zero."

"Chief fifty meters, now."

"Torpedo is closing," Veldmon hissed through clenched teeth.

The propellers bit deep into the water. The crew reached out for anything that might support them when the bow of the German submarine dropped.

"I can't hear anything, "Veldmon cried out.

Becker stood between the two periscopes holding on to each as the angle increased.

VEPR

The jammed plane bent backwards while water continued to flow over the damaged surface. The control arm could no longer bear the strain and the seven-ton slab of steel broke. The entire submarine shook like a toy. Hydrodynamic forces acted on the free plane, lifted it three meters before the ever-envious force of gravity pulled down the fluttering steel. Only the screw blocked its path to the bottom of the sea.

The computer machined nickel-bronze and Type 3311 high tensile steel met with the explosive force of a torpedo warhead. Four of the Akula's propeller blades sheared off under the weight and force of the falling stern plane. The remaining three blades bent at odd angles and the stern plane twisted around along its axis.

In the Command Center of the crippled submarine, the crew remained calm. Carl Blevins wedged himself between two consoles.

The submarine fell on her side as a deep rumble swept through the straining steel. The angle grew steeper and the stern bounced in a corkscrew motion. Those not braced tumbled in the air only to crash to the unyielding deck.

A blur of stumbling and falling men, and machines screamed in protest. Lights flickered on and off with sparks and shrieks. The Akula bucked and the deck quaked as if made of rubber.

USS MIAMI

"Master-two, master-two, damn," came the voice over the 27MC.

"What is it, sonar?" McKinnon demanded.

"Conn, sounds like the Akula is breaking up!"

"Officer of the deck, periscope depth now," McKinnon ordered.

"Where's that torpedo?"

"We've lost it in the noise."

"Okay, I can hear master-one running. No, wait. I have active from the Russian weapon."

"Sonar we're going to PD. Stay on top of it," McKinnon bellowed.

The Torpedo

Confusion lasted only a second. The sea alive with noises provided a number of possible targets. The sophisticated computer sorted and filtered information sent by the simple sonar. On either side of its seeker, head the torpedo heard the rumble, but ignored the sound due to the fact the Mother Ship was back there. It pinged and analyzed the returning waves of sound. The reflection from the U-boat's hull matched the target profile. The torpedoes' computer adjusted the control surfaces, and the weapon turned east and pitched down three degrees. It listened.

Sound energy transmitted by the screws of the fleeing German Submarine struck the weapon's passive transducers. Instantly the active sonar adjusted its pulse and beam direction, and let go a surge of acoustic energy.

A possible target loomed into the weapon's acoustic eye. A blend of signals swept in for analysis. These signals were in both high and low frequencies. Unsure, the torpedo pinged again. The hull of the U-boat gave a fuzzy return, but this new object almost blanked the system. It listened again. The frequencies shifted on almost all scales while its electronic mind wondered. The computer ordered the influence section of the warhead to energize. An invisible field of magnetic energy surrounded the torpedo's nose. Sensors at the top and bottom of the seeker measured the field looking for any disturbance. In the warhead, a pellet of Dystol-7 explosive aligned with the top of a tiny electro-explosive squib. The torpedo was ready to fulfill its mission.

U-761

"Boat is level at fifty-meters." Edel wiped a bead of moisture from his forehead.

"Where is the torpedo?" Becker asked.

"Still astern, closing fast," Veldmon announced.

"We're under the berg," Hamlin called out from the plot table.

"Periscope depth," Becker ordered.

Edel looked at Becker his mouth as wide as his eyes.

"Now, chief," Becker screamed.

"Full rise on both planes," Edel ordered.

U-761 leveled for a moment then the bow rose. Suddenly they could hear the ice just outside the submarine's thin skin. It cracked and hissed as if angry at the sudden intrusion.

THE TORPEDO

Logic circuits processed hundreds of acoustic signals as fast as noise filters could send them. The object in the seeker's acoustic window flooded the receiver with sound. The torpedo pinged again. A faint return that matched the target's last bearing struck the receiver module. With only a minor command to the control surfaces, the torpedo aligned its active sonar and again pinged. This time the return was solid. The computer measured the distance and rate of closure.

Passive filters eliminated all noises except for the whirring propellers of the German submarine. The received signal matched the profile the weapon created for this target.

The Russian torpedo tipped its nose up five degrees to follow. Unaware it had been fooled by the U-boat diving under to the other side of the ice mountain the weapon hit the bottom of the iceberg. The explosion of nearly a ton of explosives shattered the surrounding ocean in a flash of orange and white. Tons of torn ice fell away and rushed to the surface. The shockwave from the expanding ball of superheated steam, plasma, and melted ice reflected off the still intact iceberg like the echo of an avalanche.

USS MIAMI

Five hundred feet below and two-thousand yards south, the shockwave from the explosion took only a quarter second to reach McKinnon's ship. The wave struck *Miami's* sail square, forcing the submarine almost on her side.

McKinnon felt the ship lurch to starboard, out of instinct grabbed the barrel of number two periscope. His feet slipped from under him when *Miami* rolled like a bathtub toy.

The XO fell hard on his side before sliding down the sloping deck until his leg caught on the fire hose cabinet in front of sonar's door. His body spun around twisting his trapped leg. A look of horror and pain flashed across his face as the tibia and fibula snapped.

In the rear of control, the quartermasters reached for the induction valves. A junior member of the tracking team tumbled over the plot tables and crashed into the BEEPS-15 radar set.

Belted to their seats, the ship control party managed to stay where they belonged. The helmsman, a wiry kid, from a small town in Nebraska, ducked as one of the yellow battle lanterns missed his head by mere inches before smashing one of the fire control screens.

Throughout the ship, men tumbled and fell. Major equipment and consoles tilted and swayed on rubber mounts. Sonar went offline, but self-protection circuits operated to keep the system's million fragile parts from shaking to bits.

The wave passed and *Miami* rolled to an even keel. A strange unnatural silence filled control. Within seconds, the first moans drifted up from the decks.

McKinnon let go of the periscope and picked up the microphone for the 1MC. "All stations, this is the captain," he said calmly, "Report damage to control."

"Sonar?" asked McKinnon over the open mike.

"Conn, sonar, I... I need to cold start the system."

"Is everyone okay in there?" McKinnon inquired.

"Just shook up a bit. I'll have us back on line in about three minutes."

McKinnon looked down and saw the XO try to pull himself to a sitting position. The captain stepped off the conn and bent down to help.

"Get the corpsman up here," McKinnon ordered.

"There goes my ski trip in February." The XO cringed in pain.

"Captain," a voice said from behind his back. Getting damage reports now," The chief of the watch called out. "Number two compressor motor shorted. Auxiliary fresh water tank, sight glass cracked. Controlled leak from shaft seals."

"Is that all?" McKinnon asked.

"The cooks say we eat off paper plates for a while."

Grant McKinnon smiled. "Good. What about injuries?"

"Mess Decks say they have lots of cuts and bruises, maybe a few broken bones. The damage control team is on the way to control to get the XO."

VEPR

The damaged Akula was only a few degrees from standing on her nose. The battered and broken propeller finally stopped. Forces of nature acted on the hull causing the submarine to slide toward the bottom. Sea pressure increased, compressing the hull and offering less resistance to the surrounding water.

Danyankov inched his way hand-over-hand toward the ballast control panel. His hands slipped but his foot found a small toehold on a chart locker and he steadied himself. He felt the ship shudder and looked at the digital depth gauge. The numbers moved faster, ninety-meters, ninety-five one-hundred meters.

He spotted a figure wedged between the radar control housing and the inertial navigation receiver. "Blevins," Danyankov shouted over the rumble of the sinking submarine.

Carl poked his head from between the two consoles.

Danyankov wrapped his arm around one of the electronic cooling water pipes. "Three buttons on top," he shouted.

"These?" Blevins pointed.

Danyankov bobbed his head. "Push the buttons." The numbers on the depth meter indicated one-hundred-thirty, one-hundred forty.

Blevins grabbed a valve handle, and pulled his body from its tiny enclosure. Blevins let out a groan when he swung his weakened legs and managed to grab another valve and pulled himself forward. Although he felt his strength drain, he pumped his legs once more and swung toward the panel. He slid his fingers under the protective plastic cover. His muscles strained but his fingers pressed the three large red buttons.

Inside *Vepr's* ballast tanks, rocket motors fired. Searing exhaust gases flashed the surrounding water to steam. Pressure from the newly formed steam forced water from the louvered flood grates on the bottom of the hull. Within seconds thousands of tons of water emptied into the sea.

The downward movement slowed then stopped. Buoyancy overcame gravity and the nose of the damaged submarine started upward. The ship approached level when the stern dropped.

"Vent forward tanks," Danyankov bellowed.

A set of firm hands pushed Blevins out of the way. He tumbled back almost losing his footing on the still slightly sloped deck. His feet back-pedaled until his hand caught another pipe and he steadied himself.

The stern dropped further. If the upward angle increased more than forty degrees, air in the ballast tanks would spill out and *Vepr* would plummet to the sea floor.

Crewmembers, at the ballast control station smoothly operated the maze of knobs and switches.

The lights for the ballast tank vents appeared as green circles. The six forward lights blinked off, then turned red. The bow of the submarine vibrated as gases and steam vented. *Vepr's* bow gently fell to level again.

Danyankov ordered the vents shut. Dazed and bloodied sailors pulled themselves up. Blevins walked to a young sailor lying face down. He knelt and gently rolled the sailor on to his back. The young sailor's face twitched, the eyes slowly opened. He spoke something in Russian.

The eyes blinked twice he sat up. Blevins extended his hand and helped the young man to his feet.

"I had kids like you in my division," Blevins whispered to himself.

37

HOPE

"How are the weapons of war perished?"

-II Samuel, I, 27

VEPR

CRIPPLED AND POWERLESS, THE Russian submarine bobbed clumsily to the surface.

"Reactor is shut down," the engineering officer reported.

"Start the diesel," Danyankov ordered. "What else is broken?"

The engineer wiped the stream of blood flowing from his nose. "The shaft is cracked, thrust bearings destroyed, reduction gears hopeless. We have partial hydraulics, but control surfaces are jammed."

"We can't maneuver?" Danyankov asked.

"The creeping motors will give us a few knots," replied the engineer.

Then a report came over the emergency announcing system, "Command center, this is compartment one. We have indications of a launch from tube-four."

"What?" Danyankov yelled into the open microphone.

"Tube four is empty," the voice said apologetically.

Danyankov spun on his heels. "Sonar, what is your status?"

The reply was sluggish, "We are operating under emergency power. We have limited broadband capabilities."

"Can we communicate with the American?"

"I can divert power to the transducer."

"Do it now," Danyankov ordered as he stepped to the microphone for underwater communications.

"You have power," sonar reported.

Danyankov snatched the microphone from its holder. "Yankee-1, Yankee-1, this is Gray Ghost."

The navigator limped next to the captain. "Do you think our torpedo...?"

"If we sank a United States nuclear submarine..." Danyankov hissed.

The navigator's head had struck the plot table during the jam dive and his right eye was nearly swollen shut. "We've started World War III."

"Get the scopes up, see if there is any debris," Danyankov ordered.

"You put a weapon in the water?" Blevins asked from the other side of the command center.

"Keep quiet."

"The hell I will," Blevins shouted back. "You better hope to God or whatever you worship you missed."

Danyankov remained silent. He keyed the mike again. "Yankee-1, Yankee-1, this is Gray Ghost...Static and watery silence.

"Captain, the sea is clear," the navigation officer reported.

Then a voice came over the underwater transducer. It was faint, spirit-like as it drifted from below. "Gray Ghost, Gray Ghost, this is Yankee-1—break. What is going on?"

With his submarine crippled and wallowing in the Arctic Ocean, Valerik Danyankov had to smile. "Yankee-1, Yankee-1, this is Gray Ghost—break. Have loss of control surfaces and propulsion—break. Accidental torpedo launch during casualty—break. We are on the surface—over."

"Gray Ghost, Gray Ghost, do you require assistance?"

"Negative Yankee-1, not now—break. What about the U-boat?" Danyankov asked.

"Gray Ghost, this is Yankee-1, status of U-boat unknown. Torpedo detonation heard near last good bearing of German submarine—over."

"It was an accident."

"Understand, Gray Ghost—break. Yankee-1 will conduct search for U-boat—over."

U-761

Blocked from the explosion by the iceberg, the U-boat rose toward the dim light of the Arctic noon.

"Twenty meters," Edel called softly.

"Ease the angle," Becker growled.

Veldmon looked back toward his captain. "Herr Kaleu?"

"What is it?" Becker snapped.

"Sounds like a submarine blowing its tanks."

"They came up to look for our bodies," Becker shouted and threw the cap to the wet, greasy deck. "What is the bearing?"

Veldmon looked at his bearing indicator. "Contact bears one-six-eight."

"Boat is at periscope depth," Edel announced.

Becker did not seem to notice.

"Captain?" asked Volker gently.

"I heard you," Becker growled. "Raise the scope."

The silver attack scope lifted to the ocean's surface.

Becker snapped the handles of the periscope down and shoved his eye to the optic window. "Give me a bearing."

"Target bears three-four-eight," Veldmon reported.

Becker swung the scope around. The small eyepiece window that framed much of a submarine captain's world moved in a slow circle. Nothing but chunks of torn ice floated in the boiling sea. As he turned the scope further, an object filled the scope's window. His brows arched and his eyes widened. "What am I looking at?" His fingers locked around the handles. The sight of the deadly efficient outline of the Russian filled the view. "Slow ahead," he ordered.

"Looking for us?" Becker hissed. "I'll show you exactly where I am." He snapped the handles on the periscope up. "Action stations, flood tube-two," he ordered.

Volker stepped up. "Herr Kaleu, it might be better for us to turn east."

Becker's eyes blazed. "Run?"

"If we miss…"

"Miss?" yelled Becker. "If we miss we die, if we run, we die. This is where it ends."

"Herr Kaleu there is another submarine out there," Volker protested.

Becker trembled. "Yes, and another destroyer, tomorrow, another plane."

Volker looked at the deck. "Maybe we should consider ... "

"Consider what?" Becker hissed, "Surrender? Those bastards lured us up with promises then shot at us. Do you want to die like a dog?"

"We can escape. We've done it before."

"There is no escape."

Volker silenced.

"Get back to your station." Becker picked up his dull and dirty commander's cap.

Volker lowered his head like a condemned man.

"I hear engine sounds," Veldmon called. "Sounds like a diesel."

USS MIAMI

"What's the bad news?" McKinnon asked.

"Not too bad," the corpsman smiled. "XO was the worst. He got a bad break we need to get him in soon as we can. The rest have cuts and bruises."

"Thanks Doc," McKinnon breathed out.

"Conn, sonar, sonar is back on line. Conn, sonar holds a regain of master-one-U-boat."

"Where is she sonar?"

"Master-one now bears one-seven-zero. It sounds like she just came around that berg."

"Conn, sonar aye," McKinnon responded. "Attention in the attack center. Regain of master-one, the German sub. She managed to avoid the torpedo. I inten..."

Sonar cut him off. "Conn sonar, master-two, the Akula just started her diesel. Captain master-one is closing on master-two."

McKinnon watched the waterfall display. "Officer of the deck, come to new course north. Get the ship to periscope depth fast."

Again, *Miami's* blunt bow angled toward the surface.

McKinnon grabbed the microphone for the underwater

telephone. *"German submarine, German submarine this is United States submarine. The attack was an accident. Repeat, the attack was an accident. Russian submarine is damaged, and on the surface. Do not attack. The war is over,"*

McKinnon tried to keep his voice calm. "Sonar can we warn the Akula?"

"Negative, diesel is masking all signals."

"Set up a firing solution on the U-boat," McKinnon barked. "Flood tubes one and three."

Miami's weapons officer stood from his console and stepped toward McKinnon. "Captain, the contacts are close. If we shoot and lose the wire ..."

"I know," McKinnon, sighed.

U-761

"Range, nine-hundred meters. Gyro angle starboard thirty, set. Final bearing, three-four-eight, set," Becker called out as the Russian submarine grew larger in the window of the attack scope.

"Herr Kaleu," Veldmon called, "Another message." Veldmon switched on the speaker. Distant and watery but still understandable a voice spoke in English.

"Do not attack, torpedo launch an accident. War is over."

"Shut that off," Becker shouted. "That was no accident."

"Firing solution set," Volker reported half-heartedly, "Open bow cap for tube-two."

"Ship is ready," Volker reported.

"Standby tube—two." Becker paused, "Tube two—los."

The torpedo left the tube with a slight thump.

"Weapon away—motor running," Veldmon reported.

THE LECHE TORPEDO

The sea filled with noise, but the low rhythmic drum of the diesel was most interesting. The noise grew stronger when the torpedo closed on the helpless Russian submarine. It turned to its preset angle and listened. The noise of the diesel filled the oil lined ceramic transducers.

USS MIAMI

"Launch transits," sonar yelled. "It's an electric torpedo."

McKinnon grabbed the rail around the periscope stand. "Range from the torpedo to master-two?"

"Two-k," sonar responded.

"Weapons officer, set a solution to the iceberg—switch tube–one to acoustic off mode."

Seconds later, the petty officer at the weapon control reported. "Solution tube-one, set."

"Open outer doors—match bearings and shoot."

At the Mk-81 weapons control console, the fire-control petty officer waited until the door open indicator went from red to green. "Standby," he said as he moved the firing lever to the right. Power flowed into the ADCAP torpedo. Another indicator on the panel lit WEAPON READY. The lever moved to the left.

A rush of air and the ADCAP left *Miami's* torpedo tube.

"Motor start," sonar confirmed.

"Good wire," the weapons officer reported.

"Weps, kick it to high speed."

A signal traveled from the computer along thousands of feet of thin command wire. The ADCAP torpedo received the signal and instantly its engine revved to maximum speed.

"Give me the count," McKinnon yelled.

"Seven seconds."

"Helm right full rudder, cut the wire, shut the outer door. Hang on everyone."

THE LECHE TORPEDO

The low thump of the Akula's diesel grew strong as the German torpedo surged on. The gyro settled and the fins made small adjustments for current.

Making twenty-eight knots, The Leche was now only one-hundred meters from its target, when a high frequency noise rushed by forcing an offset error of eight degrees. The German weapon lost the diesel engine sound for three seconds, but as the wake of the unknown object passed, the transducers reacquired the low thump of the diesel.

THE ADCAP TORPEDO

Although it was the most advanced torpedo in the world, this ADCAP was dumb. It sped through the sea straight into the second iceberg. The contact detonator survived the collision long enough to perform its one and only function.

USS MIAMI

"Warhead detonation," sonar called.

Again, a wave of pressure struck the ship. This time the shock wave found little when it reached the American submarine. McKinnon turned so only the narrow stern offered resistance to the explosion's pressure wave. The bow dipped some as the wave washed over.

"Let's pray this works," McKinnon said softly, "Helm, left full rudder. Steady course north."

THE LECHE TORPEDO

Thirty meters from the end of its mission the German torpedo's depth and yaw gyros slammed to the limit of their gimbals. The sound information went from steady to a jumble of high and low frequency signals. The low rhythmic thumping of the diesel vanished as its transducers flooded with sound. As programmed, it turned toward the lowest frequency noise. This new low frequency sound, although not as steady as the diesel was still louder and therefore a better target. Two seconds later, it slammed into the ice.

USS MIAMI

"Second detonation," sonar reported, "Same bearing as our weapon."

"What about master-two?" McKinnon asked almost in a whisper.

There was a pause, "Too many reverbs from the explosions."

"Now what," McKinnon wondered aloud.

"Conn, sonar regain of master-two. Regain based on diesel lines."

"Anything from master one," McKinnon asked.

"Just picked him up on tracker three, broad band submerged two three-bladed screws. Looks like he's turned to opening range on master-two. He might come around for another shot."

U-761

"What happened?" Volker asked as he picked himself off the deck.

The pressure wave from the ADCAP's explosion threw the U-boat around like a cork. Becker held on to the scope and managed to stay on his feet. He shook his head to clear the ring in his ears. He placed his eye against the optic window. "Missed," he said. "I'm going to open range and attack again. I…"

Veldmon cut him off, "Captain, listen, another message." Without orders, Veldmon turned on the speaker. Again, the voice drifted out of the depths.

"Captain Becker, this is Commander Grant McKinnon USS Miami. I have detonated your torpedo. Do not attack again or I will destroy your ship. Germany and the United States are now allies. I have no desire to sink you, but I will defend my ship and the Russian submarine. The attack on your ship was a mistake and I am prepared to prove that, but you must not attack. If I hear a tube flood or a door open, I will sink you. I ask you as Captain-to-Captain to give me the chance to prove to you the war's over. You and I can see our families again."

"They won't fool me again," Becker hissed. "Helm, continue to new course zero-seven-zero."

USS MIAMI

"Close on the Akula," McKinnon ordered. "Bring us within two hundred yards."

"Five-hundred yards," the plot operator called out.

Grant McKinnon squared his shoulders. "Officer of the deck put us on a parallel course with the Russian. Come to all stop," McKinnon, ordered quietly.

"Maneuvering answers all stop," the Helm reported.

"Three-hundred yards," the plot announced.

The Mk-81 operator spoke next, "Angle on the bow to master-two is port zero-nine–zero."

"Officer of the deck," McKinnon started. "Conduct a three-second emergency blow."

Every head in the control room turned to look at the Captain. The looks ranged from fear to bewilderment.

"Get this boat on the surface," McKinnon repeated.

"Surface the ship, aye," the officer of the deck responded.

A blast of high-pressure air displaced seawater from Miami's ballast tanks.

VEPR

Air rushed past their heads with the noise of a jet engine as the intake for the diesel sucked in frigid air.

"Engineer," Danyankov called over the sound of the screaming air. "How long until the creeper motors are operational?" He leaned over placing his ear close to the bridge communication box.

"The port creeper motor has a damaged bearing," the engineer called back.

"I don't give a damn. Get me moving."

Then the lookout raised a nervous hand to the south, "Periscope."

Danyankov twisted his head, "Where?"

The young lookout stuttered, "Th-the-there."

Vepr's captain raised his binoculars. Jutting from the water, its head slightly thicker than its body the periscope brushed aside chunks of floating.

"Command, do I have weapons control?" Danyankov yelled into the frosted microphone.

"No, sir," a static filled voice replied. "Data and weapons control circuits are off line. A bad power converter shorted the entire system."

"It's turning toward us," the lookout yelled.

Danyankov stood and looked around. Ice locked him in to port and the U-boat to starboard. Vepr could not move nor shoot. For the first time in his life, Valerik Danyankov knew what it was like to be trapped.

Then a huge mound of water reared from the sea. The perfectly formed dome rose almost a meter before it exploded, sending jets of freezing water over the men in the Russian submarine's bridge. The Russian submarine bobbed while the ocean frothed and boiled.

Danyankov wiped the stinging saltwater from his face. His mouth dropped open as a black shape rose from the center of the swirling hissing water. The black square shape of *Miami's* sail rose like a building. Water cascaded down the shiny surface like a hundred waterfalls. Raising slowly the long deck came out of the sea.

U-761

Becker flinched back from the periscope. The shape of the American submarine nearly blocked his vision.

Then the voice came through the hydrophone again. *"Captain Becker, this is Commander McKinnon, Commanding Officer of USS Miami, we have surfaced next to the Russian submarine. We are defenseless. Our weapons are unable to reach you. I ask you Captain to Captain to surface.*

"You can, if you decide, destroy us both. If you do shoot, the world will plunge into a third world war. Captain Becker, the war you fought has long been over. Your next action will decide if there is another. I tell you the fate of all is now in your hands, Miami—out."

Becker stood back from the periscope.

Edel wiped his hands on his leather trousers and stepped to his captain, "Sir?"

Becker looked into Edel's eyes and smiled. The secret language worked again and Edel grinned back. Becker reached out and placed his hand on his friend's shoulder. "Chief, surface the boat."

38

DINNER AND A MOVIE

"The sword within the scabbard keep,
And let mankind agree."

John Dryden:
The secular Masque, 1700

"CONN, SONAR AIR TRANSIENTS from master-one," sonar called nervously.

"Launch transients?" McKinnon asked.

"Negative. Sounds like a submarine blowing tanks off the starboard side."

McKinnon walked to the already raised periscope. "There she is," he smiled at the sight of *U-761's* knife-like bow cutting through a foaming patch of ocean. *Miami's* captain snatched the microphone of the 1MC from its holder. "All hands, this is the Captain. The German U-boat has surfaced. Break rig for dive man the bridge. Chief of the boat, drain and open the forward escape trunk."

"Conn-radio, *Miami* is receiving clear voice *comms* from Russian submarine."

"Send it to the conn," McKinnon ordered.

Suddenly a blast of static screeched through the air, followed by a voice. "Commander McKinnon, this is Captain Danyankov of the Russian submarine K-157. Well done."

The thick huffy Russian accent made some of the words hard to understand "Radio, am I lined up to go out, clear voice?"

"Conn radio yes."

McKinnon keyed the mike, "Captain Danyankov this is Commander McKinnon do you require assistance?"

"*Miami* this is *Vepr*, negative. I have my secondary propulsion on line and can steam at five knots. We are unable to submerge due to control surface failure." He paused. "What now?"

McKinnon let the microphone dangle around his neck. The answer seems easy enough. "Request you join me to meet with U-boat commander."

"I will launch a small boat to my starboard," Danyankov said.

"Understand and will meet you on this vessel, *Miami* out."

"Weps," McKinnon called. "You have the boat. Hold us here. Draft a sitrep and transmit in the clear."

"Aye sir, it will be ready in five minutes."

U-761

"All stop," Becker ordered. He took his own microphone. "Men, we have surfaced to surrender. I do not know what the future holds for us, but we could fight no longer. This is a chance at life. A life I want you all to have. We have been asleep in the ice for sixty years, maybe more. I want you all to be proud of your service and your boat. Do not resist, comply with our captor's wishes. You are the finest crew in the German Navy and I am proud of each of you. I wish you all luck and I will do my best to ensure you are treated fairly."

Becker replaced the microphone slowly and again looked at Edel. "Well, my friend, it's over."

"Captain, would you like me to be the first on the bridge?"

Becker smiled. "You know I can't allow that."

"Are you sure about this?" Edel asked.

"It's too late now," Becker slowly stepped into the conning tower. "Volker, have the off watch man the after casing."

"Yes, sir," Volker smiled.

Becker reached the upper bridge hatch and spun the dogging wheel. With a hiss, the foul air of the U-boat's interior rushed out.

The hatch flopped open and Becker climbed into the dimming light.

USS MIAMI

Grant McKinnon stood on the after deck of his submarine trying rather unsuccessfully not to shiver. The U-boat floated less than a hundred yards away. The current eased and the drifting ships managed to keep their distance.

A washing sound caused McKinnon to turn. In the growing mist, a large rubber raft approached his port side.

Chief of the Boat, Danny Norse stepped beside *Miami's* captain. "What will you say?"

"I don't know COB."

"You'll figure something out skipper," Norse smiled through the black scarf around his face. "Here comes your ride."

The black rubber boat bumped along the American submarine. The *Jacobs's ladder* unrolled neatly down the rounded side. Norse threw a heaving line toward one of the Russians in the raft To the COB's surprise, the third man from the front reached out for the line.

"Got it COB," the man said as he reeled the line around his arm.

"You speak pretty good English," Norse chuckled.

"When you live in Connecticut most of your life you pick up a few things," the man answered.

Norse lowered the scarf from his face and peered into the bobbing raft. "Connecticut?"

"How you been, Danny?" The man asked.

Norse leaned toward the boat in total shock. "How do you know my name?"

The man laughed. "I know all about you. Your favorite team is the Dolphins. Oh, and three years ago you tried to jump a golf cart over the canal in Puerto Rico."

"There's only one son-of-a-bitch who knows about that." Norse pulled the hood from his head. "Carl?"

"Yep," Blevins smiled.

"What in the name of God are you doing here?"

The boat bumped alongside bobbing in the small swells. One of the men on *Miami's* deck held out the boat hook. Blevins took the cold brass end in his hand forming a handrail for the McKinnon to steady himself as he descended into the Russian raft.

Carl Blevins smiled up at Norse. "I got sick of sitting on my ass, so I joined the Russian Navy."

His mouth fell open. "What the hell?"

Blevins burst into a deep heartfelt laugh. "Long story Danny, I'll fill you in later."

Danyankov moved to make room for the American captain. He held out his hand as McKinnon crouched into the space next to him. "Captain," he nodded with the proper air of formality.

McKinnon took the Russian's hand, "A pleasure sir."

The Russian sailors pushed off the rubber tiles of the American submarine's side. They paddled backwards and turned the bobbing raft toward *Miami's* stern.

"What do you think of this whole thing?" McKinnon asked.

"It is historical."

Carl Blevins placed his hand on Danyankov's shoulder, "Oh come on skipper you think this is cool as hell."

Danyankov rolled his eyes. "Would you like this one back?" he asked McKinnon. "And don't call me that."

Grant McKinnon burst into laughter. "I thought you could use Chief Blevins's charm." A rare but genuine smile crossed Danyankov's face. "No thank you, I've had my fill. How did you win the Cold War with men such as this?"

"Hey, I just saved your ass," Blevins called back. "I thought of transferring over till you said that."

The raft rounded *Miami's* rudder. *U-761* sat motionless less than fifty yards away.

"She is impressive," Danyankov said admiringly.

U-761

The oarsmen panted by the time the raft bumped with a rubbery squish into the side of the U-boat.

On the bridge, Becker straightened his cap and ordered attention on deck. The German sailors stood rigid in perfect military style.

Becker watched the first man out of the boat pull himself to the deck using the lifeline. The man gained his footing on the U-boat's after casing. The next man on deck was taller, his shoulders wider and his face seemed frozen in a permanent scowl. "That must be the Russian," Becker whispered.

Oberbootsmann Hamlin saluted each man that stepped on deck. Both men returned the salute. Hamlin directed them to the small ladder leading to the after flak deck. They stepped up, each seeming in awe of the flak guns. They paused only briefly as Hamlin guided them to the bridge.

Becker stepped forward and saluted. "I am Kapitanleutnaunt Manfred Becker, Commanding officer of the German submarine *U-761*. I surrender my ship and crew. I ask that you treat my men in accordance with the Geneva Convention."

McKinnon and Danyankov returned the salute.

An awkward silence ensued then McKinnon spoke, "Captain Becker, I do not accept your surrender."

The silence carried a life of its own.

"What?" whispered Danyankov?

McKinnon dropped his salute. "The surrender occurred many years ago, even before I was born. Our nations have been allies for decades." McKinnon extended his hand and smiled. "Welcome to a new century."

Becker stared in shock and took McKinnon's hand. "We are allies?"

"Captain, there are things you're going to learn that you will not even believe."

Danyankov stepped up, "In the name of the Russian people, I also welcome you."

Becker cocked his head, "You didn't say Soviet people."

"Like the American said, you have much to learn."

McKinnon shivered from the cold. "Captain, is there anything your crew needs? We will be happy to provide food and medical care."

"You have a doctor?" Becker asked.

"We have one," Danyankov announced.

"My first watch officer is injured."

Danyankov turned and spoke to those in the boat. The boat pulled away. "The doctor will be here soon."

Becker bowed, "Thank you sir." He then turned to McKinnon. "My men are in need of food."

"I think tonight is lobster night."

"Lobster?" asked Becker. "In German lobster means one's anus."

McKinnon laughed, "Or maybe it's steak night."

A shout came from the rear deck of the U-boat's after deck. "What a beauty!" Those on the bridge turned. A man in a Russian lieutenant's uniform stepped rather clumsily onto the bridge. "Look, there is the UZO, and radio direction finder."

McKinnon smiled. "Captain Becker I would like to introduce retired Chief Petty Officer, Carl Blevins."

Becker extended his hand.

"It is good to meet you captain."

"Ah thank you," Becker answered. "You seem to know about U-boats."

"Yes sir, I do. Ever since I was a kid, I studied U-boats. When I went to see *U-505*, I decided to join the Navy."

"*U-505* is Harald Lange's boat. Where did you see *U-505*?" Becker asked.

"In Chicago," Blevins smiled.

Becker's mouth dropped open, "Chicago, But—how?"

McKinnon laughed, "I told you, you have a lot to learn."

THE PENTAGON

"Admiral we have a message from the *Miami*."

Malroy snatched the message out of the officer's hand. His eyes scanned the paper as his lips moved silently.

"Hot damn," Malroy said leaning back in the large chair. "Get me a line to the Kremlin and the president."

"Which president," the officer grinned.

Malroy eyes narrowed, "Our president smart ass."

"I thought so."

USS MIAMI

The German sailors devoured the lobsters. The coleslaw and yeast rolls didn't last long either. The crew of *U-761* had an introduction to soft serve chocolate ice cream.

Becker ate with the officers in *Miami's* wardroom. He marveled at the space and the size of this wonderful vessel.

A few of the German crew spoke some English. They acted as translators for the others. The conversation in the crew's mess mirrored the talk in the wardroom. All burned with curiosity, but understood now was a time to celebrate being alive.

A few at a time, the German crew toured *Miami*. With a common language unnecessary among submariners, the Germans seemed awed by the systems, especially the torpedoes.

McKinnon invited Becker and Danyankov to his stateroom. A plate of warm chocolate chip cookies waited on the small desk for the three officers.

"You have been most kind," Becker said softly.

"Think nothing of it," McKinnon smiled back.

Becker's face turned serious. "What happens now?" he asked.

McKinnon glanced at Danyankov. "Our three countries are figuring that out now."

A soft rap at McKinnon's door broke the tense silence.

"Excuse me," McKinnon said. "Enter."

The door opened and the radioman of the watch held out a covered clipboard. "Flash traffic."

McKinnon took the message board. "Thank you," he nodded to the young sailor.

"Excuse me again I also have a message for Captain Danyankov."

The radioman reached behind his back, pulling another covered clipboard from his belt. He handed the board to the wide-eyed Russian.

"How did you?"

"I can't say," replied McKinnon with a smile.

Danyankov grunted and took the board.

Both captains crossed their legs letting the message board rest on the bent knee. They flipped the covers open and read.

McKinnon closed the black plastic cover of the message board. Danyankov followed a few seconds later. The Russian and American Captains looked at each other, the seriousness in both faces seemed to route lines in their brows.

"Captain Becker, we have received orders," McKinnon said softly.

The Russian's face seemed as cold and unemotional as a statue.

McKinnon's serious look faded and a smile cracked his lips, "You're going home."

"Home?" asked Becker.

"Yes, home," McKinnon said as he re-opened the folder and read the message. "We are to escort you to Wilhelmshaven, to arrive on the twenty-fifth of this month."

Becker's bearded face opened with a wide grin. His tired blue eyes brightened.

Danyankov nodded, "I have received the same orders." He then offered a thin smile. "I have never been to another country."

"Captain Danyankov, can you sail?" McKinnon asked.

"My boat can travel on the surface. Our screw is damaged and we will be required to use our secondary motors."

McKinnon looked at Becker. "And you, sir?"

"*U-761* is fully operational."

"Then if we all agree we can remain surfaced here through the night. Captain Becker, you and your crew can get some rest. Captain Danyankov can conduct repairs. We will begin our transit at first light. All agreed?"

Becker and Danyankov nodded.

"Then Gentlemen, it is agreed."

39

A NEW FLAG

"How are the weapons of war perished?"

-II Samuel, I, 27

A RIBBON OF PALE orange appeared just above the horizon when Becker climbed to the bridge. Although the frozen Arctic was behind them, a chill seemed to follow. Becker fastened the top button of his coat. Around him silhouetted in the struggling sun, the bridge watch scanned the star-studded darkness.

Becker looked aft. To port the American submarine kept station, two-hundred meters off the U-boat's after quarter. Becker admired the powerful ship. A wave formed over her bow as if she herself were part of the sea. On her sail-Becker liked that Americans called their conning towers sails-an amber light flashed warning all ships that this was not an ordinary vessel.

On the after starboard side, Becker made out the somewhat sinister shape of the Russian submarine.

"Morning skipper," said the voice of the retired American chief.

"Guten Morgen, Oberbootsmann Blevins," Becker replied.

Blevins moved over to make room for the U-boat captain. "Are you ready for today?" Blevins asked quietly.

"I don't know, so much... maybe too much time." Becker stared at the passing sea. The black water changed in the growing light to a shade of blue-green. "Tell me, what will we find?"

"I don't really know. As you said, it may be too much. You are about to enter a new time and a new world. I wish I could say a better world. The dumb asses that started the last world war are still around. Only the names and countries changed. It's just a different time."

"No one learned from the war?"

"Oh, we learned. We learned to make weapons that kill millions. We learned to use germs and chemicals. Now we can destroy any city in the world in less than an hour. Did we learn to stop war? Never will." Blevins paused. "You'll find out for yourself. Besides today is a great day. Any day you come home from sea is a great day."

"True," Becker nodded.

"Sailors are a strange bunch," Blevins shrugged. "We can't wait to get to sea, then when we're there we think about nothing but getting back to shore."

Becker looked worried. "This gas—this *Forever Project*, it is far more dangerous than beneficial. Look what almost happened." Becker turned toward the American. "There is a difference between life and living."

"I never thought of it like that, but I guess you're right." Blevins squinted into the new dawn.

"Does the world know about this gas?"

Blevins reached in his coat and brought out the CD. He smiled at Becker then flipped the disc over the side. "Now only one person knows, but he'll never talk."

The forward port lookout lifted his right arm and pointed across the water, "Land."

Becker turned his eyes to the thin strip of shore. The light grew some brighter while the last of night retreated. He lifted his chin and let warm rays play across his face.

"I guess this is as good a time as any," Blevins smiled.

"Time for what," Becker asked.

"Captain, will you stop your boat?"

"What?" Becker asked surprised.

"Formalities need to be taken care of before we hit port. Please Captain, stop the boat."

Becker eyed the smiling American cautiously but ordered the U-boat to halt.

Carl Blevins reached in his jacket and pulled a small two-way radio, "*Miami*, this is Gray Wolf. How copy?—over."

"Good morning," Commander McKinnon answered.

"This is Gray Wolf we are in position—over."

"Roger, Gray Wolf,—break. Look off your starboard bow."

Blevins turned to Becker. "Take a look out there." He pointed into the water.

A shape rose from the water, bubbles frothed and the small conning tower of another submarine reared from the sea. A sleek craft, more streamlined than the Russian submarine.

Becker stared in disbelief. The submarine approached his U-boat.

"That Captain Becker is the newest German U-boat."

Becker's mouth dropped open, as did the lookouts. "She's German?"

"Sure is," Blevins nodded. "Her CO needs a word with you."

Men appeared on *U-212's* bridge. They smiled and waved. Becker returned the wave.

Soon a rubber raft slid over the calm sea toward *U-761* "Lookouts to the forward casing," Becker ordered when the raft came alongside.

Becker watched from his bridge as a single figure climbed the limber holes onto the forward deck. "Attention on deck," he ordered.

The officer saluted and made his way around the conning tower and up the ladder to the bridge. His hands ran over the flak guns. Purpose seemed to remind him of his mission and the officer came to attention. He saluted Becker. "I am *Kapitanleutnaunt* Hans Brinkermon, Commanding *U-212*. It is an honor to welcome you home.

"You look old for a U-boat Commander."

"Times have changed. We need to proceed carefully." *U-212's* Commander pointed over the bow.

Every type boat, yacht, and small ship covered the once empty ocean.

Becker and his crew, ducked low as a loud whirr and whooshing sound vibrated the deck. Above their heads, three German built EURO Fighters screamed over the submarines.

"The Luftwaffe also welcomes you," Brinkermon shouted over the roar of the jets.

"Our planes?" he asked.

"Yes Captain, our planes, built and piloted by Germans."

"Incredible," mumbled Becker.

"Captain Becker, I would like to present your ship with the ensign of our country," Brinkermon reached inside his heavy overcoat and handed Becker a neatly folded German flag.

Becker took the flag letting his hands gently run over the smooth nylon. "This is our flag?" Becker asked as he looked down at the black, red, and yellow stripes. Then his head snapped up. He walked to the voice tube at the front of the bridge. "Send up the flag," he ordered.

Volker appeared out of the hatch. His hand held the flag under which they had fought so many battles and killed so many ships and men. Becker held out his hand. Volker passed him the aging and dulled Nazi flag.

Becker held the old cloth flag in his hand. Becker stepped to the side of the tower. With a sudden extension of his arm, the Nazi flag flew into the waiting sea. Becker did not notice the cheers from the other submarines. He walked to the flagstaff carefully almost reverently Becker attached the flag to the lanyard and hauled it up the staff. The slight breeze caught the folds of the flag and it unfurled.

"Beautiful," Becker whispered.

"Yes it is." Brinkermon smiled. "Now with your permission, let's go home."

Becker came to attention and saluted, "Thank you."

WILHELMSHAVEN, GERMANY

Hundreds if not thousands of boats lined the outer harbor. Flags of Germany, the United States, even Russia flew seemingly from everywhere. Helicopters buzzed like flies around the four submarines as they passed into the mouth of the channel.

Becker lined the crew on deck in the tradition of a returning U-boat. When *U-761* rounded the turn just off the sea wall, cameras flashed at the sight of the returning relic. People waved and shouted.

One group of elderly men caught Becker's attention. They stood, some with canes others proud and tall. Some were bald while others bore the silver crown of age and wisdom. These men did not cheer. They stood in line and saluted.

"Those men?" asked Becker.

"U-Boat veterans," Blevins explained.

"Becker came to attention, and rendered a salute.

U-761 slowed as the channel narrowed. Becker gasped, as his eyes took in a submarine so large it filled the entire end of the long quay. The submarine three times the size of *Miami* featured a high flat after casing and a sail that towered over the entire base. Toward the stern, the flag of the United States waved lazily in the wind.

"What is that?"

"That Captain Becker is the *USS West Virginia*. I am a friend of her CO."

The throng of people thinned some as *U-761* slid along the quay to her berth. White tents had been erected near the quay head. Becker spotted a group of long black cars a short distance from the tents. On the front fenders tiny flags of at least a dozen nations waved in the breeze.

"You see that tall man in the black suit with the slightly gray hair—the one talking with the lady in the green dress?" Blevins asked.

"Yes, I see."

"That is the President of the United States."

"What?"

"Oh and the lady he is talking to—she is the Chancellor of Germany."

Becker shook his head as if trying to clear a hangover. "The world has indeed changed."

As was tradition, the IWO (First Watch Officer) Volker brought the ship into port. Becker and his crew knew this place and docking the ship seemed routine. The U-boat slipped along the quay. Neatly uniformed American, German, and Russian sailors passed lines to the U-boat.

The band stopped and the crowds fell silent. An electric crane silently lifted a gangway through a small arc, onto the U-boat's deck.

Blevins placed his hand on Becker's shoulder. "You're home."

"Thank you for getting us here," Becker smiled.

Becker climbed slowly down the flak deck ladder. He turned to his crew and saluted.

"You men have made history. I cannot tell you how proud and grateful I am to each of you. Nor can I tell what awaits you. I ask God look down on each of you and let you live in peace. My final order is that you make the most of this chance you have. I hope to see you all again, Dismissed."

Becker walked to the gangway. Blevins close behind. At the end of the brow, Becker looked up at the curious smiling faces staring at him. Slowly he stepped down.

A uniformed man walked up and rendered a salute. His uniform was strange but the braid and stars were not. Becker snapped again to attention. "Admiral," Becker began. "I report the return of *U-761*. My casualties are one dead, five wounded. We have expended ten torpedoes."

The admiral smiled. "Welcome home." He pumped Becker's hand. "Please come with me."

As they neared the group of dignitaries, Becker again saluted.

The woman was around fifty or so. Her face was round and her cheeks bounced a bit as she walked forward. Her once blonde hair seemed dulled, but her eyes were bright and her smile warm. "In the name of the German people and I think for the entire world I welcome you home."

Becker winced as the voice sounded over loud speakers. Applause erupted, as did ship whistles and horns.

"Captain Becker, I would like to introduce the President of the United States."

The president spoke. "Captain Becker, you have given the world hope. I, along with the men and women of the United States Navy and our entire nation welcome you."

On cue, the crowd quieted. Carl Blevins and Commander McKinnon walked up with another man between them.

Blevins and McKinnon rounded the crowd through a line of ropes set up to keep the path clear.

The three stopped in front of Becker. The tall, thin man in

the middle wore the uniform of a naval officer, an American naval officer.

A look of worry crossed McKinnon's face. He cleared his throat. "Captain Becker, this is the commander of the United States Ballistic Missile Submarine *USS West Virginia.*"

The officer held out his hand.

Becker noticed how the hand trembled. He looked at the man's face. He scanned down the uniform over the right pocket and noticed a nametag. White letters on a black background read BECKER.

Manfred Becker felt his own hand tremble. Those eyes, they looked like Ada's eyes.

On the verge of tears, in a broken voice, the man spoke, "I am Commander Peter Becker, Commanding Officer *USS West Virginia.* Welcome home, Grandpa."

ABOUT THE AUTHOR

D. Clayton Meadows

D. Clayton Meadows served nearly twenty years on nuclear submarines. He served on the nuclear, Fast Attack submarines USS RAY, USS DALLAS, and USS SPRINGFIELD. His writing includes numerous articles dealing with submarine history. This is his first novel. He lives in Charleston, South Carolina.